MW00583436

THE IBIS DOOR

J.K. Stephens

Daybreak Publications

To my father, whose dreams have always been contagious.

THE IBIS DOOR

J.K. Stephens

CHAPTER ONE

*S**HE SLEPT IN A PILE OF BONES** at the edge of the cliff. The coming of day didn't wake her. Day and night were all the same to her; she slept on.*

Dawn touched a mountaintop that faced the sunrise. Light traveled slowly down the red rocks to a valley floor that stretched to the next set of foothills. As if a torch had been set to grassland, the sun suddenly lit the sweep of the valley and colored it red. Then, as if the foothills were covered with autumn trees, they began to glow with orange light. Light that reflected from rock faces and fault edges might have been streams of water falling. Even creases in the valley floor caught light on the sharp edge of each line; this light, too, looked like water, flowing through streams as intricate as the branches of a tree.

Yet when full daylight arrived, there were only parched cliffs, bald foothills, and a valley floor that was dry as earthen pottery.

The barrenness of the place was striking. But to one who knew its long history, the most peculiar thing of all was this: there was no music.

In Reykjavik, Iceland, Freya turned restlessly under her comforter and then lay still, gradually separating herself from the dream.

Her strangest ever.

No music?

So many weird dreams lately. Maybe it was because of the volcanoes.

**

Ozzie's beat-up 2045 pickup rattled through the entry gate, spraying dust and gravel, and he hit the mushy old brakes hard to make it skid into an arc so it stopped next to the inner fence. He cut the engine, swearing, and sat for a minute looking at the faded sign on the top rail that said "Main Lodge."

Ha. The Main Lodge was really a run-down farmhouse, sitting at the entry to a campground outside Las Cruces, New Mexico. Right now it looked as dismal as a prison: faded wood siding, front yard full of unmowed dry grass and field flowers, a couple of enormous cottonwood trees just beginning to lose some leaves as the nights grew cooler.

He had loved this place, growing up. *But just when it's time to go see the solar system, dammit: someone has torn up my ticket.*

**

Freya lay in the dark, reaching out with her imagination to touch the stone walls and timbers of the basement room that had been hers most of her life. Her back, arms, and legs ached from firefighter training. Heat from the cat, Banzai, was making her curls sweaty. She nudged him away. At least the air was cool — the thick walls held heat and cold in balance, never too much of either.

The time display said it was after midnight. She pushed a handful of curls out of her eyes and turned a little to find the cat sitting upright on the pillow by her head again.

Last week she had put up a holopost on the worldweb about telepathic cats, hoping that maybe someone could explain why Banzai seemed to be trying so hard to communicate with her recently. For weeks he had been insisting on her attention and demanding to look into her eyes. He didn't want to play, didn't want to eat. And he spent the night sitting right by her head while she slept.

There was faraway rumbling that sounded like thunder. The dish of coins on her dresser rattled briefly. *The volcanoes.* She shuddered and pulled the comforter tighter around her, trying not to think of them.

**

Ozzie stared through the windshield westward at the

pinyon trees dotting the foothills, feeling smothered suddenly by all the farmland around him. *This doesn't make sense. Suddenly Grand Galactic wants "robotics design experience"? Why?*

On the memo that Mr. Brunelli, White Sands Space Academy's overworked student advisor, had showed him this morning, Ozzie's name ("Oliver S. Reed, age 16") was at the top of the *To* list. The *From* was Grand Galactic, the world's leading spaceline. Expecting it to be good news about his apprenticeship, he read fast. His jaw dropped. He looked up from the memo and saw his own outrage reflected in Mr. B's face.

Grand Galactic, located just to the north in "Space City" — Las Cruces — always launched its first outgoing merchant ship of each new year with the last year's most outstanding graduate of the White Sands Space Academy on board as part of the crew. The winning graduate would start as Captain's Apprentice on the Earth-Moon Line — and for Ozzie's graduating class it would be the Earth-Moon-Mars Line because Mars would soon be opened up for trade. The apprenticeship came with a promotion to Lieutenant Captain in a year or two if everything went well.

Even if I screwed up all this year, I'd still be at the top of the list for this when I graduate next June. I've earned this apprenticeship. It's mine.

Was mine.

Now they wanted bot-design experience? This was

totally news to him. And news to the Academy, Mr. B said. Mr. B had a right to be furious that Grand Galactic had changed the requirements. No one studied robotics *design* at the Academy. And now without it, he was crash-diving without a parachute.

He swore some more, sadly now, adding some of the strings of swearwords that Malo in the campground always used. He just couldn't end up stuck here being a farmer, like most of the neighbors, or end up like his father, running the campground instead of doing what he really wanted.

Low clouds above the hills scattered the sunlight. *Chores!* It was late. Had to finish them before dark. He longed to go running in the desert instead, but no time for that.

A rusty hinge on the truck door squealed as he flung it open. His boots hit the ground. His thoughts burst out as small explosions. *Some people can afford to BUY apprenticeships.* He slammed the truck door shut. *We can't.* He stalked toward the barn. *Besides, none of the bought ones are as good as this one.* He slammed open the barn door. The cow mooed anxiously and the horses shied. *Too late to apply for a college scholarship.* He snatched up the shovel to clean out the stalls, but he stabbed it into the dirt floor instead. — *Well, who wants to go to college, anyway?*

He stared at the horses without seeing them. Instead, in his mind he saw the enormous assembly bay where the *Liberty*, his ship, was being built and fitted for the first Martian trade flight, right now.

**

Freya looked at the time display again.

At dawn tomorrow — actually today already — just as yesterday, she would wake and walk to the Icelandic Firefighting Technical School ten blocks away, a hastily furnished place with a sign that had been repurposed from somewhere, painted over with white and hand-lettered.

Last week the news was all about another old volcano starting to break open and leak lava in the north part of Iceland. Like the ones before it, this one was on the MidAtlantic Ridge, the fragile line where two slabs of the earth's crust met. The ridge sliced across Iceland from north to south. Along this line the volcanoes had happened for millennia, but never like this. Last week's was the second old one this year to go live, up near the northern coast. And there were others last year, one old, one new.

She tried to block it now, but the holovideo newscast was burned into her memory: frightened sheep farmers driving panic-stricken herds away from the lava flows, the grassfires burning out of control, a farm woman crying as she watched her old family home blacken in the flames.

Would hers burn too? Freya almost never cried, but

she felt tears gathering in the outside corners of her eyes.

**

What are they thinking? I'm not training to be a robotics designer. Ozzie had studied bots for years, knew how they worked, could repair and modify them — because of course any trader had to maintain his equipment. But inventing robots to do technical work? Rigging emergency bots in a pinch? *Come on.*

His school, the White Sands Space Academy, turned out merchant space officers — spacetraders — fit and fast-acting, trained in navigation and mechanics, currencies, buying and selling. Ready for apprenticing. The demand was big. The job might be scary if you thought about it much, but what a job.

People actually moved here from places like New York City and San Francisco, even Hong Kong, to get their kids into spaceflight training early. They always told him he was lucky to be born here.

Lucky. He stabbed and tossed a hay bale with the pitchfork, doing battle with Galactic. He tossed another and another, way too many.

"I can start the apprenticeship without bot-design experience and learn it as I go," he had told Mr. B. "Let's ask Galactic. There must be a way."

The answer from Galactic made him furious: no, no way. He and Mr. B had fought this one hard all day, while

Ozzie was marked absent in every class, of course. Mr. B put in several appeals to Grand Galactic on his behalf. He even pumped the part about how Ozzie was the only student ever to manage the school store at a profit. *You'd think that would make a trading company more interested.* But it didn't budge Galactic.

Ozzie stood a moment, panting, smelling horse sweat and hay and manure. The horses watched him warily, chewing.

He felt doomed. In the quiet of the barn he heard a sound like rumbling, like doom closing in on him.

No. Just the blood beating in his ears. He turned impatiently to shut the ancient door, and the cow and horses jerked their heads from their food, waiting for it to slam.

The cow's ear twitched once, then froze.

He sighed. "Sorry, guys. Not your fault." He grabbed a scoop of feed for the chickens and closed the latch.

**

In the dark and silence the house seemed to tremble. Freya shuddered again. She thought she could hear the lava rumbling, deep in the earth.

It was a year since the new volcanic eruptions had started, in 2064. She and Mamma had been doing pretty well till then. A few months ago in April, just after another sleeping volcano came alive, she decided she would go crazy if she didn't do something to protect her home and Reykjavik. Even if it was worthless, she had to do something. She left school with more credits already, at 16, than she needed to graduate, and signed up for the firefighting program: free training in exchange for two years of service, at a small salary that started while you learned.

Her teachers and the headmaster of the school had protested that she was a promising student who should continue. She demanded early graduation anyway, and left. She and Mamma needed the money, too, to pay for a better roof — one that wouldn't burn so easily.

**

Ozzie hated garden chores. He plunged down the rows of the fenced vegetable garden by the barn, weeding murderously at first. But the fussy task slowed him to a mournful pace. It was lonely out here.

He ripped out a final weed and tossed it at the compost pile. With a dozen hard yanks he pulled up some beets and carrots for dinner.

By the time he dumped the carrots and beets into the sink inside the house to soak, he was worn out enough to be able to think in a straight line instead of so many jagged ones. Ozzie tossed himself heavily onto the front porch steps and considered his options.

**

Freya sat up and opened her book. When she touched

the page it flooded the comforter with pale-blue light. Sometimes reading could put her back to sleep, but now she coulnd't stop worrying, even while she tried to follow the story.

She was doing her own research and she had her own ideas about why the fragile Icelandic crust was breaking and spilling lava. But no one knew for sure. She would be training for fireboats and land vehicles, city and open-land work, while Icelandic and European researchers worked around the clock trying to find out the cause for the volcanic activity.

So many things happening that made no sense. And then two days ago her cat began to speak to her — so she could actually make out what it was telling her, for the first time.

The coins rattled again in the dish on the dresser. Longer than before, this time.

But Banzai's purring was insistent now, close to her ear. She fell asleep against him, with the book still glowing onto the comforter as her eyes closed.

**

Who are all these people who know so much about designing robots? Ozzie stared southward at the familiar fields with the familiar trees marking their boundaries. The sun hung just above the hills. The sleepy Mesilla Valley looked isolated from this angle, but really it was a sort of vegetable garden for the sprawling city of Las

Cruces just to the north, whose population had doubled four times in thirty years because of the spaceflight industry.

Georgie leaped into his lap, rubbing her gray-tabby nose and scratchy whiskers into the front of his red Space Academy T-shirt. No one was looking so he took her face in two hands and nuzzled the top of her head with his cheek, as he had when he was younger. She purred. He sighed and set her on the top step.

Ozzie pulled his holophone out of his back pocket, slid it out of the case, and unfolded the clear plastic holosheet on his knee. He touched the sheet to open, waved his fingers through the icons that flew up. He leaned back against the steps and searched on "robotics design" to see what the big deal was.

Georgie rubbed her head against the side of his face. He petted her absently as he poked through the icons. She wrapped herself around his head, purring, nuzzling him. Her tail was in his eyes. She seemed to want his attention a lot all of a sudden. *C'mon, give it a rest, cat.* "Too busy, Georgie," he said, and pushed the cat's butt to the planks to make her sit down.

Suddenly up popped this holo of a girl called Freya in Reykjavik, with a posting about cats. Reykjavik, Iceland? The country with the volcanoes and the northern lights? How did this happen? Nothing here about robotics.

His phone was really outdated and it wasn't the first time something screwy had showed up lately...he almost brushed the holo away, but he stopped, looking at her.

She had put up this holopost a week ago, according to the date on it, asking if anyone else had a cat that seemed telepathic. *She acts like the whole world is her living room.* She was getting telepathic information from her cats, she said. For the first time today, Ozzie smiled. That was absurd. But she was kind of interesting.

Something got into him, and on impulse he posted a reply: "Yes, my cat Georgie talks to me all the time." He sent that off.

Ozzie chose Search again, and this time he said "robotics design" clearly enough into his phone that even this antique piece of junk would understand. Out poured symbols and text, robotics video choices, corporate listings, government listings, an image of a guy his age with a trophy...That one he flicked with a finger and it bloomed into a holo of the guy with a story beside it on the sheet.

Interested in spite of himself, Ozzie skimmed the story: Out in California, Jet Propulsion Laboratory, recently sold by the government to private investors...had a robotics contest for students, with a prize...Grand Galactic had even helped to fund the prize.

There was a pop-up about some kind of U.S. robotics group in New York City and he eagerly put himself on the Send list for it, only to find that there were dozens of similar groups.

He took a deep breath to slow himself down, pulled

up the Jet Propulsion Lab contest site and fingered through it.

Here were rules about the contest and partners. Each contestant had to be a team of two. There was a bit about posting now for a partner if you didn't have one. *Well, there's a possibility.* Maybe you could team with someone and help so much that you got some credit for it.

He checked the "Need a Contest Partner?" postings and found one from a Norman Garcia in Pasadena, California. Up came Norman's holo signature, showing a guy with bronze skin and straight black hair, shorter than Ozzie's, and features that seemed to be borrowed from three or four continents and arranged uniquely for him, topped off by freckles like precise dots on his cheeks. Wearing glasses and a grin that looked like he'd just said something funny. Ozzie was curious so he read on. The guy was pretty fit-looking, but his bio said he was a full-time nerd, a fan of electronics and holo games.

Ozzie took another deep breath and entered his holo signature in the box under the Want to Be My Partner? heading. He didn't mention that he had no experience. They'd have to deal with that in the live call. He flicked the icon to send the message.

**

While Ozzie sat waiting for Norman to answer, he watched the tiny breeze move a cottonwood leaf across the water in the pump tub below, thinking of what Reykjavik might be like, and about living here in New Mexico with his dad for all of his life, while other people lived in Reykjavik, Iceland or Pasadena, California or at Moon Colony Three...

His phone sounded. Norman calling. No, not Norman. He read the display on the case as he picked it up. "No Caller ID"? That was impossible. IDs were automatic. You had to have one for the connection to work. Was this phone malfunctioning in some new way?

While he stared in surprise the call went away.

He looked out past the barn toward the south to see if Dad was headed back from the campground, half-lidding his eyes against the brightness of the setting sun. It painted long shadows across the valley. No sign of him yet.

His phone sounded. A text message.

He stood and slapped the holosheet on his palm, scowling over it and waving his fingers into the icons. It must be Norman. He took a deep breath. This was the moment of truth about being partners in the robotics contest.

A message appeared on the screen. Not from Norman.

From Freya in Iceland, already, with her holo ID standing beside it. Wasn't it the middle of the night there? He wondered if he'd waked her. Or if she was up all night watching the northern lights or something.

He couldn't help examining the holo ID again instead of reading the text message. And he suddenly felt hopeless, for the second time today.

It wasn't that she was so pretty, but she was so...something. He wasn't sure what.

She had that kind of gingery light hair that could be red or blonde or brown, hard to say from the holo. She had freckles. Mostly she had this look. Not like you'd expect. Not "I'm cute." Not "You should think I'm sexy." More like, "I have this great secret to tell you right away, it can't wait a second." She seemed to be so eager she was off-balance and she seemed to be wound so tight that her eyes leaked electricity. *She looks like a dancer, or a cheetah, ready to leap and run.*

He sighed. He looked around, feeling as if someone was watching. *Is Dad back, and I didn't hear him come in? No. Just Georgie here.*

Why did he clown around with her about that cat stuff? She had probably texted right back to tell him off for being a wise guy. Or for waking her up.

Her holotext said: "Thanks to you for answering me! I have something strange to talk with you about. Hope you do not think I'm psycho..."

Psycho? For the second time today, Ozzie smiled.

CHAPTER TWO

FREYA WOKE LATE and had to leave in a hurry to get to firefighting school on time. She grabbed her phone and lunch case and ran. That's how she missed Ozzie's return text until after the day's training was over, and after she had detoured on the way home to the Vestur thermal pool to ease her aching muscles so she could sleep better. After she had swum laps, lazily, letting the heat and the pressure of the water pull some of the stiffness out of her arms and legs. And after she had settled into one of the hottest spots and rolled a towel behind her head at the curved lip of the pool. She lay back looking up at the rising steam and the first stars long enough to let the events of the day rise away from her too.

The day had gone on forever. It included such delights as the chemical canister strapped to her back that was so heavy it made running awkward. The equipment was designed for men, who carry from the shoulders more easily; she and the other women in the program — and the others were tall and sturdy, and at least five years older than Freya — would eventually develop more strength for their sizes than the men had, just by training with the heavy stuff.

And there was dragging, reeling, unreeling, re-reeling the heavy old hoses till every muscle in her body had been misused and abused and her gloves were tearing. The equipment might soon be updated, "if they had the time and resources." And it might not.

The tekryl boots they had issued to her were the best quality you could get: the biodegradable plastic was thick and porous and flexible as velvet. And they did fit. It was just that they were new; they had not fully formed to her calves and ankles so they blistered her feet.

She was slender but tough, and a strong swimmer. Still, the men in the training program laughed at her and called her cute names, betting she wouldn't make it through the training and into the Fourteenth Reykjavik Fire Company with them.

What else can I do but keep going? I have to make it.

A man, then a woman, climbed out of the water and sat on a bench below some lights to dry themselves.

She would keep on researching as fast as she could. And what about the people who should know much more than she did about the volcanoes? They were doing things as fast as they could too, she guessed. But that ridge, that crack down the center of Iceland, was always

17

too much *there* and too scary.

Steaming in water heated by the lava below, she imagined she could feel the MidAtlantic ridge curving southward overland almost 320 kilometers from the northern shores of Iceland and hooking wickedly to the west, cutting right next to where she was now. Despite the hot water, she shivered. If new volcanoes could start in the north they could start anywhere along the ridge, even close to the city. Or old ones could become active again. Iceland was full of sleeping volcanoes, and now something was disturbing the earth's crust here.

A few other pool visitors entered the cement deck at the other end: a mother and three little kids in bright bathing suits, for an after-supper swim. She thought briefly of Mamma. Although she was late, Mamma wouldn't worry about her.

The frightening image that she kept away from her mind pushed forward now. She saw her grandmother's house — Mamma's house now — burning, lava flowing down the streets of Reykjavik, and fear rose in her stomach. Sometimes the hugeness of the volcanoes, compared to the small efforts of the firefighters, made it all seem impossible to her.

But gradually the steam took everything away, upward. The sulfurous smell was a primitive comfort. People from other places thought sulfur stank — she knew from talking on the worldweb — but to her it was familiar and she liked it. Her skin drank the minerals in.

Finally she thought to pull the phone from her bag on the pool deck and turn it on.

Sleepy now from the hot water, in memory she saw again how his holo looked, an American guy named Ozzie: a suntanned face with a stubborn jawline and nose and thick eyebrows that matched his scorched-looking light hair. His hair was brushed back, growing below his ears. After the dream that woke her last night, her phone had waked her a second time with this guy's message. His cat talked with him! How interesting. She had texted when to call her, and fell asleep again.

His reply from last night came in now, with his holo ID again: OK, he would call after her training. But no call from him yet.

It was pleasant here, and despite the worn paint and the cracked cement, it was clean. The place was never crowded anymore. Now that it was twilight the horizon showed an orange smudge to the north: the stain of the volcanic fires, always there if you looked.

Her phone signaled. She turned to face the pool's edge and accepted Ozzie's call. Sound Only, though; she must look pretty beaten-up right now. "Hello," she said.

"Hello, Freya in Reykjavik. You wanted me to call?" She liked his voice, something about it. She rearranged herself so her chin could rest on her arms on the poolside. "Are you in the *bathtub?*" Ozzie demanded. He sounded astonished and delighted at the same time.

"No, silly. At the town pool." She had the background

19

noise filter on, so it seemed to her that the noises must have traveled some other way. Maybe by echoing in the layers of ancient sea rock below America...

"Isn't it a little cold there for that?"

Was he born yesterday? But how different life must be in Las Cruces, New Mexico. No volcanoes, for one thing. And not so many hot pools. "It's a thermal pool," she said simply. "It steams, you know?"

"Oh. I get it." An awkward pause. "We have some of those here, off in the mountains mostly...You really are reaching out, to send a post worldwide."

"I do it all the time. I holopost all over the world."

"Why?"

"To find things out, to ask about things in other places. Don't you?"

"Well sure, I have holo'd Mexico City, and California, and even to New York for some parts once. I holo my friends all the time."

She chuckled. "And I thought *I* lived on an island," she said. "I talk all the time to people in at least 50 countries. My friends have always done the same — in touch all over the place. I guess it's because our island is small and we want to be part of the bigger world."

"You're not the only one." He sighed.

Now, what could this guy possibly have to sigh about?

"But. About your cat, Ozzie: what has he said to you?"

"She. Georgie is a she. Well..." He paused for a few

seconds. "It's hard to tell. She's trying to get my attention all the time, but I can't make it out...How 'bout your cat?"

"It was the same for me! He's always trying to speak to me. Recently though, I suddenly could understand what he was saying."

There was a brief silence, then the cautious question: "...And, what was that?"

"He said I needed to find out about Osiris."

Another silence at the other end. Then, "Osiris," he repeated, sounding like he had just lost track of the conversation.

"I'll tell you more about that in a minute," she said. "Let me explain, Ozzie. There's a problem, see. It shows up mostly here in Iceland because the earth's crust is new and thin here. We have had new volcanoes erupt in the last few years, and old sleeping volcanoes going live. You know that, right? Several in one place, so close together. That is a bad sign. I have studied and pursued information everywhere about it because I love Iceland and also because it's not just Iceland — if it's happening here it could begin elsewhere too: tearing of the earth's crust. It has happened before, long ago, and if it does again...

"I need help with a plan. And so strange, the cat seems to be giving me information. It might seem *crazy*..."

She heard noise near him. An electronic alarm or something.

"My next class. Can't talk more now, sorry, have to go," he said.

Fear hit her stomach. He was going away. What she said was too freaky for him.

But then he added in a rushed whisper, "Can you talk late tonight? I mean... early morning for you, like... 7?"

"Make it six and I can," she said, breathing again.

"OK." And he was gone.

**

Freya and her mother sat at the kitchen table with the teakettle between them. Once this had been Freya's favorite place, in all the world the spot where she felt happiest. She had loved visiting her grandmother here as a little girl: the grooved wooden walls and neat painted cupboards, the thick old table, the worn floor. All her life it had smelled as it did now: of coffee, wood, and bread, and faintly of fish.

It was late and she was tired, filled with laziness by the minerals in the pool. Tomorrow would start early. She needed to be alert for the morning call from that Ozzie guy. Maybe he could help.

Her mother leaned toward her, holding the teakettle, ready to pour a second cup. "Yes, thank you," Freya said, although she didn't want any. Sharing tea made her mother happy for some reason. Around Mamma's green eyes the skin crinkled; she smiled as if Freya had given her a treat.

Her freckles and eyes are like mine, but mine are paler. Mamma's hair was the same red-blonde as her own but more buttery-colored and it had a few silver threads running through it.

Freya's eyes wandered away to something more restful: the herbs that grew on the kitchen windowsill in little pots marked with their names, as always: basil, chives, and thyme. She realized she was tapping impatient rhythms on the table with her fingers, and stopped. *There seems to be a reason for this tea party. What is it?*

Mamma held her hot cup to her cheekbones: one side then the other, closing her eyes blissfully. Finally she began, "We have a guest tomorrow night. I want you to help me with dinner for him."

"Oh Mamma, *now* what?" Tiredness made her thinning patience crumble. How flighty and silly her mother was. How could she be so hopeless?

Because her father had disappeared before she was old enough to remember him, Freya had done home chores since she was grown enough to walk, to help her mother keep house and accommodate the renters: dusting and scrubbing, painting rooms, and caring for the vegetable and herb gardens outside the back door, in the little walled yard. Sometimes she cooked too — but now that she was pulling hoses and chopping at blocks of wood for hours a day? What could her mother be thinking?

23

Mamma was talking about the man, the one she had met at the market today. "He said he will hire me to paint his portrait if he likes the samples I have in my studio."

"You mean, if he likes the way you cook and thinks you're available." Knowing she shouldn't, she added, "...*After* you feed him dinner, and *after* I have to help you cook, listen to your conversation, and watch him make eyes at you."

Mamma looked fiercely at Freya for few seconds. Then her face sagged a little in defeat.

Freya was sorry. But inside she defended herself, stubbornly. *Her portraits aren't that good. Her songs are better. Why doesn't she sing?* She loved her mother's music. She hated her man-friends.

As if the thought had been said aloud, Mamma said, "Freya, I am not looking for another man-friend." She spoke with precision. Her beautiful voice was as clear as if she were performing, her lips puckered a little, her eyes crinkled with merriment that she could not possibly feel. "He has told me he wants me to paint his portrait. You know that we need the money, so I'm glad for this opportunity. I can't do it without you."

**

A little later, as Freya pulled off her clothes, cleaned her teeth, and fell into her bed, she saw her years with her mother playing before her like a speeded-up holovid: what her mother couldn't do defined what she had to do.

24

Her mother needed help, and no matter how tired she was from training, Freya would need to help. It had always been that way.

Before Freya could turn out the light, Lindis called from Sweden. Hopelessness about Mamma made Freya glad to talk, tired as she was, to an old friend.

"Yes, we're all fine," Lindis said. "We are chickens and cowards here, runaways from the volcanoes. You are the brave ones — I heard about the latest lava. How are *you*? Still writing poems?"

"Tired, honestly," Freya admitted. "Remember dancing all night at the cafés? Just a year ago. Now I feel like an old lady, off to bed early."

She talked about firefighting school and her absurd struggles with the fire equipment today, yesterday, the day before, until they both laughed at it all. For a few minutes life seemed to be easy again and she wasn't worried. She was as safe in Lindis' voice as if she were in Sweden, too, right now.

Lindis was on the study path to be a doctor. She was shocked to hear about the arduous firefighter training. At the end of the account she sighed.

Freya hated to end that way, so she tried to seem more cheerful: "Well, I plan to read and sing my stuff someday in the cafés here when the volcanoes have quieted down. I just... don't know how long that will be. What do you think?"

Lindis said, very quietly, that she didn't know either.

After they ended the call, Freya pounded her pillow a few dozen times. Then she stared into the dark a while and let a few tears drop onto it.

**

When she was almost asleep, she remembered Ozzie and the morning call again. He was likely to think she was an idiot. But she needed someone to talk to about this latest idea of hers, and if he thought she was crazy and went away, then that would tell her something about him. And she would find someone else.

Two are better than one, she had decided. Two can solve things.

And you always must start somewhere. But how likely that he will be the kind of person who can help me? She nodded to herself: *As likely as a snowball in a sauna.*

CHAPTER THREE

OZZIE SAT HUNCHED OVER HIS PHONE in a study booth at the Academy library, flipping icons into the air with one finger and scribbling notes. Finally, some time to look into things. He had turned up the liquid lighting in the booth to cover his flying icons. If the librarian caught him, she'd demand an explanation he didn't have time for. It was the last segment of the day, Mandatory Free Study, and he had to get home for chores on time tonight. Had to be able to finish his Advanced Navigation problems in time to talk to her — to Freya. She might be nuts but she was interesting.

This morning his call to her had been cut short by the start of Advanced Navigation. "OK class, pull up your Navigational files and let's get started," Ms. Wilder had glared so meaningfully at Ozzie that he signed off, folded his phone and stowed it without thinking. But then he felt outraged by the teacher and glowered back. *How can I pay attention to Navigation right now, with my whole future on the line?*

All through the school day Ozzie chewed nervously on the tekryl On-Off button at the end of his battered laser pen, waiting to find out more from Norm. He even left his phone turned on during the lunch hour meeting of the Senior Traders Career Club.

No one in the Traders Club seemed to have heard the new word from Grand Galactic about robotics and apprenticeships. Ozzie guessed that Mr. B and Ms. Chang, the principal, were working fast to solve the school's problem — that their course of study didn't cut it in the real spacetrading world anymore — before they let the news loose. He should feel flattered that they trusted him to keep his word and not mention it, but right now he didn't care.

Ray, Lucia, Jen and Phillip, and the usual others, chattered over their sandwiches as usual, about trade route improvements and meeting extraterrestrials in person someday. All that was trivial to Ozzie, now. He kept thinking about robotics design. Even gym class and Weightlessness Training barely took his mind off it.

So now he was finding out the answer to his question: *Why?*

The article he had found in a worldweb search said the opening of Mars to trade and tourist traffic meant that trading ships would now have to deal with the wild winds and electronics of Mars, during landing, takeoffs, loading. Well, he already knew that. But the news story went on: about Grand Galactic's decision that it was a safety matter for a trader to be able to design emergency robotic systems on the fly.

Like you'd really be designing a bot in an electronic storm. It made no sense.

And that wasn't the only thing in his life that didn't make sense. It was one of the reasons he wanted to be a spacetrader: to go to the Moon, the asteroids, a thousand places — to see a million new things and end up with a way to understand them.

He sighed. *OK, no wonder robotics design has become a requirement.* It was his bad luck that the rules had to change right now.

Where is Norman-the-nerd? Ozzie sent another holotext to Norman, vowing to find another partner if he didn't hurry up.

On second thought, he checked the Jet Propulsion Lab contest site, under "Need a Contest Partner?" to see what new postings had shown up. A guy named Seth Raker had entered his name on the list of people looking for partners, a little after Norman Garcia. The postings since yesterday showed that Seth was "considering" about eight partner offers without committing to one of them. And Norman had received six or more offers since Ozzie's and exchanged schedules and phone numbers with them all. There was no message from Norman to Ozzie, though. Ozzie's heart sank.

But wait, this was odd: as he followed the messages

in order he found that all of the people who had contacted Norm were now in orbit around Seth, and he was just keeping them there hanging, waiting for his word. Not one of them was talking with Norm anymore. It seemed like Seth was playing some game. Maybe trying to force Norman to make a partner offer to him?

Weird. Time to get this plan to lift off.

A text came in from Mr. Brunelli. It invited him to come and work on the "robotics problem" today after classes were over, at 4:00 p.m. That was soon. But he wasn't going to have time for that, he thought grimly. "Can't today," he texted back.

**

"Norman?" the voice on the phone called out toward some other part of the house. The voice sounded Hispanic, a little like the rancher's wife down the road, Ms. Carmen, whose house always smelled delicious: of masa and chiles, beef and cilantro... The familiar accent was encouraging. "Norman! Your phone!"

There was a long pause. Ozzie sat on the bleachers behind the Academy, watching some wild geese flapping their way into a V-formation in front of the afternoon sun. The farm chores were waiting for him at home.

The voice spoke to Ozzie again. "I'm sorry, Norman is so hard to get out of his games sometimes...Who is calling? Ozzie?? ...Does he know you?" The voice had become cautious. Must be his mother.

"Yes, he knows me. Well, not really," Ozzie said. "I've only messaged him so far. — Thank you for helping me to reach him," he added hastily, hoping diplomacy would keep her on his side. "I'm calling about the robotics competition. He was looking for a partner. I want to help him in the contest."

"Ohhhh." Her voice warmed. "Well, Ozzie, I *think* he's coming to the phone. I *hope* so... Where do you live?" She chatted with him, trying to be friendly and mostly being motherly. One of the kids had brought her the holophone, she said, because it kept going off and no one was answering it. Ozzie could hear something sizzling on the stove, and in the background, a loud holovideo playing, two kids squabbling and an adult shushing them, then a quarrel between male voices that had a political sound... Now and then she stirred up whatever she was cooking, making it sizzle some more, and called out for Norman again.

Tonight was Dad's turn to cook. Ozzie was hungry.

There was a new burst of political squabbling, mixed with explosive noises from the holovid. Busy place there.

Finally, without any introduction: "Yeah?" That had to be Norman.

"Ozzie here. Did you get my message?"

"Uh...Think so," the guy said. He sounded like he was still deep in Level 13 of some virtual world. Ozzie recognized the symptoms. After a few seconds, Norman seemed to reconsider his answer. "Uh, what message?"

It took a while to pull him out of Level 13, but Ozzie and Norman finally connected in the real universe. Norman was astonished that Ozzie wanted to be his contest assistant when he had absolutely no robotics design experience. But Ozzie had his arguments mustered already. He had taken lots of robotics courses in school, including two years of Bot Maintenance. He was studying robotics design online. (Well, he was, wasn't he? And he would be cramming robotics from now till they met, that was for sure.) He had top marks in the spaceflight program, so he was no slacker at technologies and mechanics. He could send a letter of recommendation from his advisor, Mr. B, to confirm that.

He added that he was a hard worker with a lot of stamina. Norman was horrified and deeply sympathetic when Ozzie told about his farm chores.

And didn't Norman already have a good idea how to win the contest? (He admitted, modestly, that he did.) Therefore, Ozzie urged, the ideal assistant should be someone who could support and help execute Norman's winning idea, not someone who thought his own idea was brilliant.

Sold. He bought the plan. As Uncle Lou always said, Ozzie was a convincing salesman. At that time a sudden clashing of plates and silverware brought things to a rapid end. Offering to put Ozzie up at his house, Norman said, "Supper's ready. Talk to you in a day or two," and signed off against the background din.

The food there is probably a big improvement over Dad's and my cooking, Ozzie thought.

He made a mental note to call Norman instead of waiting to hear from him, betting that he would be imprisoned on Level 14 or 15 by tomorrow.

CHAPTER FOUR

O ZZIE DRIED THE LAST PLATE. He despised dishes even more than working in the garden, but it was his turn if Dad cooked. And he was too relieved about his deal with Norman to mind doing dishes tonight.

Dad sat at the kitchen table scowling a little, still getting over the robotics news. Ozzie had waited a day to tell him, hoping to solve the problem first.

This goal isn't just mine. Ozzie knew Dad had been proudly anticipating the day when he could see Ozzie lift off as Captain's Apprentice on the first Grand Galactic Earth-Moon-Mars merchant liner.

"Robotics design." Dad shook his head. "What a setback. I was sure you'd get that apprenticeship."

"Well, I still could." Now that he had an agreement with Norman-the-nerd, he had a chance at it again.

Ozzie had an impulse to cheer his dad up. "Want to play tonight?" Ozzie waved the dish towel in the direction of Dad's guitar, over there in the living room.

"No, probably not."

"How come?" Ozzie asked softly. *Speaking of goals, how about your own?*

"I'm out of practice. Other things to do."

Ozzie wished he could lighten things up for them both. He said, "Hey, I've met this girl."

He wasn't sure he should be talking about this at all. It was kind of private. Besides, that was *all* he had done: met her. By phone, that's all. But too late; Dad's face lit up with interest. "Well, she lives in Iceland." His man-voice broke into a kid voice a little on the upswing and he coughed to cover it.

Silence. His dad was half-smiling at him now, absently.

"*What*, Dad?" Ozzie was impatient. *Are you laughing at me?*

"I knew someone from there once."

Ozzie jealously imagined himself speaking that way someday: slow and deep.

"Interesting place." Dad added, looking at something in the air.

"Had a girlfriend there?" Ozzie goaded.

Dad snapped out of it and looked at Ozzie. "Yes. Long time ago. Before I knew your mother." And he smiled.

Ozzie couldn't help it. That particular smile always got to him. His hand went to the ring on the chain around his neck and he turned away, wishing for the hundredth time that he could tell what he knew.

Even guys with girlfriends didn't wear things like the chain, but Dad had never asked about it. At school Ozzie had smart-mouthed and even fought a few times to establish his right to not explain them to anyone. On impulse he stuffed the ring inside the neck of his shirt.

He suddenly wanted to be gone. "I'm going to the campground to talk with Malo about some things. I'll be back late." He hung the towel up deliberately. *Forget the Advanced Navigation homework. Who cares?* Then he raked his hair back with his fingertips, faced his father's curious gaze bravely for a second, took a jacket and his gun, and went out the back door.

**

The idea of talking to Malo, the leader of the campground gypsies, had come to Ozzie only because he wanted to end the conversation with Dad. But then he might just go see Malo, too. He had hours till it was time to call Freya.

Ozzie thought about Freya in Reykjavik. *I shouldn't have told her Georgie was telepathic.* But that one was too hard to resist. He grinned again. *Well, I wasn't totally lying... just mostly lying.*

He knew the campground road well enough to walk it in pitch darkness, but tonight there was a rising moon, squash-yellow and full. The rutted dirt-and-gravel road followed the dry bed of a stream that flowed only after rain or snow and ended up about a quarter mile from the house. Now the moon gleamed on the flattened sand of the stream bed.

This road belonged to Dad. After Grandpa Reed died Dad and Uncle Lou had divided Grandpa's farm, and Uncle Lou took the flat and fertile part because he liked farming. Because Dad was a musician, not a farmer, he took the house and the pretty part that wasn't good farmland to make a campground out of it.

A twig snapped near Ozzie, and he froze, raising the gun in his hand.

A fat raccoon scuttled away.

Dad and Uncle Lou had trained him to use guns and knives for defense, but so far he had never needed to. Dad once said that the world had changed, and today the risks were things that you dealt with personally, like being robbed or beaten, or having shortages of food sometimes. Outside their home areas, at least in New Mexico, people traveled armed and mostly in company, kids with adults almost always.

Ozzie knew, from years of family talk, how many other things had changed around here since Grandpa Reed was young. When the spacelines really got going in the 2020's, the missile range of the old White Sands area was bought by some investors and the White Sands Space Academy opened there. Now this valley and the next were the places where most American spaceflight companies were located. Las Cruces, which had dozed beside the Rio Grande for centuries, became a high-tech center and port city in such a short time that the older locals were never going to get used to it.

A shooting star soared upward above the trees to lose itself in the Milky Way. He couldn't help smiling, just looking at it. Not a shooting star at all, of course, going in that direction. Probably a utility launch from the spaceport, headed for the asteroids with mining equipment.

In History of Exploration, he had learned that the Space Boom was like Europe after the time of Magellan and Cortez: once the governments, with their huge treasuries, had funded the first waves of trading ships to the New World, private trading companies formed and began to take over, inventing technology and paying for exploration.

And here I am, out on the farm, standing right at the doorway to Space Valley, USA. Time for me to walk through the door and launch.

He rounded a curve and saw the familiar welcome of a small campfire, then a second fire beyond it, both of them dissolving everything around them so they floated in the darkness. They didn't seem to exist in real space, but he knew that from this curve they were about a hundred yards away.

The fires had been there like signposts all his life, marking the roadway. He had helped out here since he was a kid, becoming an expert at cleaning bathrooms, hauling trash, and checking the wooded spots to report wood snitching. He heard this was like the campgrounds outside most big cities — a place for the ten percent of the population that was always in motion. They were workers following the harvests, war veterans, refugees from unstable countries, students off to see the world, and sometimes just people looking for something... To him it was like another dimension.

Nearing the fires, Ozzie pocketed his gun and felt the other side of his jacket for the knife.

**

Malo motioned him closer.

Malo's old cow was tied to a stake near a tree. Wash hung from a line. The gypsy tents were pitched in a circle around the first fire because the gypsies were the first and most respected residents here, the unofficial leaders and peacekeepers among the campground people. A few people were seated at the fire, but it was quiet except for the flapping sound of the flames and the popping of sap in the firewood.

"You came to talk," Malo said when Ozzie was near. It was a statement, not a question. His dark eyes reflected the flames.

"I guess I did," Ozzie decided. He paused. No shows of courtesy were required by the gypsies, but among themselves it was customary to look quietly at the person you addressed as if you were taking them in, before you spoke much. Most of the local Anglos thought that was creepy. Ozzie didn't mind. He and Malo looked at each other for half a minute.

Then Ozzie began: "What do you know about telepathic cats?"

Malo's eyebrows raised. He smiled. He walked to the fire, pulled a coffee pot off an old grate, and filled two mugs so they steamed. "Cream?" he asked. He poured and stirred cream from a bottle into both slowly, handing Ozzie his. Even in the firelight, which robbed colors, the cream was yellow with butterfat. Probably from this morning's milking. No refrigerators out here.

He and Malo sat cross-legged on the ground, cradling their mugs, sipping the rich brew and watching the fire. Ozzie knew from experience that he should wait.

After a while a black and gray tabby cat walked out of the darkness, sat in the firelight near Malo, and began to lick a front paw. It moved its head in an oval pattern as if that was the way to get the right cleansing effect.

"String, this is Ozzie," Malo said. The cat paused. It licked one more time, a leisurely lick. Then it stopped and looked directly at Ozzie.

[Delighted], String said. Ozzie stared. The cat's mouth hadn't moved. Ozzie turned to Malo.

Malo chided, "You didn't answer her. You'd better."

"Pleased to meet you also," Ozzie said, hastily. He was so stunned his voice squeaked on the end. He coughed politely. "Malo? How did he talk to me?"

"She. She did it the usual way: telepathically. Now, I called String first because she is the easiest to hear and to speak to. She heard you say the words, but this time say it telepathically. Say it to her in your mind."

[Pleased to meet you,] Ozzie thought. She nodded her head once, deliberately, then began to lick the other paw. "So you called her here telepathically?" he asked Malo.

Malo nodded.

Weird. Considering that, Ozzie sipped his coffee and gazed at sparks spiraling upward for a while.

When he looked downward again, String seemed to have disappeared but a new cat was prowling back and forth before the fire — an orange tabby, with white where the stripes looked like they had been blotted off. "Raina, this is Ozzie," Malo said.

Raina stopped pacing, looked at Ozzie and then away, looked at Malo, and paced again. Malo nudged Ozzie.

Ozzie opened his mouth, shut it, and thought at the cat, [Pleased to meet you.]

Raina stopped mid-stride and looked at Ozzie for a few seconds. [The pleasure is mine.]

He heard it! Not as loud as String, but he knew he had really heard it. [Thank you,] Ozzie thought politely in return. He turned and raised his eyebrows at Malo, seeking instructions.

Malo nodded approval. Raina was already prowling away.

"Now," Malo said, "one more thing." He sipped

41

meditatively for a little, so Ozzie did the same.

When Ozzie's cup was nearly empty, a pair of cats slipped like shadows out of the nearest tent — Malo's tent, Ozzie guessed, although he had never been invited inside. He had always imagined Malo's place to be filled with the smells of exotic spices, hung with ornate rugs, lit by brass lamps.

Both cats were black except for blazes of white. One wore the blaze on its forehead, the other on its chest. Chest-Blaze ran off after something in the trees. Forehead-Blaze walked to a spot about a yard in front of Ozzie's knees and sat facing him calmly.

An image came to Ozzie: he was leaping from a tree. He hadn't been thinking about trees or leaping, so this was odd. Malo said, "What message did you get?"

Oh: it was from the cat. "Leaping from a tree," he reported, intrigued.

"Yes," Malo said. "Good. Now another."

Ozzie listened again, watching the perfectly still cat. At least it seemed perfectly still — its heart must be beating, but not a hair seemed to move.

"It said, 'There is a mouse in a burrow beneath the third tree,'" Ozzie reported, without thinking at all this time. He scowled. *Wait. How do I know that?*

Malo grinned, looking at the cat intently. "Is that correct, Star?"

Star melted from a black statue into a thick stream of black that flowed to Malo, purring as it rubbed against his knees. His fingers scratched her back deeply and she accepted the attention luxuriously.

Malo smiled. His teeth were very white. "Good work, Ozzie. Now you know all I know about telepathic cats."

He stood, took Ozzie's empty cup from his hands, and sort of flowed away into his tent. The others around the fire seemed to have melted away some time ago. The gypsies were like cats, Ozzie thought. They never made much of leaving or goodbyes.

Then the thought struck him: *maybe I was telling the truth after all about Georgie.* What if that cat really *had* been trying to talk to him all this time?

CHAPTER FIVE

I T WAS MIDNIGHT and the moon sailed high above him. He had returned to the bright sand of the stream bed to put the bordering screen of trees between him and the campground for privacy. And the open space here was protection from surprises. The night was mild so he lay on the sand that was still warm from today's sun, as if he were getting a moon-tan. He was puzzling about cats when her call came in.

Freya started off at a run. Her voice, he realized, sounded a little like a young boy's. Her English was good. Not perfect, but she was a whole lot better at it than he would be at Icelandic.

She had been having strange dreams. And her cat stayed close beside her often, gazing into her eyes as if he wanted to speak to her. Recently she had actually heard him.

Ozzie felt a little guilty about Georgie. Were there messages from Georgie that he had ignored?

But she must back up and tell more of the story, she said. She told him about firefighting and why she had left school — because of the volcanoes, two new ones this year. Had he heard about those two?

Yes. But when he did, the new Icelandic volcanoes were just a geological wonder, without emotion. Now that they contained fear and pain for someone he knew, they became vivid and toothy with evil.

She was frightened for her homeland but also... She read a lot, she said, poetry and legends from all over the world, and philosophy. When the volcanoes began to frighten her, she had studied more, read most of the Reykjavik library on the subject of geology and studied on the worldweb, holoposted to ask everywhere for knowledge. "Because something is wrong. Iceland is most vulnerable, because the earth's mantle there is thin and new, but this problem threatens the geophysics of the whole planet." She paused.

"Do you see what I mean?" she said.

Suddenly unwilling to be caught seeming dumb, Ozzie said firmly, "Yes. Yes, I do."

"Good," she breathed. "Have you heard of the Lost Continent of Atlantis?" she asked. "And the Great Flood?"

"Heard of them," Ozzie said cautiously.

She continued with her tale: There had been psychics for centuries who had visions about Atlantis and the Flood. The most recent two were an aborigine guy in Australia and a Lakota Sioux from America, who both had similar dreams and spoke about how the mighty continent of Atlantis sank into the ocean thousands of years ago, causing the Great Flood. "You know the flood that many legends talk about — the one that Noah's Ark happened in?"

"Sure, yeah," Ozzie said. *At least I think so. Better check the worldweb on it.*

On went her story. This aborigine and the Lakota shaman said that there was a lot of technology in Atlantis, although people today think we are the first inventors of sophisticated electronic technology. Atlantis had it, before the planet was sent back to the stone age. And Lemuria had it — a big continent where the Pacific is now. Because of crystals or electronics of some kind, vibrations were created that caused the earth to resonate too, on a dangerous frequency that began to break and tear the earth's crust, causing earthquakes that became too much.

"Then, the Earth's crust heaved like a shook blanket," she said. "So Atlantis and Lemuria went under, the American continents rose more, the floods were huge. Those who survived were those who took to boats and stayed afloat. The native people of the Americas were mostly Atlanteans who made it. But Atlanteans had no understanding of their own technology, so all the technology went down into the ocean with the continent and the only people who survived on the lands were those who were smart enough to learn to live with the earth, as hunters and farmers."

She paused again. Ozzie was silent.

She was really something else. He had never heard more concentrated thought process out of any one person in his life, not even his father. And Dad thought a lot.

"I am sorry to blurb this out at you," she said. "To say so much all at once. I feel like I need to hurry, you know?"

He assured her that he knew. That he didn't mind. And he really didn't — he could listen to her for a long time without being bored. He added, helpfully, "that's 'blurt,' too, not 'blurb.' You say, 'Blurt this out.'"

"Blurt. Thank you," she said, and rushed on.

It was worrisome, she said. The technology that was being used had dangers that had not been put through proper testing. They seemed to harm some species, and it was possible that the volcanoes, too, were a result of microwave technologies or other vibrations that were being created by electronics or mining or oil exploration.

She had written and called the Icelandic government, but they were sure that her idea couldn't be right because they were following studies done by Berkford and Oxbridge that said it was impossible.

She had learned that there were technologies to make people and living things safe by realigning unharmonious vibrations, by re-routing the noisy waves from electronics into the ground, and other things. The problem here was that the ground itself was being injured, not just living things. And none of the solutions she had found were big enough to cancel out disruptions that were so big they caused volcanoes.

Ozzie couldn't think of a thing to say.

"Maybe you already knew about this part?" she offered politely.

"No, no. This is interesting," he said, thinking, **You** *are interesting. The most interesting person I've ever met, even more interesting than Malo.*

She breathed again, a relieved sound. Then she plunged on. She had researched the earth's crust then, studying how electromagnetism and microwaves affected it.

The representatives of her government had been kindly, but not not helpful. She had written to Paris, to the headquarters of UNESCO, the United Nations Educational, Scientific and Cultural Organization, asking if they could look into it. No answer. Another volcano since then. She was becoming frightened.

"Couldn't you leave Iceland for safety?" he asked. Immediately he knew that was the wrong thing to say.

"Leave Iceland!" her voice flew at him with its teeth bared, waving a Viking sword. "It's my home!" and then more gently, "But don't you see? This tearing of the crust only begins at Iceland. It will affect much more, I'm sure of it. Look what happened with Atlantis."

He told her he saw what she meant. He considered all

this for a few moments, doubtful that it would happen as she described. That it could be that bad. But then he sighed, feeling sorry for her distress, anyway. He said, "So what will you do?"

She named the things she had tried: contacting technology companies, asking for responsible testing. Contacting officials of the US Government, formerly the seat of advanced thinking in the world. No replies.

She then began to study vibration and the effects of energy waves. Back to the library, the worldweb, holoposts... "Then I thought of music," she said.

Music? Ozzie sat up. The moon had moved about a thumb's width across the sky. Her voice was so interesting, but it was making him feel safe, or at rest — or something else that was just as unfamiliar to him. He was sure he had fallen asleep. *Music?* He was lost. "Hmmm," he said, trying to seem thoughtful, to buy time. *How did we get onto music?*

"Music is waves also, see?" she said. "Sound waves can affect animals and plants too. So maybe music affects the crust of the earth as well, I was thinking." And that, she said, was when her cat, Banzai, began to talk to her. Just two nights ago he said something she could really understand clearly, for the first time.

"He said I needed to find out about Osiris," she said.

Ozzie blinked. *Osiris.*

But this girl was a research freak. Armed with that clue she had started hunting again on the worldweb, in the library, studying Osiris.

"According to legend Osiris tamed the floods and turned Egypt into a great civilization. For that the Egyptians called him a god. I'm still trying to find out what exactly he did," she concluded.

It was like a bedtime story to Ozzie, who was in fact sleepy by now. This one was a tall tale with heroes, flaming lava, towering floods, and mighty deeds. Told by this voice on his phone, an entrancing voice tinted with the longing accent of the Nordic world that he recalled from old flat-films. In his imagination the longing was for days gone by, and heroic deeds, and for freedom.

And the voice belonged to a ginger-haired girl in Reykjavik. He savored his good fortune — just to have her talking to him.

"Ozzie?" He returned to earth and found that he was sitting in the moonlight smiling idiotically to himself. "Ozzie. I must go train now... I have to go soon. Again tomorrow?" she urged.

"Sure," he agreed. Why not? Maybe she was his girlfriend now, and she would come to visit him in New Mexico, where his friends could be amazed and jealous when they met her.

After they had signed off, he walked sleepily home down the moonlit stream bed, and in his imagination, he was a merchant prince, captain of his own ship, trading in minerals and treasure from the asteroids, Mars and the moon — and she was his brave consort, who traveled the vast reaches of space with him and dined in his cabin each night.

CHAPTER SIX

WHEN DO WE START FIGHTING the *real* fires?" Freya said in exasperation to the fire company captain. Another long day ahead, hauling hoses.

"Soon enough," he said, and shook his head grimly at her. His eyes seemed to be measuring her against something. "Freya. All of you. This morning there is steam coming out of Hengill, to the southeast. Do you know how long that one has been cold?" Freya's mouth opened in horror. He tapped the training room display screen. It lit in response to his touch, with the day's volcano news streaming on it.

But she already knew the answer to his question: *Hengill has been cold for all of Iceland's recorded history.*

**

All morning Freya pulled hoses like a madwoman, frightened and angry at the people who knew too much to find out why this was really happening.

Arni joined their team in the afternoon. He had volunteered to return home to Iceland, his birthplace, from Sweden, where he had worked as a firefighter for two years. He was maybe 19 or 20, big, ruddy, and cheerful. His eyes twinkled at Freya without any apology. He joked easily with the older men.

For her he was an antidote for Hengill. His confidence made her worry less. The hoses seemed lighter when he was around.

**

Freya arrived home filthy. Mamma seemed to be unaware of the news about Hengill steaming 25 kilometers away. Even when Freya told her, she shook her head as if she couldn't be bothered with such things.

So Freya showered and dressed, and spent a rushed hour helping to cook Mamma's specialties for her new portrait customer, followed by a "visit" with the man that was every bit as mind-numbing as Freya had predicted it would be. How could this man be such an idiot that he was thinking of his portrait when lava was brewing in a gigantic kettle only twenty-five kilometers from here?

**

At the end of supper she drank chamomile tea because her mother insisted. It gave her an excuse to plead that she was sleepy and leave the table, but still her muscles ached and she slept restlessly.

Vague dreams nagged at her, in which lava churned and volcanoes opened their relentless mouths. She fell, then, into a deep black sleep, one that she shared with dead things only: long-ago ancestors, ancient heroes and demons, and she was ancient like them, all old and dead in a dead and frozen earth.

Then it thawed again and steamed like the hot pots, became a deep well, and she swam upward out of the dark pool where the demons and dragons were. And she dreamed something as clear as a holovid:

It was night and she felt sharply how young she was and how lighthearted. The air was sweet with blossoms and full of insect songs, the boom and hiss of the flying creatures, the sound of water in the irrigation ditches as she and her lifetime friend walked together by the city wall. Like distant singing, there was a throbbing beneath the sounds that was woven through all of them.

Her friend was now her love...

She was surrounded by the beauties of the place, the music everywhere, the iron-reddened soil, the thick green leaves and feathered ferns, the grace of winged lizards and the songs of the small lighted dragon insects that put magic into the nights. All of it was like an old song that was laden with the memories attached to it by long use, full of the spirit of the once-living...

Freya woke. Her insides were twisting with painful confusion. She was lost. Who was she?

When she smelled the old wood and stone of her room she knew herself again. She was not really the owner of this dream; it couldn't be hers. Nothing in it was familiar. Even the music in the dream was just an idea of music — nothing she could really hear.

So why was she dreaming it?

Beside her head on the pillow, she heard Banzai's whirring breath and smelled the whiff of fish he wore around his mouth.

CHAPTER SEVEN

H E WALKED EAGERLY toward the campground, anticipating her call.

Tonight the sandy stream bed shone whitely when there were spaces between the streaming silver clouds that slid across the moon.

To avoid discussions, Ozzie had pretended to turn in for the night and then eased quietly out of the house after Dad turned out the lights. He was riding on an adrenaline wave following the triumphant deal with Norman and last night's conversation with Freya. He anticipated more of her tale tonight: what luck. Things were looking up again.

She called at a few minutes after midnight. — Six a.m. for her, and she had just managed to wake for work, she said. Her voice sounded blurred. "Not sleeping right. Crazy dreams," she reported. "And you?"

Ozzie told her, then, about his day. His week. In fact, since she hadn't asked yet, about his life: his dream and his training to be a trading-vessel captain. "And the best jobs are in space travel and space trade these days," he said. He told her about the robotics problem, and about his exciting solution to the problem, a partnership with Norman Garcia.

"So," he finished grandly, "someday soon I'll be trading on the Earth-Moon-Mars route, rich as a king, living like a gypsy." He smiled happily to himself at the idea.

Maybe he expected her to volunteer to ship out with him as a merchant prince's consort, bound for a life of excitement. Or hint that she'd like an invitation to tour the asteroids. Maybe he thought she would admire his ambitious plans. He wasn't sure what he expected. But what she said was a surprise to him, anyway.

She said tiredly, "Ozzie, I need your help. Something has to be done about the volcanoes before it's too late. It's too hard for one person. Two together — we could figure it out, I think. You are smart and you aren't afraid. Will you help me?"

"Well, I need to go get the robotics know-how to get that apprenticeship on the Earth-Moon-Mars Galactic line before someone else grabs it up. Then I'll be glad to help you. I'll help you while I do it, in fact. If I can."

"Thank you. But see, Ozzie, maybe you won't have an apprenticeship, or even a spaceport to take off from, if the volcanoes go as fast as it seems they will. The frequency of new activity is increasing. Yesterday, an old Pacific volcano began to flow again. It's not just my country that is at risk. Isn't this more important right now?"

Ozzie was tempted in spite of himself. Her plea was fascinating, and so was she.

But who said she was right? Just her opinion against the whole scientific world?

"I can't, Freya," he heard himself say, as if from a big distance. *Forget my plans? She must be nuts.*

And from a distance he heard her say stubbornly, "But maybe you could, Ozzie."

He mustered all his salesmanship and tried to fascinate her in return. He told her about the ancient stone buildings and tunnels on the moon that were being explored a little more each year by lunar archeologists. And about the ruins of ancient cities on Mars, the teams who were just starting to map them, and the newly-found fossils of giant plants and animals there. How could she not be drawn by these wonders? But he felt her ebbing further and further away. He fought against the tide to hold her here, now with exciting tales about mineral treasures on the asteroids.

"I have to go, Ozzie," she said. "Time to go train." And then, sadly, "Let me know if you change your mind, huh?" And she was gone.

**

He stumbled a little on some roots as he left the streambed to cut through the trees to the road. He felt as if he had lost something valuable.

But what? It didn't make sense to be chasing after this girl's idea, which could be totally a delusion, when he had good things going here: the chance at a real ship and the best, most exciting life anyone could ask for.

CHAPTER EIGHT

TODAY IT WAS FIREBOAT TRAINING. The boat was a made-over fishing tub fitted with pumps to pull in water and equipped with water cannon, high and low, to spray at fires and act as thrusters. Freya was running the side-thrusters to keep the boat in position so the rest of the crew could shoot water cannons at a target, an unused storage shed in New Harbor.

She kept the fireboat steady in the water, standing in the stern between two hydraulic levers and shooting water behind her on both sides in streams like ski poles. She used them to balance the boat and push it forward against the back-thrust caused by the high cannons.

Water was something she was good at, and for the first time in this training program she was enjoying herself. It was a welcome relief from the heavy carrying, chopping, and hose-hauling of the last few days.

She needed more rest, she knew it. She would just get

through this day. Maybe she could sleep long tonight.

She saw herself in the past, swimming all day and all night at the summer solstice parties. *How long ago? Just a year.* She felt old and tired now.

Ozzie whatever-his-name-was. He doubted her ideas about the danger of the volcanoes. *Who wouldn't, when no one else in the world seems to agree with me?*

And maybe she was wrong, after all. Maybe, as some scientists said, this was just a little wave of volcanic activity that would taper off as it had begun and all would be well. She imagined Iceland calm again, with its raw beauty and hot pots, but no threats from lava.

The men guiding the forward cannons shouted about a good hit, then called back to her to cheer her on. She shouted "Nice one!" and nodded big so they could see her through the spray.

She pictured that Ozzie-person in his American school, learning about exciting things, preparing for his future. She recalled holovids about American teenagers, who always seemed to be having fun, even though the rest of the world was struggling these days. Racing their aircars. Hang-gliding across the mountains. Suddenly she longed to be able to go have fun in America where there were no eruptions — maybe escape forever from volcanoes and the doom they seemed to predict.

Salty spray stung her eyes and she shook her head hard to clear them, squinting ahead through the bright mist at the target. An ocean liner's wake had hit the fireboat and it rocked deeply in the waves. She lost her hold on one handle. She grabbed at it, but it swung wildly away from her grasp, and the boat rocked even further the other way. Fear shot through her; what if she let it capsize?

Straining to hold with her right hand, she pulled with all her might to reach the left handle. Again the boat rocked crazily. The men at the bow shouted in alarm. The handle reversed and struck pain into her hand as it swung by. She was losing her footing on the wet deck.

Fiercely she slapped at the handle on its next swing, and barely got hold of it with her fingertips, drawing it into her palm by sheer will. She hauled with all her might, leaned left and leaned right, pulling the levers to steady the boat, then held her rear thrusters in balance again so the boat stayed pointed at the storage shed.

Her heart was slowing down. She watched more carefully now. But stubbornly she continued to go over what she had studied and what she had concluded, running it backwards and forwards, looking for holes in her thought.

By the time the wake of the liner passed beyond them, Freya had decided again that it must be true: *We are in danger,* she thought sadly. *And Iceland is worst but no part of the world will be the same if the earth's crust ever really starts to break.*

**

Ozzie put his wrench down and gazed out at the purple and blue San Andres Mountains at the edge of the plain. He dragged his fingers back through his hair. Around him, 40 jumpsuited students were scattered over a few acres of fused-sand plexi surface, each working on the air system of a small shuttlecraft. They stood, or crawled over, or stuck out of, or like him, were sitting beside, their Senior Mechanics projects — their personal shuttles for the semester.

His course tablet displayed the lesson "Advanced Mechanics: Shuttle Maintenance. Unit 2, Air System Maintenance and Repair." The morning sun was bright and hot on the back of his black jumpsuit. He rummaged through his tool kit — it was really his own, a gift from Uncle Lou's family last year — and found the needle-nosed pliers. He hand-adjusted a few switches to new settings so he could open up this part of the system.

His phone signalled.

It was Norman-the-nerd from Pasadena! Ozzie flipped open the phone sheet as he moved to the side of his craft away from the instructor, and hit the Voice Only button for speed.

"Hey," Norman said. There was no noise coming from his house this time. But his holo ID showed up and there he was, frozen in a big soft knit shirt, sweats and running shoes, and a grin. His hair was rumpled.

"Hey," Ozzie echoed. Not certain how much time they'd have, he didn't wait to ask: "Norman, know a guy named Seth Raker?"

"Call me Norm, OK? Yeah, I know him," he said without joy. "He's the competition. According to the people who love to predict these things, I look like I'm tied with Seth for third place. Do you know him?"

"Tied? Why third place?"

"I dunno. I guess because there are a couple of very brilliant geeks who are predicted to win first and second," Norm said. His wise-guy voice matched the smile on the holo.

"But we want first, don't we?"

"Sure, I guess. But for me, all I care about is getting a scholarship to engineering school. My family can't pay for it, I know *that*. If I go to engin school I can get a top-flight job as a corporate robotics guru, maybe get a job at the Moon colony, so they pay me the big bucks and I can buy all the toys I want. Also maybe buy my mom a big house, like the rock stars do."

He didn't ask what Ozzie wanted. What Ozzie wanted was so huge to him at that moment that he couldn't say it anyway.

But it occurred to him that he wasn't sure how *much* robotics experience it would take to get him that spot on the first Grand Galactic Earth-Moon-Mars flight. First place in the Jet Propulsion Lab competition ought to do it, he guessed.

"Well," he said, "What do you need to do, to get a scholarship to engineering school?"

"Not much, to be honest," Norm yawned. "I've already got two offers that are hinting that they'll pay all my college costs, based on my record. They're saying that placing at JPL this year should clinch it. So third is fine. Especially if it means I beat out that jerk Seth."

Shooting for third will get you fourth, Ozzie thought. *And no one has promised you any scholarship yet... Maybe this guy hasn't touched down in the real world recently.* "OK, let's shoot for the top," Ozzie said. "Have you started any work?" Ozzie doubted it.

"Not really," Norm said. "But I've actually been working on this in my head since last year — I took second last year — and I have such a good idea that I didn't think I even needed a partner. But then they made it *mandatory.*"

Ozzie had to work to keep the relief out of his voice. Second place! Not bad. And at least Norm was thinking about it. "Great, man. Let's talk more about your idea soon. When do you want me out there? —No, wait, text me. Instructor's coming!"

**

When supper was over that night, Ozzie turned from the dishes to look for a minute at Dad, who was sitting at the kitchen table going through the day's mail. Things were scattered on the table top: a notice about local irrigation rights in bold letters, a letter that might have been from that cousin of his in Colorado, bills and a seed catalog and a livestock magazine. Next to it was a pile of paper money and coins, weekly fees from the campground residents. Beyond him, in the living room, his guitar was propped against a chair. It hadn't moved in months.

"Dad."

"Yeah?"

"That woman in Iceland that you knew before Mom. Did you sing with her?"

Dad gave him a look, but all he said was "Yes."

"And Mom, did you sing with her?"

Another long look. "No, I never did." His head turned slowly toward the guitar in the living room and he studied it with his hawk-like, stubborn gaze as if it had just gone three-dimensional. When he looked back at Ozzie, his eyes seemed to say, "What a surprise, to find a guitar here."

Ozzie blinked. Something had just happened but he couldn't say what.

He pushed back his hair. "I need to go to California pretty soon." He tried to make it casual, as if he always went to California or somewhere. Actually, he'd only been out of New Mexico once that he remembered, for an Academy field trip to Denver. Dad said that when he was young, ordinary people travelled more. Even more, when Grandpa Reed was young. It was another thing that had changed; the world seemed to have been a little messy for a few decades.

Ozzie explained about how the contest launch was October first, and how Norm's mother had invited him to stay at their house in Pasadena. They would need to work together on Norm's design to have it ready for the competition judging in mid-December. As his advisor, Mr. B was arranging his leave of absence from school, "and I'll finish my Last Year work in spring and summer terms, Dad, then do my exams and final projects. I got Benjie Lopez to take over managing the school store from now on. He's excited about it."

Dad had probably overheard bits of planning already. He must have known this was coming. But he just nodded and looked at Ozzie. "Norm's mother promised I could do chores there to pay for my food," Ozzie said, "so she says we don't have to give her any money. They have younger kids I can maybe tutor, and a yard that needs work, and house-painting..." Dad nodded again. "I can use my savings for the train ticket." Another nod.

"Oh!" It suddenly came to Ozzie. "My chores here. Let's see...I'll talk with Qualen in the campground. Maybe I could pay him for it a little at a time..."

"No," Dad said. "I can do the chores till you get back." He continued to look at Ozzie.

"*What*, Dad?" Ozzie was impatient. *I can't read your mind.*

"Just impressed by your plan," he said. "Mr. Brunelli called me earlier and said he was too. Give me Norm's mother's number. I'll call her, just to... say hello."

CHAPTER NINE

D ON'T YOU NEED A BREAK FROM IT?" Britta said. Freya looked up from her holosheet and saw the two older girls, Britta and Grindl, watching her with amusement.

The girls were friendly enough. But instead of joining their chatter at lunch each day she read the geophysical reports on her phone, plastering the holosheet onto the lunchroom table as she ate each day.

Freya just shrugged. *They seem to be oblivious to the actual danger they're fighting. It's like a game of sand-volleyball to them.*

Freya's legs and back ached less than yesterday; she was growing stronger and sturdier. Arni, the new guy, joined them at the table and flashed his handsome grin. She was drawn to him like hunger. His eyes seemed to promise something — maybe safety. He smiled and leaned toward Freya as if he was about to say something.

Her "lunch call" rang in, a distraction that she found she was looking forward to each day. She shrugged apologetically at her table mates and left to sit outside on the cement steps.

It was sunny there, breezy and cool. This old building, and the ones across from it, were worn but clean. She was fond of this part of Reykjavik, on which the city's history of wool and fish, shipbuilding and trading were written.

She had accidentally met a new friend — although Freya still didn't know how the holopost had come to her. The day after she talked with Ozzie, her phone showed a post from Alexis Wu, a British girl who had never heard from a cat at all. She was just looking around for a way to get some major robotics experience to help her get ready for a career. Freya passed on what she knew from Ozzie: about the Jet Propulsion Lab contest, his partner Norm, and people who were posting to find partners. Alexis didn't waste any time finding out more.

They had texted or talked, after that, for the last several days. About Mamma and the renters, about firefighting, about Alexis' school. Alexis lived with her parents, several younger kids, and her uncle and aunt's family in a reclaimed row house in a rough part of London. A house that had a little courtyard garden, like Freya's house did, and a cat.

"I am *deluged* with homework for tonight," she said today. "At least I can do some on the way home, on the lightrail."

Freya thought of how long ago school seemed to her already. "Homework is a part of school that I don't miss."

"Shocking to me that you have finished school with no university plans," Alexis said. She had a piping Britishy voice. "But so brave of you. My family insists that I study hard to do better. You know, the old Asian-parents thing." She added, "I've won an award or two! But they won't be happy till I get a fat job for some corporation and make lots of money for the family.

"—And of course it's my duty to," she added hastily. "But I have a bit of rebellion, also." Her act of independence was holotexting all over the world. "We came from China when I was one. They say it's unsafe to talk freely to strangers, but it makes me feel safer to know people everywhere! —You know what? My parents only got themselves and me out of China alive because of the kindness of a 'friend' who didn't really even know them. It's weird that they still distrust strangers."

Freya told about her day: chronic fright but nothing new, just more and more rumbling underground. She couldn't expect Alexis to understand how scary.

"Hey, Freya, good news. They've let me in!" The story followed. She had arranged with a robotics contest entrant, Seth somebody, to be his assistant. "And the letter came today!"

It took a little work to get through all her modest dodging, but Freya learned that she had not only applied to enter the Jet Propulsion Lab contest with her new partner, she had also requested a scholarship to help her with travel and lodging so she could be in California for the months of work leading up to the contest. The letter said that it all would be covered because of her "excellent scholarship and competitive success" in England. Freya thought of Alexis traveling to California, where Ozzie would be, and she felt a little left behind.

"Good work, Alexis!" she said anyway.

"It's kind of horrifying," Alexis confided. "I'll be in America, competing against rich, bright kids who probably know everything there is to know about robotics. But I want to go anyway. Because even if I lose — and I probably would have no chance of winning, so it's good that I'll just be this guy's assistant — just competing in the contest will help me to land a better job in Britain. As long as I don't make embarrassing mistakes while I'm losing." She giggled.

Freya had never known anyone who actually giggled.

CHAPTER TEN

MR. BRUNELLI CALLED OZZIE INTO HIS OFFICE to say that the leave from school had finally been approved, including Ozzie's robotics study program in California for extra credits toward graduation. Mr. B would be telling the other students about the Robotics Problem tomorrow, now that the school had created new courses to get the younger grades prepared for the new requirements. He sighed. "But for the ones in their last year, your class, all hell is going to break loose. They're going to be scrambling, just like you." Ozzie shook the hand Mr B. offered him.

**

He traded the antique 15-speed bike in the barn to some of the campground gypsies for a sleeping bag, in pretty good shape, and a real good backpack.

Before Ozzie left the camp, the news of his plans had already reached Malo — without a ripple of obvious conversation anywhere. *Are the gypsies telepathic?* Ozzie wondered. Malo came out of his tent to wish him good luck.

**

It was before dawn when Dad drove Ozzie into Las Cruces in the aircar to catch the U.S. Rail for Los Angeles. Georgie made an astonishing fuss about wanting to get in the car and go too. Georgie hated cars, usually. While Ozzie tried to remove her, she yowled miserably and clung to the truck seat with her claws, hissing at Ozzie. In spite of her protests, she was left behind.

**

An actual journey somewhere. It felt like good medicine. *Going to California alone is exciting, even if I just went and bought a burger or something and came back.* But it was better than that. He was going to learn to be a robotics genius and keep his claim to the apprenticeship. Anticipation made him impatient as he watched the conductors prepare the train to leave. *Let's go.*

This train route had been built thirty years ago, at the start of the Space Boom, as a commuter channel to and from Los Angeles. That made it one of the newest rail lines in the country. Ozzie had heard one of the local farmers tell his dad that the roads and rail systems and public transportation were being maintained, in spite of funding shortages, as a final attempt by the national government to prove how much it was needed. But many of the roads had already been taken over by state or local governments, like the highways in New Mexico and Nevada. In Europe all of them had been, the man said, and there were more toll roads. "Let the ones who use 'em, pay for 'em," he said.

The guy in the next seat was snoring softly. Ozzie put his earbuds in. With only about 15 days till the contest launch, he needed to be ready and there was so much he had to learn — so he could do something to help Norm that was worth getting credit for. He had loaded advanced robotics texts and a science dictionary on his notebook. He took out his holosheet and spread it on his knee to help with the 3D illustrations, then settled deeper into the reclining seat to study.

The ring-tone of his phone startled him. Maybe Dad? Did he leave something behind? "No Caller ID," the case display said. Weird. There it was again. He almost took the call, out of curiosity, but then the train started.

He looked out the window to see if he should wave at Dad as the train pulled out. He couldn't see him from this side.

The cars curved away ahead of him for a hundred yards or more, and they had begun to move. As a kid Ozzie had watched trains leaving this station. He had ridden one to Denver, but that was one of the vintage models. This train was slick: shining silver, as beautifully aerodynamic as a spacecraft.

He turned on his player and sighed. It was tempting to think about spending the whole time looking out the window at the Arizona desert, but he had things to study. Ozzie had forgotten that the train went 180 miles per hour, so he couldn't see much anyway. It was just a blur.

CHAPTER ELEVEN

S OOT HAD BLACKENED EVERYTHING, even her eyelids. After a day fighting practice fires, Freya was barely able to strip off her charcoal-dusted clothes and shower before she fell into bed and into another fathomless sleep. After hours of dark unconsciousness, she rose toward the surface again. And again she dreamed.

She sang to him and he sang back to her. There were others all around them, but she saw only him. The place was draped with flowering vines. Small lamps hung from curving poles. The night was dark and warm; the lighted lizards were still flying. This was the Ceremony of the Moons, and it made their lifetime friendship sacred. They would live together and be a pair for the rest of their lives. Life was for two, the saying went.

Like her, he was a singer of stories. His voice

harmonized with hers. He wore a flat, curved yoke of woven greenery around his neck on his bare chest, as a symbol of ongoing life. She held a shimmering phosphor flower and an ankh in her hands.

Their happiness was huge. It seemed that it could never end...

She woke smiling in the darkness. Then she felt the comforter cool against her cheek and shook her head a little to clear it. *Another one. Whose dream is this?*

As before, the music had no notes. It was just an idea of singing. And the ankh? She saw it vividly again: a rod with a small loop at the top and a crosspiece where the rod met the loop. She had seen ankhs in holovids about ancient Egypt. The place in the dream must be Egypt, in some long-ago time... But it still seemed to her that she was being given someone else's dream to dream.

Banzai sat beside her head, his determined purr rumbling in her ear.

Now that she was awake Freya sat up and checked her phone. There was a late text in from Arni: "Want to go to the Belna Café this weekend?"

Today she had talked with Arni about her volcano research and the cat. He laughed at the idea that the cat talked to her. "You are such a bright one, doing all this study," he admired and teased at the same time. "And your cat is lucky that you listen to him so hard."

She would answer tomorrow. She'd better do more

research this weekend instead. That's all she would be thinking about anyway.

Freya lay back, needing to sleep. She closed her eyes and saw Arni. Then Ozzie, and she heard his voice. She was lonely, wishing someone could help her with an answer to the volcanoes.

A message rang in — another response to her holopost about the cats.

There had been answers from many people. Some of them just wanted to go out with her. "Got a place where I can stay in Reykjavik?" one texted. "I hear it's a party city!"

My beautiful city. Maybe it once was, she thought miserably. *But I'm too tired and obsessed to party now, even if it was the most fun party on earth.*

The message showing now was from Marvin, in Edinburgh, who had eight cats and six of them talked to him, he said. She took the call.

CHAPTER TWELVE

C OMPARED TO OZZIE'S TOO-QUIET HOUSE in New Mexico, Norm's place in Pasadena was bedlam.

Outside, the house had salmon-colored stucco walls and a roof with curved tiles. There were palm trees and flowers sunning themselves in the yard even now, in late September. Very peaceful out there. But the living room, where Ozzie's couch sat, was noisy from 7:00 a.m. till about midnight.

It took getting used to, but it was friendly.

Jet Propulsion Laboratory, nearby, would be holding the contest launch event in a little over a week, on October first. He had been here in Pasadena for a week and already the pressure was on. He slept on the couch with the dog and worked with Norm in the evenings after Norm returned from school.

He was starting to like having Norm's little brothers crawl all over his back like puppies to wake him in the morning. And the uncles and aunts who stopped in at all hours to talk or borrow things or bring food. And Norm's sisters, ten and twelve, who smiled at him shyly, asked questions and listened politely, and (most wondrous of all, to him) did the dishes, tended the backyard chickens and weeded the vegetable garden themselves. Without him.

Partly to protect himself from any close encounters with dishes or weeding vegetables, Ozzie insisted on being put to work right after Norm left for school on the first day. No, he didn't need to rest. Yes, he had important robotics things to think about, but he could think while he worked.

Norm's mother wagged her head at him in wonder and pleasure, and sent him out to mow, lop branches, and tame the shrubbery in the overgrown front yard.

Ozzie studied long hours after his chores each day. He liked starting with chores, though, to wake up.

Ozzie and Norm had sized each other up pretty quickly, without dislike. This was a business arrangement, Ozzie thought with a practical air, and Norm would be fine to work with. He seemed to be one of those brilliant people who might forget to breathe someday, but he had a sense of humor anyway. And as for what Norm thought of him, Ozzie was pretty sure Norm thought he was mentally deficient. Ozzie would have to work hard to keep up his end of the deal and actually help the guy in some way.

After school the first day, Norm called Ozzie in from

the yard. "Time to start the think tank," he grinned. So they holed up in Norm's cluttered bedroom, where there were more electronics than there was sleeping space. Robotics charts and tables of figures were pinned to the walls. Three desktop holo devices were all going at once.

Ozzie had crammed on robotics design heavily so he wouldn't seem stupid, but he still felt very stupid as Norm went over his idea, pointing to places on a crude holo-design he had drawn, rotating it to show all angles. Ozzie wrote down anything that he didn't understand to catch up on during the next school day.

The second day at Norm's he walked into the shaggy backyard ready to take it on as the enemy, and found it wasn't really something to conquer — there was so much green and growing, oranges getting fat on the trees and the warm sun glazing it all. But he lopped, trimmed, groomed it anyway. While he worked he thought of Freya and the volcanoes sometimes. Wondering what she was doing in Reykjavik today.

Mrs. G. came to watch a little and smiled oddly at Ozzie, as if she had just met a new species of 16-year-old male and couldn't quite decide what it was.

That night, think tank again, with Ozzie smarter and faster on the uptake, able to ask some not-too-dumb questions. Norm looked a little relieved. More things on Ozzie's notepad to study the next day, and another go at it that night, the third think tank evening. Norm smiled once that evening, so Ozzie knew he was getting somewhere.

The next afternoon Norm had to go work at Dingo's Pizza after school. Grateful for the chance to catch up to Norm by studying, Ozzie stayed inside to pore over robotics texts and watch design holovids on his phone.

Norm's Uncle Leon stopped by to visit and ask how the project was going. He sat on Ozzie's sleeping bag with his legs up on the coffee table and said, "Norm has been making pizzas for three years. He actually flings them better than anyone there, except when he starts inventing things while he works. A time or two he lost control of a pizza and the Dingo's manager had to put him on probation."

Ozzie laughed, picturing that. Norm was brilliant, but it was true. He seemed to be sort of an airhead.

"When he has his license he'll start driving, delivering pizzas. Dingo's specializes in old-fashioned hot deliveries by humans..."

Ozzie couldn't believe anyone bothered with licenses in California. Around Las Cruces no one paid much attention to how old you were, and if you had a vehicle your parents let you use, they figured you could drive it.

"...But his cousins think that will be a disaster because he's so absent-minded he gets lost, even with a GPS. Maybe he won't deliver any pizza to anyone." Uncle Leon laughed and went to the fridge for a squeezepak of beer.

"Norm wants the tips so he can go to CalTech for

robotics," he called from the kitchen.

Norm came home that night smelling of garlic and declined to think-tank because he had homework. He went upstairs to find comfort in a few holo games, first.

But there were several more think tank nights. By the night before the contest launch event, Norm and Ozzie had Norm's concept for the invention clear between them, and the technical principles involved in its construction were all installed in Ozzie's mind. Ozzie couldn't say whether this was the most innovative and brilliant thing ever, but he understood it and it sounded brilliant to him. He sure hoped it was going to be impressive. And they had their story down: this is what we're doing and why. He liked Norm. Norm clearly didn't think he was stupid any more.

They joked and watched a space opera holovid to celebrate, with pizza from Dingo's that Norm had made himself and overcooked, unfortunately, so they let him take it home.

It was only when he turned off the light and lay down on the couch to sleep that Ozzie noticed: his neck chain and the ring were missing.

CHAPTER THIRTEEN

THEY OVERSLEPT and made a hasty start, without breakfast, in the morning. On the hoverbus for Jet Propulsion Lab, Ozzie finally had time to think about the missing ring.

The bus wound through the quiet Saturday-morning version of Pasadena, gathering a few more passengers from little clear tekryl sheds, then shot down a thoroughfare to the end of the line in front of JPL. All the way they rode in silence, and Ozzie rummaged through his memory to try to find a place where the chain and ring might have gone. For weeks he had been so busy that he couldn't even remember the last time he knew he had them.

Norm and Ozzie walked into a large room whose brushed-steel walls were lined with long, clear tekryl tables. Holomarquees above the first three tables said "Information for Contest Entrants," "Registration — Have Your holoID Ready Please," and "Partner Photos

(Optional)."

He and Norm must be early. People their age were trickling in, a few accompanied by families. A girl in jeans, elaborate braids, and a college sweatshirt walked by with an armload of literature, and pointed at some of the tables. "Look, free stuff!" she said.

Ozzie looked where she was pointing. Some tables represented areas of interest, like one for Robotics for the Hungry, and another two for Engineers Against Atomic Waste and What's the Latest in Robotics? These carried big-screen holovids or holo slideshows and free data slivers, each with a petabyte or two of holo and info on the topic, and icons for downloading if you preferred to suck the whole mess of data onto your phone. And some paper literature for people who liked pulp. "Data download?" a robot asked as they passed. "No thanks," Ozzie answered. He'd rather be a little more choosy.

There were sponsor tables too, where companies like Hydroponic Harvest and Aves Aircar were displaying or demonstrating wares. A small tribe of younger brothers and sisters, about ten years old, were busy downloading everything in sight and snacking hungrily on the free food.

Chairs surrounded clear round tables in the center of the room. There were enough seats there for a hundred or more entrants. The whole place was full of electronics, light and reflection and metal.

The registration table was one of the few human-staffed ones. Ozzie and Norm registered with one of them, showed their IDs, and signed out a hand-sized tablet that contained electronic forms preloaded with their holoIDs and ready to fill out for contest entry.

Ozzie turned to look for a table and nearly stepped on the foot of a little girl.

Or not a little girl, just a small girl. Small compared to Ozzie. And probably his age, actually, he realized as she came into focus. He looked down into her face. She was Asian, with glossy black hair pulled back behind her head somehow. She wore a red school-uniform tunic over a black-and-white striped sweater and black leggings, short black boots. Clearly she was used to dressing for some other climate, for cold that she wasn't going to find here in Sunny California.

Her eyes were frozen on Ozzie as she stepped back. Then she looked at Norm. She seemed to be getting her bearings slowly, like someone who had just arrived from another planet.

Norm must have been bored, because she seemed to fit right into some need he felt for entertainment. He said, "Welcome, nerd-girl, to California and JPL."

A lopsided smile made a bow of her mouth in slow motion, as if his message was gradually arriving. She answered in a high, British-sounding voice, "Thank you very much, nerd-gentlemen." When she smiled her eyes formed new-moon curves, her irises dark as raisins above very pale cheeks. She was pretty. Norm stared a couple of seconds, then recovered. Ozzie liked her. He wondered if she had a boyfriend.

"I'm Norm. This is Ozzie, my colleague and contest partner." They both extended their hands with great solemnity to shake hers.

"You are Ozzie? Then I should be bringing you greetings from Freya, who helped me to get here. I'm Alexis."

Freya? Ozzie was astonished, but before he could say a word, a spiky-blond figure, a little taller than him, appeared behind her.

"You're Alexis Wu? I'm Seth Raker. Your partner."

Alexis turned. Her braid, Ozzie discovered in a couple seconds of observation, looked like the tail of one of those fancy black goldfish — it was woven in some intricate fashion and bound with a fat stretch band, from which it spread out and floated down her back.

As an afterthought, Seth added, "Here's Marna, my girlfriend."

Now, if Marna were a fish, she would be something spiky to match Seth's spiky bleach-blonde hair. Her shirt was distractingly tight. She chewed her gum slowly, half-smiling, as she looked Alexis up and down. Then she took Seth's arm very deliberately. My property, no trespassing.

Seth sneered over Alexis at Norm, then Ozzie. To Alexis, he said, "Who's the guy with the country-boy hair?"

"This is Ozzie." She turned to begin introductions. "From New Mexico. And Norm is his partner…"

"Ooo. Interstate team." Seth shoved the words at them heavily. His voice was smooth and average and his words were precise. But he was afraid, Ozzie realized.

Norm stuck out his hand. "Norm Garcia," he said, waiting for Seth to shake. When Seth didn't, Norm dropped his hand and said, "We have a phenomenal design and we intend to win." He grinned his biggest wise-guy grin. "We have a good team here. I like Ozzie's approach to technical problems. (Another grin that seemed to be designed especially for Seth.) He just makes it happen. That's his approach: 'Let's make this happen.' "

Norm had a great voice when he got going, Ozzie thought — smooth and melodious, like one of those preachers in the old flat-films. He also had this annoying grin that Ozzie had seen him use on his sisters. And now on Seth. It was perfectly calculated to irritate others. And he delivered it perfectly, too.

As a show of partnership unity Ozzie added his own prepared speech: "We have many exciting technical problems to solve, like how to move with precision in difficult environments — and other issues that may be pivotal points in this competition — but you know," he said airily, "that doesn't worry me much. Norm is brilliant and we're good at working on the fly."

Seth stood there a second, his sneer becoming tight-lipped as he took Ozzie in. Then he turned away. "Well, *good luck.*" He tossed it back over his shoulder like a rock.

Alexis' fishtail swung a little as she followed him away.

"So she's the one who holo'd me," Norm said, thoughtfully, watching her go. He scratched his head, and that left his hair rumpled.

"Who, her? About what?" Alexis knew Freya? And she had contacted Norm?

Norm looked embarrassed. "She sent me a message a few weeks ago. She wanted someone to take her on as a partner. You and I had already made a plan. But... I didn't know if it would work out. I didn't know you then, really."

How does this girl know Freya? Ozzie wondered. *And if she got her info from Freya, why did she call the person Freya told her was my partner?*

**

Norm and Ozzie filled disposable plates with snacks from the Hydroponic Harvest table and the Celestial Candy display, and sat at one of the round tables with some other people they didn't know who were about their ages. "We just need to put our data on this tablet to register for the Freestyle Challenge," Norm said, "and upload our parts list from a data sliver, too. The information goes directly into the main contest computer."

For JPL Freestyle, although you now had to be in teams of two, you could make any kind of robot you wanted and have it do anything. You only had two and a half months to build your design, though. It was the toughest contest, because you made up your own challenge and you were scored against your own specs: how ambitious they were and how well you did what you set out to do. "Almost every year there are a few entries that just plain blow up in the air or never work right at all," Norm said, "but the ones that do work are pretty clever ideas."

Norm's was very *very* clever. The robot he had planned was about twenty inches in diameter and 3 feet high. It could propel itself off the ground and get to the exact location you entered, as far as 50 kilometers from where it started. It could move over uneven terrain there and collect surface samples of soil and rock. It could even drill thin cores a meter long out of rock and place them neatly in a basket at the back, like arrows in a quiver. It could operate in low gravity or rough weather.

Once it got where it was going it could attach to the ground by forcing hot rods from its foot pads downward into the surface dirt or rock, melting the stuff so it welded to the rods. That would hold the bot in place for sampling. Or hold it down if crazy winds were blowing, or if there was such low gravity that it might float away. When the sampling was over, or the winds died down or whatever, the bot could re-melt and retract the rods. Norm called it the Hot Rod because of this feature. The trick to it was programming the bot so it could choose the correct options to use depending on what its sensors told it about the environment.

"There are lots more complicated robots than this, already in use," Norm said. "But for student work this is *way* advanced. And the things it does are partly new and sort of trendy — just what people are interested in, these days."

Ozzie was sure this bot would be a hit (if it worked) now that the asteroids were open to mining and exploration. Their robot's new features would make it much easier to get rock samples and find the best areas for mining. And now that there was a colony on Mars, which had a reputation for crazy storms, that might be another place to use the thing.

They turned in their registration tablet as fast as they could, along with their secret Concept and Requirements Specifications on a data sliver in a sealed contest envelope, and got in line at the Parts Request table — which was becoming the most popular place in the room now that the food had mostly disappeared.

"Are you worried about our list?"

"Nah." Norm shifted from foot to foot, bored. "I spec'd parts that are easy to get or I broke them down so they're easy to make of other things." When Ozzie's eyebrows went up appreciatively, he said, "I'm no fool."

Their list went through without a hiccup. The parts would be delivered by Airdrop Express next day. They each took a squeezepak of water from a tall ice tub and went out to catch the hoverbus home.

Ozzie felt like he and Norm had the world by the tail. They were on their way toward a brilliant robot already.

As Ozzie and Norm neared a couple of entrants at the bus stop out front, one muttered, "That's him. With the hair." Ozzie stopped and faced him. "You the guy from New Mexico?" the speaker said.

"Yeah. So?"

"We heard you know *nothing* about robotics," he jeered, "even though you think you're so hot, and you're here faking to swing this contest to your partner."

Ozzie felt exposed as an amateur. It was a little too close to the truth. He could feel his face getting hot. He looked at Norm. Norm gave a shrug that meant "who cares what they think?"

But Ozzie said, "Who says so?"

"Someone told my partner."

"Whoever it was doesn't know anything. Who told you that?" he asked the other one.

The other looked sullen. "Seth."

"Ha!" Ozzie hooted. "Seth is afraid he'll lose to my brilliant partner, that's all. Tell him I said so if you want."

Seth stepped out from behind a pillar, acting as if he'd just arrived on the spot. "Yeah, Ozzie? Count on this: I'll make sure that *you* lose the contest, no matter what.

And *I'm* going to be Captain's Apprentice on the first Earth-to-Mars Grand Galactic trader."

Ozzie felt his throat tighten. How did Seth know about that? Suddenly whatever he had by the tail was beating him black-and-blue. This guy was sure he could take that apprenticeship spot; maybe he could, if he was so sure. If they let students from other schools compete...

He felt sick. But he laughed again, anyway. It was a trick he had learned from the gypsies; they laughed to unnerve their opponents.

CHAPTER FOURTEEN

I T WAS SATURDAY morning again. Ozzie paused as he screwed one piece to another, and looked over at Norm. He was lucky to have such a genius as a partner. And such a great design. *Why did Seth have to show up to ruin things?* Every time he thought of Seth it was like a dark cloud moving in. Otherwise this would have been more fun. It was bad enough that this was kind of a desperate gamble to try to get back his apprenticeship, without adding a fight with some demented creep.

To himself he began the long string of comforting swearwords that he had learned from Malo. He added some special flourishes. Summary: Seth was a sack of crap.

He reached for the ring on the chain at his neck. The reminder that it was missing just added to his discomfort. He felt like his good luck charm had left him; not that he believed in such things.

THE IBIS DOOR

"Norm. Why does Seth hate me so much? He doesn't even know me."

"General principle. He hates anyone who's really good at something — like me." Norm flashed that grin. "Hates me too."

Ozzie sighed and looked around him — at the walls hung with rakes and old bike inner tubes, the shelves of tools and cans of ancient gas-car supplies. They sat in Norm's garage on a pair of dented folding chairs, going through the parts list and putting together the parts that were made of smaller parts. — To simplify things, Norm said.

They had small screwdrivers, vintage soldering irons and other tools scattered on a clean old bedsheet on the dirty garage floor. It had taken the rest of last weekend just to empty the place out into the back shed and sweep it up some.

Now, after another week of school and Dingo's for Norm, house painting and robotics cramming for Ozzie, they were working on the project for real, full-time for the weekend. The contest deadline was December 15. *And who knows how long this will take?*

Ozzie had suggested that they stick labels on each little assembled bit before they put them aside in a box so they didn't have to keep rummaging through them all as Norm was doing. Norm declared that the idea was outstanding, brilliant.

Even with the door raised, the garage smelled heavily

of oil and tires and musty, heated wood. They had Devastation, the electric metal group, playing on Norm's phone since his was set to local broadcasts. Abruptly the phone made an explosive noise. Ozzie jumped. "Call coming in," Norm said absently, looking for a matching screw. He had poured out all the screws so they were mixed in with everything else.

The explosion was Norm's ring-tone. When Norm finally accepted the second try by the same caller, it turned out to be Alexis. Ozzie could hear her voice on speaker, and then she holo'd herself in, live. "Hey, what's up?" Norm said in surprise. It was as if a smaller version of her was in the room with them.

Ozzie combed back his hair with his fingers. Today she was wearing a T-shirt and jeans, dressing a little more for the weather. Her mouth was perfect; it almost looked painted on. Her hands were fidgeting with the hem of her shirt. They were softly formed like those of a child. She seemed shy because her eyes were downcast. But when they rose they were surprisingly matter-of-fact.

"Am I disturbing you?" she asked.

Ozzie let Norm answer. He was the boss here.

"Interrupting, but not disturbing," Norm grinned annoyingly at her.

Again that lopsided smile curved her mouth. "I'm sorry. I have no one else here to talk to, and I'm new to all this... I need to talk to someone."

"Sure, that's OK," Norm said. "Go ahead." He began to rummage again for the missing screw.

Ozzie decided that most of their robot idea wasn't visible yet so she couldn't pick up any of their design secrets even if she was tempted to. He slid the parts list under his chair with his foot, just in case, so it would be impossible to read. "Mind if we work while we listen?" he said.

No, she didn't. She took a deep breath. "America is very different from England," she began. "People speak differently, manners are different, and I'm Chinese-British so that's another difference..." She ticked these things off on her fingers carefully.

"Yeah." Ozzie figured she'd get to the point pretty soon, but he could understand how things could get difficult, with all those layers of difference. Maybe she was homesick? They could invite her over for a holovid or something.

Norm screwed two pieces of metal together, adding a couple kinds of washers and a nut in what looked like an important sequence. Alexis looked at him in a smitten way. He began rummaging again.

Finally, she continued. "So working with Seth — Seth was sooo nice to me at first. He said that he was lucky to have such a pretty assistant." She giggled, stopped. "He even held doors open for me and offered me snacks. He told me about his family and his life. I felt a little sorry for him."

Norm snorted.

"Really I did," she said. "His family is filthy rich.

So rich they took him to the Moon for his tenth birthday! But his mother is so drugged she hardly knows him. His father is a California Congress-guy who is always off on his political career. Neither of them pays much attention to Seth. He actually hates them — you should hear him. But he goes on and on about them anyway, like he's haunted by them.

"Well, I told him about my family too. I thought we could be friendly, you know, while we work. I didn't come expecting to be treated like a movie star! But..."

When she paused too long Ozzie looked up and saw that she was fighting tears. He froze, as if by concentrating he could help her win the fight.

She won, and said, "After only a week he treats me like a servant, his lackey. I have to get him lunch while he works, fetch him a drink when he wants, make coffee. He told me how little I know every evening last week till I started to think he was right. But I've won the Royal Robotics Cup twice!"

Norm's head jerked up and he stared. He whistled. "No kidding?" His voice had a "why didn't you tell me?" ring to it. Sounded like Norm regretted missing Alexis as his partner. Ozzie's sense of worth sagged. *And why did Alexis call Norm in the first place?* He still didn't know.

"Last night," she said, "I was tired, and I *did* make a mistake, and he screamed at me, the nastiest foulest stuff, as if I was some HongKong street-girl!" She was getting steamed up. "I didn't know if that was just the way Americans really are, or *what*."

"They aren't," Norm said, unconcerned. He stood, tucked his turtleneck into his sweats, stretched, and plugged in the old soldering iron.

Ozzie said, "Seth is a pig, Alexis. He can't treat you that way. He deserves to be clobbered."

She giggled, and even in the holo he could see her eyes glowing at him. My-Hero sort of look.

"You know what he told me, Ozzie? He said he told you he's going to take that merchant ship apprenticeship that you are going after. He was bragging about it. But he really doesn't want to do the job at all. He said he'll take it just so he can check the box on his resume and then go do something else. He just wants to keep you from getting it."

Norm went on labeling another assembled part.

Ozzie felt a little sick again, like he'd just taken a punch in the stomach. Someone who didn't really even know him hated him enough to try to do that. It made him want to work furiously, right now, to make sure they won so he could protect what was his. He grabbed for the next part and began hastily to attach it to its mate.

But Alexis was still standing there. With an effort, Ozzie put his attention back on her: "So... what are you going to do?"

"Not sure." A long pause. She seemed to be thinking.

"Thanks for listening, guys. I'm glad you're more civilized than my partner is. Don't worry, I'll figure out something. Back to the slave camp with Seth." She winked out.

CHAPTER FIFTEEN

THE HEAT FROM THE FLAMES was intense, even inside her insulating coverall. Freya was with the other Fourteenth Reykjavik Fire Company trainees, attacking a fire at the outer perimeter of the newest volcano. They were doing open land drilling now, terrifying but also oddly thrilling to her. She and the other trainees worked safely in a line at the edge of the flames with chemical canisters strapped to their backs. Arni, their group leader, had made sure he was near her.

If she was good enough, they had told her she could get pilot certification, to drop airborne water and chemicals — better than dragging them around on your back like this.

A stiff wind began to blow the fire at them. They moved to close ranks, backing away and shooting flame retardant into the fire as they went. But she was a little far from the group. A sudden wind sent a fork of flame shooting across the sun-dried shelf, separating her from the others. She swung her arm to spray blindly at the grass that fed this new curtain of fire. No one else was visible. Panic rose in her throat, threatening to choke her. She fought the wall, backing quickly along the curtain away from the core of the fire, trying to see her group through the leaping flames.

A large arm and leg, then a masked face, appeared through the flame wall, grabbed her arm and yanked her into it. Being dragged directly into the fire: horrifying, even as she felt her own coverall and helmet deflect the heat. But in a few heartbeats they were on the other side, joining the rest of the group that backed away from the perimeter of the fire, fighting on to contain it.

Finally airborne water arrived to put out most of the grassfire. They had managed to hold it in place long enough. Panting and sooty, they all unhelmeted and as the others walked to the truck she turned to Arni to thank him for helping her.

"Those heavy canisters." He slid them off her shoulders and let them drop behind her to the ground. She felt the relief of dropping their weight — lighter, too, because the danger was over; then she felt his strong hands against her back as he pulled her close. He kissed her hungrily, and she kissed him back just as intensely, pumped full of adrenaline from the fright.

But then she was confused, as if she had waked to find herself in the wrong place. She pulled away slowly and gathered up her things.

**

Now she sat beside him near the others on a large chest of equipment on the fireboat, washing bread and cheese down with bottled water. Arni was telling a funny story about his uncle in Sweden when a text came in from Alexis. Freya made an apologetic face and began to read.

Alexis said that she and Seth were working together. "But he's being an ass. I don't know how this is all going to come out. Hey, I met your friend Ozzie here, with Norm, right away. Impossible not to like them. We all watched an old, old flat-film Saturday night at Norm's. His mother had to drive them to get me because a 16-year-old isn't allowed to drive in California! But it was fun."

"My friend Alexis," Freya explained to Arni. Then, because of something left-out in his look, she waved the text up into the air so he could read it.

While he did she looked longingly across the harbor at old Reykjavik, dreaming of the old harbor full of pleasure boats, and the new harbor busy with trade. Iceland restored so the land was stable again and people came back from Denmark and Scotland, or wherever they all had gone, to live here again. Thousands more people to speak to in the language she loved. When Arni had finished reading he watched her silently. "Do you wish you could go there?" he asked at last.

"Where? California? No." But he was right that she was wishing. Her sense of duty was struggling against her own personal wishes — the need to do something about the volcanoes against the wish to agree with people like Ozzie, Norm, and Alexis that it didn't matter or there was nothing she could do. *I would love to just have a boyfriend and a job, and read my stuff on the weekends at some cafe.*

**

And she said so, to Alexis, later. It wasn't something she planned to do. It just all spilled out. While Mamma was busy painting her new patron after dinner, Freya holed up in her room, saying that she wanted to study. She called to wish Alexis luck but really it was because she wanted to be understood by someone.

It was noon hour in California, lunch break in Alexis' study day, and she took the call as Freya thought she would.

Freya sympathized when she heard the latest about Seth. "He sounds disgusting."

"Yes. But I just need to make it through this contest to the end with no fault. I can do it." Then Alexis said, "What about you? What do you want?"

"You know how you dream of getting that corporate power-job? For me, I dream about reading and singing my poetry in Iceland someday, in the cafes when the volcanoes have gotten quiet. About seeing the world and meeting amazing people. Also about a brave guy, someone epic like in the legends, to love... Silly, huh?"

"No." Alexis said. "Why don't you do what you want, then? Yes, the volcanoes, but don't you have the right to get away from them for now?"

Freya wanted to tell the whole long story, so Alexis would understand and say that she did. But instead of all that, Freya told Alexis a shorter version of the story she had told Ozzie: about her research and the danger that the volcanoes would become a worldwide disaster.

Alexis listened. She was quiet for a little after Freya had finished, so Freya thought her attention must have wandered. But then she said: "You're scaring me, Freya. — But wait, let me tell you why: because what you're saying sounds like my weird nightmares...

"I've always been frightened that someone will destroy things and my kids will never grow up. I've actually had bad dreams about it all my life: The world goes up in flames or something...My children are burning...Horrible. The same nightmare again and again.

"My real dream, my own dream that I never say — because the other one is my *family's* dream — is that my great corporate job earns me the right to have babies and a garden full of vegetables, farm animals, ducks and cats and dogs. Things growing all around me, trees and green grass... and children who live long enough to grow up. That's what *I* want. I guess I'm not the typical techie, am I."

**

That night, after Freya slept like a swimmer deep in dark water, she rose to the surface to find a clear sky and stars that shone on the busy Old Harbor, which had moved somehow so it was right here. It was full of pleasure boats strung with colored lights. She lay on her back and floated and the water began to steam. It made her feel so refreshed that she dove deeply again, drawing strength from the pressure, the heat, and the rich minerals, so that she became owner of the dark secrets of the earth's past...

Much later she resurfaced and dreamed again:

She felt older and a lot wearier than before. It was nearly dawn. The hills were jagged, outlined by the moon that had just dipped behind them. She could see trap-plants, whose lush flowers must be full of insects by now, closing for the day to digest. The air was heavy with their perfume. One by one the glowing lizards alighted on branches and their glows winked out. As she and her Other walked along, singing from habit and no longer from inspiration, vehicles began to light the red dawn sky, rising in dozens from the port. Their mission, she suddenly knew, was war. Knowing filled her with terror.

A thundering impact threw them off their feet. As she fell she saw flamelike lights stabbing the sky and nearby earthen walls sliding into the water. The fall

knocked her breath and the song from her.

Freya awoke, wet with sweat and tears — still struggling, as she came up out of sleep, to get up again and sing.

Cool air calmed her, coming from the white basement walls. *Another dream, so real.* All but the singing. As before, the dream contained just the ghost of music instead of music itself.

Banzai sat on her pillow. He gazed down at her in the dawn light. "Smart to tell Alexis," he said unmistakably, without making a sound. "You will need her too."

CHAPTER SIXTEEN

OZZIE LOOKED AROUND HIM, feeling doomed again. It was another sunny Saturday morning, with the whole weekend ahead of them to work on their winning robot. Out by the sidewalk the roses were still nodding on the bushes, although it was almost Halloween. He couldn't think of any reason for this feeling, except maybe Seth.

He and Norm had the garage door open and the sheet on the floor was covered with a fresh assortment of parts. The original pile of tiny parts was gradually clumping together into bigger and bigger chunks of robot. Ozzie had learned so much that by now he could do some pretty complex assembly directly from Norm's notes.

Norm went inside for a bathroom break, two glasses of iced tea, and his phone for music. In the sudden lull Ozzie listened to the neighborhood noises: the kids squealing, hovercraft and gas cars moving on the nearby streets, birds singing in the trees. Not at all like the sounds back home — which he didn't miss too much, usually.

The cat from next door came into the garage and sat at Ozzie's feet. When Ozzie met its eyes, it blinked slowly, started to lick a paw, stopped, and decided to just look back at him. Ozzie had seen this one before, a light-gray tabby with a white chest.

[Time is short,] it said.

Ozzie was startled. It had talked to him. Then he felt silly; why should he be surprised — after Malo's demonstration and all? He'd better say something, or be rude.

[Hello,] he thought politely at the cat.

[Greetings, and from your friend 'Georgie,' who sends word.] This cat gave Georgie's name as if it were surrounded by giant ridiculous quotation marks.

Word from 680 miles away. Passing the message from cat to cat like the pony express? This thought wasn't for the cat, but the cat answered Ozzie anyway: [No. I'm helping her, that's all. She said you weren't listening.]

Ozzie blushed. He looked around. Good thing Norm wasn't back yet to see him turn red.

[Thank you,] Ozzie thought. [Your message?]

[Look at the newsfeed. Volcanoes. Please.]

[That's all there is?]

Norm strode around the corner into the garage,

singing loudly with the sound system on his phone. "Look, man. Two giant ice teas, lemon and sugar. Isn't that little Belinda a peach?"

Ozzie turned back to the cat but it wasn't there anymore. He leaped up.

"Yeah, she's a peach. My turn for the bathroom," Ozzie called over his shoulder, already on his way inside. He had stopped looking at the daily newsfeeds when he left school for California. Just forgot to. He shut the bathroom door, sat on the edge of the old bathtub, and waved up the newsfeed icon. He entered the topic "volcanoes" for speed, and stared at Belinda and Monica's array of bubble bottles and kiddy makeup on the bathroom shelf while the images winked on.

Up came a bunch of choices, holos, posts. There, a list called "Volcanic Activity 2065." He flicked it up into 3D and ran his eyes down it, his stomach turning heavy as if he were swallowing bricks, line by line. Three weeks ago two utterly dead volcanic peaks in the Pacific had begun to ooze lava. Last week Volcan Arenal in Costa Rica started to spit smoke. Yesterday — oh no — Crater Lake in Oregon began to steam at the center. All boats were cleared from the lake, all locals and campers evacuated... *Freya. Freya of the talking cats — maybe she was right. Holy crap.*

Norm was soldering away when he returned to the garage. "Hey Norm, thanks for the tea. Need to talk with you about something. But let's don't stop — give me something to put together while we're at it, OK?"

"Want to talk with me? Hey, buddy, got girl trouble?" Norm grinned. "You can talk to Uncle Norm, sure." His solder smoked and he pulled the soldering iron away from a partly-assembled group of components. "Here: finish this."

But before Ozzie could open his mouth, Norm's phone exploded, Norm waved to accept, and Alexis arrived in the middle of the garage in holo, looking awful. Ozzie stared.

"Got the Saturday blues again, dear?" Norm said, pulling another length of solder from the spool.

"He hit me," she said.

Ozzie was up out of his chair, outraged.

Norm's eyebrows went up. "No. Really, no kidding?"

She turned fully to face them, nodding miserably. Ozzie could see the livid slap-mark already forming on her face.

"Where are you, Alexis? Are you at his house?" Ozzie said. "We'll come get you."

"Left there." She said, trying not to cry. "I'm at a bus stop near his house. I snuck out."

"Tell us where. Hide if you need to. We'll get you." She disappeared.

"How?" Norm demanded. Ozzie knew that Norm's mother had taken the hovercar for groceries. His dad was across town working on someone's vintage AC system. Nothing here but the antique gas vehicle that

Norm called The Heap. (Where do you get names like The Heap and Hot Rod? Ozzie had asked. From hundred-year-old flat-films, Norm told him.) Also, they didn't have one California driver's license between them.

"Where's the remote for The Heap?" Ozzie said. Norm found the hook that the dusty thing was hanging on and presented it, looking doubtful. But Ozzie had the old car started up and they were off before Norm could think of anything funny to say about illegal drivers.

They found Alexis in the expensive part of town a few miles away, a block from the hoverbus stop, in the entryway of a former drug store or something whose sign now said "Palms Read." They hustled her into the back seat and Norm handed her a tissue from the musty-smelling glove compartment of The Heap. She blew her nose as they drove. Norm tried to joke but mostly looked back over the seat at her, awe-struck by so serious a drama: the slap-mark, the tissue, the tears.

Near Norm's house, Ozzie's phone signalled. Swerving as he got it wrestled from his pocket, he saw it was Freya. "Norm, I'd better take it," he sighed.

"Stop over there before you wreck us," Norm pointed. "The historic neighborhood Dairy Swirl! We will get some — for medicinal purposes only." When Ozzie stopped at the curb he leaped out and pulled Alexis from the back seat. "Come. You are needed at the Dairy Swirl," he insisted, and she was weak-willed enough at the moment to let him pull her toward the Serve window.

The window was a square hole that opened into the cone part of a giant fake ice cream cone.

"Hey, Freya. What's up? You OK?"

"Ozzie, another volcano has started on the fault line, in the sea north of Iceland. The third new one here! I'm frightened, I admit it. But besides that, Ozzie, we can't wait any longer to do something about this. Do you see?"

It was as if their last conversation, nearly a month ago, had never ended. She had just given him a month to witness Exhibit A, that was all.

His head hurt. He raked his fingers through his hair, trying to think. It was too weird to think about. There were his plans, which he was still trying to salvage. There was the robotics contest. How could he do anything about the volcanoes right now?

Why couldn't things be the way he thought they were before? Just him and the trade route to Mars and the asteroids. Wasn't that exciting enough?

He sighed. "What do you think we should do, Freya?"

"I think I've found the way to an answer. We need to go to Egypt. To find out about the music of Osiris."

"Why?"

"I've been researching: In the legend of Osiris it says that after the flood he calmed the planet with persuasion, music and song. I found a recent Lakota shaman-dream, from just three years ago, that said the same: that after Atlantis was destroyed, someone who had a gift for it put things back in order somehow —

113

using waves of sound. Music. Osiris could actually do some kind of 'magic' with waves of sound."

"So he sang to people and they did better?" Ozzie was skeptical of this solution.

"Yes. No. Maybe, but there is more to it than that. The pyramids seem to have been large generators. They resonate even today at certain frequencies that correspond with musical notes. I think maybe they were built to vibrate to calm the earth's crust. The Egyptians had some unique instruments, too: who knows what all the tools were that he used to make his "music"? And it is clear that vibrations can disturb the surface of the earth..."

Clear to you. But the famous scientists don't get it, right?

"...So why couldn't vibrations heal it? If we can find the right music, whatever Osiris used, we can counteract whatever is disrupting the earth and starting to tear the crust."

Could this really work?

But then, does anyone have a better idea? According to the newsfeeds, the top people in the world were scrambling, with lots of resources. And they weren't getting anywhere.

"So 'we' means you and me?" His eyes widened as Ozzie finally caught up to that idea. Traveling to Egypt together? In some corner of his imagination he was delighted by her boldness.

"It will take more than one person, and it would be best to have a team to do this search fast enough. Besides, safety in numbers." She took a deep breath. "Can all three of you come?"

**

Surprised at himself, Ozzie agreed to call a meeting right there, at 11:00 a.m. on a Saturday in mid-October, on the back table in the Dairy Swirl parking lot. The surface of the table was painted red, probably 100 years of layered red coats, so thickly that the knots in the wood hardly showed.

Freya holo'd in live, standing on the red paint, but extra-small so she didn't attract much attention from the people at the next table. Norm and Alexis licked their cones in unison, and Norm's medicine seemed to be working so far because Alexis looked a little less miserable. But that might have been because of Freya. No one mentioned Alexis' recent escape from Seth.

"So you're Freya," Norm said. He pushed up his glasses and blinked at the little holo curiously. She wore blue jeans and a T-shirt with some writing on it that Ozzie couldn't understand. And running shoes. Her pale gingery hair, fine and curly, was pulled into a knot at the back of her head, but wisps escaped around her face.

You wouldn't notice her in a crowd, Ozzie thought. But close up she was hard to take your eyes off. And then she started to talk.

115

"Hello Norm and Alexis. I need to speak to all three of you about a large danger to the earth's crust."

She'll never get them interested with a lead-in like that, Ozzie thought.

Ten minutes later Ozzie realized that she had just finished speaking. He didn't remember the words but all three of them were mesmerized. Norm and Alexis were sitting with the stumps of their ice cream cones dripping on their fingers and their mouths half open.

He looked at her standing there and suddenly melted with some kind of kinship and admiration that he had never felt about anyone before. It made him long to help her, although he knew the others wouldn't be willing. And he couldn't right now, of course; he needed to get that apprenticeship first. Then he could *really* help her.

"Freya," Ozzie said. His mind was straining to grasp something, he wasn't sure what, and failing that, he sought for familiar things, solid things. Alexis began to shiver; maybe she was in shock, a little bit, from being hit by Seth. They'd better get her warm. Get the car home before Norm's parents worried. And before they got a ticket. Thinking of these things was a refuge from Freya's wild proposal. "Freya. Let me get these guys and the car home. We'll talk and we'll call you back, OK?"

"I. Don't. Want. To go home," Alexis said dreamily, emphasizing the words as if she were making a very meaningful statement.

"Why do we have to actually travel to Egypt to find

out? Can't we just look things up on the worldweb?" Norm said.

Ozzie stared at the two of them, amazed that this plan wasn't totally out of the question for them.

Freya said, "We have to test and feel the vibration, the resonance, ourselves. And we have to talk to people who are there. Maybe they aren't *on* the web."

Norm didn't argue, didn't joke.

"Call me in two hours," Freya said.

Alexis looked at her watch and countered: "Can we make it three?"

Freya nodded agreement and her holo vanished.

Ozzie stared. But Norm and Alexis just dumped their sticky cone butts in the can labeled Trash, washed their hands in the old water fountain attached to the side of the giant fake ice cream cone, and looked resolutely at him.

Freya had just hijacked his friends.

CHAPTER SEVENTEEN

OZZIE DROVE THEM HOME TO NORM'S HOUSE. While Norm offered Alexis a warm jacket and heated her a pouch of instant soup, then installed her in the back yard to rest, Ozzie was stuck with the task of explaining the right number of things, and no more, to Mrs. G.

About Seth hitting Alexis, and having to take the car to save her from further injury by Seth (omitting the extra time at the Dairy Swirl and the talk with Freya there) and how they hoped Alexis could stay awhile today, until they could take her to her lodgings. After Ozzie had run these things by Mrs. G. she was so sympathetic that Ozzie decided to lay a foundation for the *really* delicate part. A little advance diplomacy, just in case it happened. He sure hoped it wouldn't.

"Meanwhile we have heard from a fellow student who needs us to go out of town to help with a research project," Ozzie began.

Out of town where?

Egypt.

Mrs. G was astonished of course, but Ozzie hinted that this could be a real opportunity for Norm and Alexis and him. Could in some way enhance their futures in robotics and space. (According to Freya, the actual way to put it would be "this would determine whether they have a future at all or not" but Ozzie wasn't going to say that. He didn't even want to think that.) He left Mrs. G to puzzle over these revelations amid the sliced meats and cheese she was piling into sandwiches for lunch.

**

"Where's Alexis?" He found Norm at work in the garage again.

"Out back," Norm answered. Good. He liked her but he didn't want her seeing what they were building and then telling Seth about it. Norm was busily arranging the morning's products in a box, labelling each newly assembled item as Ozzie had showed him.

These familiar things looked different to Ozzie now, as if they were overshadowed by doom: each thing they had made was priceless and quaint and the garage was a memorial to their contest entry eons ago. He wondered if Norm felt that way.

"Tally ho, adventure calls, eh?" Norm grinned up at Ozzie. "Better get this all stowed safely enough to keep the little brothers out of it for a week or two, right?"

Ozzie guessed that no, Norm didn't exactly feel the way he did. But for Freya's sake at least, it was all right with him that Norm was cheerfully embracing her idea.

And why not? Ozzie labored over the thought. He felt torn. It would be an adventure, maybe. Only a week or two...

"Good thinking, Norm." He went out back to find Alexis.

Alexis was sitting in a garden chair, bent over her holophone and fast-flipping icons into the air above the holosheet. She was so absorbed in waving them up and sorting them with her fingers that she jumped when Ozzie said, "Doing OK now?"

She stopped, looked around, and sighed with pleasure. The backyard chickens were clucking softly. "This place is like heaven. Look at it," she said. The high back fence was thick with bougainvillea that spilled like a magenta waterfall toward the ground. Avocados, dozens of them, grew on little fat trees in the back corners, and rose bushes flowered in pots beside the orange trees.

Ozzie was about to say that he knew, he'd pruned it all himself, but she was looking at her phone again. She pulled some hair behind her ear, flicked an icon toward her with one finger, made some notes on the surface pad, and said, "I was right. We can get cut-rate tickets using the U.S. Student Standby pass. Britain has this too. I have a temporary US pass, issued for this robotics trip to

California. You and Norm could have passes without any fuss using student IDs, it says here. $36 USD each with the pass, roundtrip. Next: hostels in Egypt."

She looked up at Ozzie and said, "I think we can do this. This is my feasibility study." She flashed a little smile.

"And Seth and the contest?"

"I hope all the gods pee from a great height on Seth." She kept on fingering icons into the air.

Ozzie went out to the front step — his thinking spot at home — and sat looking at the street, the shrubs in front of the neighbor's house across the street, and The Heap parked out at the curb. He thought of all the remaining reasons why it would be hard for the three of them to go to Egypt, now that Alexis' travel-planner wizardry was getting rid of transportation and lodging problems. How would they get food and operating cash, for instance? *And what about the contest?*

The cat showed up again near his feet, looking at him.

[What?] he thought, impatiently.

The cat turned its back on him and walked to the curb, pausing, ready to step down and cross the street.

[Wait, what do you want to say?] No answer. Ozzie took a deep breath and began again. [Hello,] he thought politely.

The cat turned and sat at the curb, gazing at him. [Please,] Ozzie thought. [Do you have a message?]

The message came.

Ozzie sighed, thanked the cat carefully, and went out back again. Alexis was just rising and gathering her things from beside her. "Hey, did you tell anyone we may be going somewhere?" he said.

"Yes. Told Scumbag Seth we're taking a trip to Egypt so I won't be able to help him just now, *sorreee*."

Ozzie nodded, groaning inside. The cat was right. Whose team was she playing for, anyway? *She probably doesn't even know.* "Alexis, don't tell *anyone* else *anything* about this without talking to me first, OK?"

He went to the garage to help Norm put away their prize-winning project, to help make sure not a piece was dropped or a paper left carelessly lying. He found one small bit of robot that had managed to creep under the sheet. They changed their minds and put the entire boxed-up project in the shed, locking it with Norm's best padlock. "No one ever uses the shed," Norm said. They each took a key and put the keys on their belt rings. That was Ozzie's idea, for redundant security.

**

When Norm, Ozzie, and Alexis entered the kitchen together, Mrs. G stood at the island counter behind a stack of sandwiches that was still in progress, with her husband, two brothers, and assorted friends standing and leaning against the counters around her. Each was eating a sandwich. They all stopped chewing and talking, looked at the young people, and looked at Mrs. G.

The uncles were glancing sideways at Alexis to see if the slap still showed. *Poor girl,* they were thinking. *Very wrong.*

Weird, Ozzie thought, that I know what they're thinking. Is practicing on cats doing this to me?

"Norman," Mrs. Garcia began. "We have been talking."

That seemed obvious. Ozzie tried hearing what she was thinking, as an experiment, but he couldn't. Besides, she was saying something out loud that he wanted to hear.

"If this research is important for your future we want you all to be able to go," she said. "And maybe it would be good for Alexis to be away for a little while."

Norm looked questioningly at Ozzie, who nodded "yes" very slightly — Yes, he'd told Mrs. G about the Egypt idea.

"So we have asked for donations. Your uncles," she beamed at her brothers, "have been very generous. Our other friends, here, have been too. We have money for you for the trip."

She nodded to Mr. G, who hastily put down his sandwich, wiped his moustache with a paper napkin, and pulled from his work pants a thick stack of paper money. He handed it to Norm. Then, at a loss for words, he shook Norm's hand.

CHAPTER EIGHTEEN

ALL THREE OF THEM — Norm, Alexis and Ozzie — sat close together in a row of chairs, balanced on Freya's bedspread like those statues in front of a temple in the tourist pictures: the row of seated Egyptian kings at Abu Simbel. Holding her list of things they needed to discuss, Freya watched their holo soberly as it came into focus.

Her house was vibrating delicately — the rhythm of the volcanos that had become a ceaseless shudder — and the coins in the dish jingled without stopping. Noticing them now, Freya clenched her teeth.

"Guess what?" Alexis said. "I've got flights from Burbank to Egypt all figured out! And hostels there too! Cheap!" She giggled.

Norm added, "My family took up a collection. We have cash."

Freya struggled not to show her amazement and delight. She gazed at them.

Ozzie's brow was furrowed. He looked at her warily as if he saw into her, doubting her. How strange that Ozzie-with-the-talking-cat was the hard one to convince. It made her heart twist a little. She bent to check off several items on her list.

"Thank you hugely, all of you," she said. She began to read the list off to them right away, afraid to give any sign of her own doubt. She had doubted they would decide to join her, and doubted they would find a way to get to Egypt. She wasn't going to tell them how much doubt she had.

To Alexis, she said they would need hostels in Cairo, in Giza as close as possible to the Great Pyramid, in Memphis near the ruins of the old city, and in Edfu, south of Luxor. Maybe other destinations, too.

"Norm or Ozzie, have you traveled outside America? No? Alexis, did they check your passport entering America?" Alexis admitted that she didn't even have one.

"I have researched, because it's changing a lot: They seldom ask for visas and passports anymore, unless you look suspicious. Lucky for you: for students entering Egypt, they are usually not required today."

She told them she'd fend for herself and take whatever flight she could find, that as a firefighter her ID would permit her to move between countries. They all had sleepsacks and backpacks, right?

Alexis didn't.

Then they would need a pack and sleepsack for

125

Alexis, as well as some other gear for their research. She went down her list of items: a compass, protein bars in case of local food shortages, a wooden recorder (the musical kind). She would send a list to them to buy the things they didn't have.

"I hope the food is good there," Norm said. "I saw on a Geo Online holovid that in northern Africa and the steppes of Asia nomads still roam around with their herds, and barter and fight with each other..."

"But they're not totally primitive, Norm," Ozzie said. "Most of the nomads call each other up on mega-battery holophones to gossip. And a lot of them have sons who have gone off to make their fortunes on the asteroids. Really."

"...Well anyway, the Egyptian food they showed was amazing: locusts and dates and this thick goat stew..."

"Wow, amazing, Norm," Freya said. They needed to hurry. Hurry seemed to be in her bones these days. "What else do you think we need?"

"I'll need to have a leave from school," Norm started up again. "That's nearly impossible, so my mom said she'd get me a doctor's excuse. Is 'excuses' on your list?" He grinned.

Alexis and Ozzie looked uncomfortable. "I'm not even mentioning it to my parents," Alexis said. "Better to beg forgiveness than ask permission."

Ozzie nodded.

He was thinking about weapons. Freya heard it. *Like*

the cats, she suddenly realized. Strange. Maybe she was learning this from practicing with cats? She wondered if she could do it anytime she wanted.

"Ozzie, can you arm and train Norm and Alexis for self-defense?"

Both Ozzie and Norm looked surprised, for different reasons. Freya said, "Norm, people mostly travel with weapons. You didn't know?"

Alexis nodded soberly, backing her up.

"I have a knife that I've been trained to use." Freya continued.

"I do, too," Ozzie said, with a questioning look at Norm and Alexis. They shook their heads. "OK, knives for two. Training tomorrow… where?"

"I don't know where you can even *get* that kind of knife in California," Norm said. "Let alone where to practice."

Alexis knew. "In Chinatown you can get them, I'll bet. …Chinese people are very practical," she explained. "And sometimes you need a knife, that's all." She shivered.

CHAPTER NINETEEN

THE TRAVEL BROCHURE they were given during the flight to Cairo had a palm tree on the cover, and a pyramid, with a nomadic-looking person on a camel in the foreground.

It said, "The 25-year-old United Egyptian Republic, peaceful since the Middle East Treaty that formed it in 2040, is still picturesque and steeped in the region's long history of arts, agriculture, and nomadic life. It is home to the ancient mysteries of the pyramids. Boasting most of the latest technologies, the area also preserves many customs of its past; for example, for religious reasons there are still women who prefer veils."

Ozzie had watched every holovid on Egypt that he could find on the worldweb, and from those he added to the travel brochure description: "the area preserves many customs of its past, like warring desert nomads, pickpockets and other thieves, camels and reeking markets…" Now that they had made up their minds to make the trip, it sounded great to him.

Help Freya, sure. An adventure, too.

But we'd better get back to the contest in time to win it.

**

The pale pink Kasr Al Nile Hostel was run-down and its stucco exterior needed fresh paint. They climbed the stairs to their third floor room, a small one with four raised sleeping platforms built two and two against the side walls, topped by thin mattresses. No ceiling fan was there to ease the heat and stuffiness, so Norm opened a window.

Their room seemed to have stored heat, like a battery, from all the hot days of the year and both the floors below it, so its walls radiated like an oven.

He and Norm and Alexis were stuck in downtown Cairo for the day waiting for Freya to fly in from Reykjavik. Ozzie figured they'd better use the time to learn to get around in this part of the world.

On the long flight he had searched the worldweb for how to say six basic things in Egyptian Arabic: hello, goodbye, I'm sorry, do you speak English, please and thank you. He made them practice as they flew. It would do no good to rely on electronic apps for translation; in a pinch they needed to be polite to the core, at a moment's notice. Now the three sat on their beds dripping in the heat, sipping bottled water, staring at the cracks in the walls and reciting the six phrases — while Ozzie grew hungrier and hungrier because of some spicy cooking-meat smells coming through the open window.

Alexis was the first to know them cold. She mopped her face and did an Advanced Number Puzzle in a pulp-book while Norm and Ozzie finished their lessons.

"Do we really care how to say these things in Arabic?" he complained.

Ozzie said, "Do you want to get your head knocked off out there?" In America casual often worked but not always, and here it might be deadly. Dad said that when he was real young you didn't have to be so careful about being polite, but in the 2060's polite was what it took to keep things cool, most places.

Once their amateur Arabic was pretty good, Ozzie made sure they were all armed and they went out into the dazzling sun to look for food in the Khan Al Kalili bazaar. He couldn't wait to see it. "It's not too far from here and pretty easy to find," he told the others, as a sales pitch. "The leading tourist stop in Cairo."

**

By the time they arrived at the bazaar it was midafternoon and they were starving. "At least the awnings and buildings make some shade here," Alexis said. The narrow, pitted streets were crowded with people and with storefronts spilling brilliant wares out onto the walkways. Like the streets, the buildings looked as if they were used a lot and never repaired, worn smooth instead of being fixed.

Some guy Ozzie couldn't spot was singing in the sort of high, up-and-down voice you hear in tourist holovids. There was a mixture of local and European music coming from sound systems in stores. The music and noises all mixed together like the people around them, who swarmed and buzzed like bugs in the heat: lots of European-looking tourists and expats, many more darker-skinned locals. A little kid wearing a toy antigrav backpack, held in tow by a woman wearing a headscarf and veil.

There was as much modern dress as traditional clothing. But the traditional costumes fascinated Ozzie: long black robes or skirts and scarves on women, long robes and turbans or skullcaps or fez on men. Sometimes the old and new were combined. One young woman boldly wore a fez above European slacks and a bead-encrusted top.

The place smelled like cloth and brass, spice and sweat, and more distantly, something tempting that was cooking. Ozzie's stomach was delighted and tormented. Where was the food?

Vendors stepped into their path and beckoned to them, urging them to see slippers or metalwork or trinkets. Some glowered at them.

Ozzie tested his Arabic on a harmless-looking rug

merchant. He nodded to show respect and greeted the man: *"Ahlan wa sahlan."*

The merchant broke into a rich smile. *"Ahlan bik."*

"Bititkallim ingilizi?" (Do you speak English?)

"Aywa."

Good. Then Ozzie was free to say in English, "Thank you, sir. We are hungry. Can you help us find the food bazaar?"

Norm and Alexis were being good students. They listened carefully till the vendor finished pointing, then thanked him almost in unison: *"Shukran gazilan."*

They had launched their first Egyptian encounter safely, and it was a good thing because the second was a near-wipeout.

On the way to the food, Norm got so interested in the snarled-up 50-year-old telecabling strung overhead that he ran, full-frontal, into a merchant. It looked like an assault. The merchant growled and reacted, going for something in his jacket pocket — a weapon, no doubt. Immediately Alexis was at his side holding up her hands. *"Aasif! maAlish!"* she pleaded sweetly. (Excuse me! I'm sorry!) She scowled at Norm and shook her head as she pulled him away from the Egyptian, to show that her friend was clearly too stupid to be dangerous.

Then she led him away without looking back. Ozzie's heart was in his throat. He knew she must be scared to turn her back on the weapon but she didn't let it show. She knew that even on the streets of London there was no law that would protect them and no one would defend them in such a case. Ozzie moved away after her, also apologizing to the merchant and shaking his head at their stupid friend.

Brilliant but stupid — no kidding. And Ozzie had hardly gotten his heart to stop thumping when Norm proved it again.

They were following the directions that the rug-seller had provided, short-cutting down side streets and weaving among the stalls of spice and fabric. Alexis walked beside Norm, keeping an eye on him, as Ozzie followed. Suddenly Norm's hand shot out toward a sort of table or counter and he popped something from a decorated dish into his mouth.

Ozzie leaped to his side. They were huge stuffed dates, so luscious-looking that Ozzie's own mouth was instantly watering. And Norm was in trouble, seriously.

Ozzie spun Norm around to face him, fist in Norm's face. "That was my date!" he blazed, shoving his free hand into his pocket and pulling out a U.S. half dollar. "That was my date!" he scolded at Alexis, as if it were her fault too, while he put the coin firmly into the vendor's free hand. The vendor already had a knife raised in his other, ready to deliver the ancient punishment for theft. "That was *my* date," Ozzie explained disgustedly to the vendor, pointing to Norm and then to himself.

"Give me fifty cents for that date!" he demanded of Norm, hand out.

Norm blinked at this nonsense, but when Alexis jabbed him hard from behind he handed over a fifty cent piece. "I thought they were free samples," he muttered.

Ozzie handed Norm's coin to the vendor as well. The vendor lowered his knife, looking a little puzzled. But he examined the coins and pocketed them contentedly.

Having overpaid the vendor twice, Ozzie now studied the date dish with great deliberation. He lifted his selection toward the vendor and the gathered onlookers with a happy smile that said, "All disputes are settled because I am now a satisfied customer of this excellent date-seller."

Alexis had Norm by the arm and had steered him many stalls away by the time Ozzie licked his fingers and followed. Ozzie kept the satisfied smile on his face till he was well away from the date stall, then he rolled his eyes. *Jeez, Norm,* he thought, breathing again.

**

After they ate, they walked. This was Cairo, "Mother of the World," home of 20 million heirs to the mysteries of ancient Egypt. Now that they had Norm reined in a little and they had thoroughly scolded him with reminders that this was *not California*, Ozzie felt pretty carefree moving with the wave of pedestrians.

They rode the tide in the late afternoon light, listening to a chorus of vehicle horns and the gas cars thumping through the potholes. They went up and down narrow streets crowded with hovercabs and hoverbuses, old gas vehicles, motorcycles, bicycles. Pedestrians walked, unconcerned, on the pavement alongside the speeding traffic, and sometimes when it slowed a little they wove within the traffic.

"Not like Pasadena, you're right," Norm said.

"Except for all the holes in the streets." Ozzie grinned. Las Cruces had pretty well-maintained streets, probably because of the space boom. Ozzie thought wistfully of their robot, in a box in Norm's garage.

But Cairo pulled him back: the tide of people flowed onward past storefronts and markets of various kinds, and wherever they went the sidewalks seemed to be lined with tables of bread, tables of trinkets or moon rocks, electronics or phones for sale. Further off there were old towers and medieval churches, the tall minarets of vintage mosques dwarfed by towering chrome-and-steel commercial buildings.

Norm and Alexis argued cheerfully and showed each other holovids as they walked. "Egypt seems to be a pretty retro place," Norm said as they walked into the hostel entrance at dusk.

"You should see London," Alexis countered. "It's even more retro."

"Than Egypt, home of the *pyramids*?" Norm wagged his head at her to show how outrageous that idea was.

"Well, you're right in one way," her lopsided smile started upward. "But if you pick up worldweb holovids you know that like China, England has relaxed back into its local customs. These days there are more local lifestyles and attitudes there than fifty years ago — in spite of all the technologies, right? It's weird.

"So anyway, in the way I'm talking about, Britain has gone retro faster than many places. People are reviving the old songs and traditions, things like Maypole dances —"

"Maypole dances." Norm grimaced.

"—you know, where the kids dance around this pole with long ribbons on it — and there are solstice festivals, winter and summer again, in most British cities. Very old customs."

Norm looked at her sternly. "Next you'll be saying they are sighting Leprechauns," he snorted.

Ozzie's phone sounded. "No Caller ID," it said, when he pulled the phone out of his pocket. It winked off.

CHAPTER TWENTY

TO GET THEM TO ARRIVE ON TIME, Ozzie had to herd and goad the other two, but somehow they managed to meet Freya as she deplaned at Cairo Airport the next morning. After the holos she was unmistakable: she strode through the jetway door toward them with a long-legged gait, her loaded backpack making her tip forward a little. She wore plain blue jeans, running shoes, and a flame red T-shirt that said "Fire and Flood — Summer Concert 2064."

As she neared, Ozzie found that at last he could see for himself the exact shade of her ginger-colored hair. Some of it matched the pale freckles on her nose. Thick light lashes framed her eyes, and the irises were intense pale green. Once a girl at school had showed him a gemstone called a peridot that she wore in a ring, and Freya's eyes were that color.

"I am very pleased to be here with you. We have so

much to do." She smiled. Her voice sounded boyish and forthright, just like on the phone.

She shook hands with Norm and Alexis, leaning toward each a little as if she were a sprinter at the mark. Alexis embraced her. Ozzie was last in the row and last to take her hand. When she let go, his fingers were tingling oddly.

"So you decided to come get some help with the contest, huh?" The voice was smooth but it rasped somehow, as menacing as a hiss. All four whirled toward it.

Seth. His unmistakable spiky bleached hair, swarthy skin, and of course his sneer. He held the handle of some expensive hover-luggage with one hand, as if he had just landed too.

There was stunned silence, from which Norm recovered first. "Who invited you?" He deliberately grinned his most annoying grin. Ozzie knew who had invited him. It was Alexis, more or less. *Damn.* He moved to stand beside Norm and grinned with him.

"I just thought I'd stop by to see what help you're getting," Seth said. "When Alexis said you were going to Egypt I knew you must be coming to cheat on the contest. Some kind of bootleg robotics data here? Is that it?" he jeered.

Alexis looked daggers at him.

Freya said, "We're not here to cheat on anything, Seth."

He looked her up and down. "And who are you? I'll bet I'll prove you *are*," he said.

"You won't," She pronounced his name again as if it was something disgusting: "...Seth."

He eyed her, this time with wary admiration. Seth was right about that, anyway, Ozzie thought. She really was...interesting. But you wouldn't want her as an enemy.

"Ozzie, Norm, and Alexis are here as my research associates on a project that has nothing to do with your contest or robotics." She spoke from way up high somewhere, as if he were a small impolite bug at her feet. "We will be researching in public places, like the Egyptian Museum."

Ozzie winced inside. *She just told him where to find us. Hope he missed that.* And he hoped the part about "nothing to do with robotics" wouldn't get around in California. Norm's relatives might want their cash back.

Seth's eyes narrowed. "*You* are a researcher? You, some kind of Nordic beggar? What a joke."

Silence; Freya's eyes were icy. She said: "Seth, *you* seem to be the beggar: you are trying to feed on us. Why don't you find yourself a real life?" She turned and stalked toward the exit.

How did she know that about him? Ozzie thought. That he vampires other people? Good one, anyway.

He and the others turned too and walked behind her. Ozzie was silently howling with triumph. No one looked back and Seth didn't follow.

**

Their room door shut behind the others. Freya allowed herself a little sigh of relief. She sat in the quiet and took in the cracked, patched walls and the dusty plant in one corner, the faded murals that marked the walls as having a far nobler past. The sleep platforms strewn with their travel things, the smell of the wooden beams and furniture that had been baking for years in air like a sauna, the sounds of someone singing and the traffic, smells of food she had never tried... This was the room that Alexis had got them. She liked it.

She was near the open window, where there was some breeze and she could look out at the streets three stories below. She was recharging her holophone at the recharge pad installed in the wall there. An Icelandic friend had told her that most hostels were like this: shabby but wired with electronics for travelers. She checked the newsfeeds and would research a few things on the worldweb while the other three found something to eat in the market. Tomorrow they must be ready to start.

In came a delayed holotext from Arni, full of affection. "Travel safe," he said. His warmth warmed her too. She sent him the same back.

They were all as she had thought they would be: good people, friendly and decent. Ozzie was strange —

he had many contradictions. He had come and somehow he had helped his friends to come. But he was so wary of her. He might not be any help at all.

Well, she was glad they had gotten rid of Seth.

**

The three returned noisily, with something containing goat meat to keep Norm happy, and rice and greens — and spicy tea to wash down the hostel's questionable water.

There were no chairs so they sat in a circle on the floor around the food containers.

"I can't believe we're all here together, not in a holo," Alexis said. "We did it!" She brandished a pressed-fiber sporkful of rice and fish.

"Yeah," Norm grinned, pushing up his glasses. "And if we don't get the touristas or anything we'll make it through the week." Freya looked up from her food box. "...Or, two," he corrected.

Freya had resolved to be professional. She knew she was sometimes impatient and hot-tempered, especially when a things mattered a lot to her, like now. "You really did do something amazing to get here," Freya agreed.

"How about you? Did you have trouble arranging to get away?" Alexis asked.

"I had to talk fast to get leave from my training program, but they gave it to me, *with conditions*...My mother was surprised, but when I showed her that I had the funds saved for the ticket and more, she wished me well and asked me to bring her a scarf from Egypt." Freya couldn't help smiling wryly.

Alexis helped herself to more food. "Hope we can find what you want fast, Freya. I don't want to work with Seth any more! so I'll need to get started with another contest partner soon.

"Hey, speaking of fast, a newsfeed from the moon today said the 945th trading run just left the moon for port in New Mexico. That's a lot of runs in so few years. Excuse me for ignorance, Ozzie — not my field. How is it they do it so fast? I clearly remember that when I was little it was a very long round-trip to the moon."

"Just old technology," he said. "We have better drives now. The Earth-to-Moon leg can now be done in two days," he said. "Earth to Mars direct now takes a couple of weeks. And I'll be doing a full circle including the asteroids, with stops to unload, trade, and load, in a few months' total time." Freya watched him: how his eyes lit when he talked about all this.

"You will be one rich trader, Ozzie. Hey," Norm said, "Is it possible that all those moon launches are damaging the earth's crust?"

Ozzie frowned.

"I don't think so," Freya said. "I looked into it but statistics don't seem to show that there's any link between space activity and seismic stuff."

Ozzie put his trash into a sack. "That reminds me,

Freya: you'll want to know some Arabic here to stay out of trouble. The three of us have learned a little...But it can wait till after you eat."

"Thanks, Ozzie." *Good idea.* She smiled at him. He wanted to protect them; that was valuable. It also drew her to him, in spite of herself. Were his cheeks flushing?

"Speaking of trouble..." Norm said — and Alexis rolled her eyes, adding that they would have to tell Freya the stories about some of *Norm's trouble* — "Is there a chance of fighting in this area? We don't want to get shot at. It used to be War-Games Central, didn't it?"

Ozzie shook his head. "Yeah, years ago. But I doubt that's a danger now. That kind of large-scale warfare requires high-powered national governments that can pay the huge cost by fooling with the currencies. The governments aren't that strong now."

Freya added, "Besides, to have a big war you have to have groups of people who are out of touch with each other, so you can talk people into the idea that all those other people over there are bad and they need to be killed. No one can believe it anymore, really."

"Right." Alexis collected all the remaining trash and stuffed it into the sack. "What country or race can you despise enough to attack when you are receiving holos and messages from them? And who wants to pay for that?"

"*I* don't wanta." Norm made a face. "Well, there are still plenty of nasty local hate-fights in some places.

Guess someone is willing to pay for *them*."

Alexis nodded slowly. "And according to what I've picked up on the worldweb there are a few governments that still have the right to push the button on existing 'machines of destruction'." She made a comic face and quotation marks in the air with her fingers.

But her eyes, locked on Freya's, weren't really laughing. Freya understood: she could see the fragile garden, Alexis' children, and the bad dream that surrounded them as clearly as if Alexis had showed a holo.

Freya wet her hands in the cup of hostel water and wiped them on a paper napkin. "I think if we solve the volcanoes there will be time for people to solve the rest," she said. "Today is October 21. I need your ideas. But here is my plan so far…"

CHAPTER TWENTY-ONE

THE FOUR SAT in the Egyptian Museum of Antiquities Public Events Room, in various stages of listening. Norm and Ozzie were beginning to fidget. Alexis looked like she had left the room mentally and was counting up something in her head. Freya, at the end of the row, nodded occasionally, concentrating.

Stacking chairs were arranged in multiple curved rows facing musicians wearing ancient Eqyptian costumes, and they were playing copies of ancient Eqyptian instruments: drums, a harp, flutes and an odd-looking lute, castanets, bells and jingling rattles they called sistrums. Other performers sang or clapped. To Ozzie, the music was eerie. Kind of wild and mysterious. He liked it. But maybe in small doses, he decided.

The program sheet for the performance told the whole story, as far as he could tell:

About ancient Egyptian music we know much yet we know almost nothing. From tombs and temples

we have examples of actual preserved instruments and wall-paintings of the instruments being played. We have the words of many musical pieces. But we can only guess backwards from these records and from more recent Egyptian music to try to imagine how the oldest music itself sounded. This performance is our most authentic attempt to present the music of 5000 years ago.

They had spent the day walking through the museum, all of both floors, calling a huddle anytime they found an ancient musical instrument or a piece of stone or papyrus that showed one. That was pretty often.

It was a lot of nerdy note-taking.

It was nice to sit and listen to some music as a change from all that, Ozzie thought. Nice for a while. He liked the sound of the instruments. Exotic. But after twenty-one pieces he was tired of ancient Egyptian audio for now.

How many more items on the program? Ozzie looked. Two. He could wait it out. His mind began to drift toward the robotics competition. Maybe he and Norm could save time by doing some work on paper while they were here. He'd ask, after this. He looked behind them, curious. Were all the seats filled for this performance?

He froze as his eyes snagged on Seth's spiky hair. And two police-looking fellas, one on either side. Seeing Ozzie turn, Seth smirked and pointed Ozzie out to his companions.

Ozzie turned away, feeling queasy.

After the final applause Freya rose and walked quickly forward to talk with the musicians. Ozzie turned to Norm, next to him, who was turning off the sound recording function of his phone. "Don't look now," Ozzie whispered to Norm and Alexis, "But Seth is behind us. Follow Freya." They filed out of their row and moved up the aisle by weaving through the exiting audience.

Freya was hefting a lute while the musician stood by and pointed out its features, let her pluck the strings and listen. The musicians seemed to be happy to have so much attention and no one was mentioning germs. So Ozzie joined in, and Norm and Alexis got permission to try the horns, harps and rattles.

Ozzie recalled Freya saying this morning, as they left the hostel to walk the ten blocks to the museum, "This program was why I wanted to be in Cairo on this date. It is not often that you can hear these instruments played live." Well, it was even more interesting to hold them and try them than to hear them played.

The next time he turned his head, Ozzie noticed with dismay that Seth and company were still here, standing a few yards away now. Norm was clowning with a sistrum, while the sistrum man watched tolerantly, when Ozzie saw Seth and the uniformed men arrive at Freya's elbow. They wore badges that said Cairo Municipal Police. One of the policemen said, "I'm sorry. We must detain you for some questioning."

Freya turned to face the three. "Why?"

"We have been given information that you are a vagrant and your friends are smugglers."

Freya looked at Seth. Ozzie saw the flinch in his eyes just before he sneered.

"We are no such thing," Freya said hotly. "Whoever gave you that information is slandering us." The two policemen looked wary. "I am here doing research and these three are students who have come with me to Cairo as research assistants."

When she opened her wallet and pulled out her ID, Ozzie craned his neck to read along with the policeman: the card had a red and blue Icelandic Flag at the top, very classy-looking, with the legend Icelandic Firefighters Association in gold letters, and below that, in black type, Corporal Freya Ilsesdottir.

Good one, Freya. And like Ozzie, she had done some study of Egypt, if she knew about the particular local dislike for slander.

The police looked at each other, then soberly at Seth. "She is an official in Iceland," one began, warningly.

"They're lying," Seth spat. "Probably some are fake IDs."

"We apologize for this inconvenience," one of the police purred to Freya. "Of course you don't mind if we check?" He wore a blast-gun at his hip.

Freya didn't hide her outrage.

**

An armed museum guard stood with her back to the outer door, as their babysitter. *Disgusting,* Freya thought.

The waiting-room chairs were hard, and there wasn't much to see: Some uninspiring stuff on the walls. A nondescript office door that needed fresh paint and said "Yarad Malouf, Dept. of Security."

Norm was checking his phone for mail. His stomach growled loudly. Alexis' mouth curved slowly into its lopsided smile. She was working a number puzzle in a pulp-book she had pulled from her backpack. Her phone signalled. "My father," she stared aghast at the ID.

Ozzie was listening to Freya. She was trying to answer his question, but she could tell he was getting impatient.

"...So," he interrupted, "looking at the musical instruments was a waste of time?"

"Of course not," she leaned toward him to emphasize it. "We had to look and listen to find out."

Norm looked up from his phone and flashed his wise-guy grin at Ozzie. It clearly meant "I didn't have to do either one, look *or* listen, to figure out that they couldn't stop a volcano. Did you?"

Ozzie couldn't help smiling back.

"Look," said Freya, annoyed. "It was possible that there was something powerful about these instruments that could do all sorts of things. You have heard about a high note breaking a drinking glass, right?

"There could have been something like that going on

here. But let's look at this together. Help me think. You may think that you don't know enough to observe something here, but what you already know isn't what matters. The famous volcanologists who already know so much have come up with no answers. They don't seem to really see everything or they would find a solution. So. What did *you* observe about the instruments?"

She sat back with a sigh, her arms folded, waiting. She still wished that she knew so much more. She hoped one of them would think of something remarkable.

Alexis said, "Well, what I observed: That the instruments were clever and I liked the sounds and all, but they didn't seem very powerful."

"OK, how do you mean?" Freya encouraged.

"Uh. Well, they didn't blow my mind," Alexis giggled. "Or, um, give me chills or make me feel very emotional, even."

"Me too," Norm said. "Me neither, I mean. They didn't have a big effect on me, you know?" He spread his hands and flashed that grin again.

Freya ignored it deliberately and looked at Ozzie. He gazed at the framed reproduction of a tomb painting that was hung on the opposite wall.

She recalled how carefully she had to listen to hear the messages from her cat, when Banzai first was trying to get her attention. She wondered if Ozzie had really heard much from his cat, because listening to a cat took a certain level of attention. If he had listened *that* carefully to the instruments as well, she imagined he really could have heard whatever it was that the instruments were doing.

"Nice, but not much there," Ozzie concluded at last.

"But is it possible that there's some magic in the real instruments that these copies don't have?" Alexis asked.

Norm snorted.

"We can't rule out anything, *including* magic," Freya said. "It's possible. Or that the originals were just constructed a little different than the copy-instruments we heard. Or that the music that our musicians were playing today was so different from the music the instruments were designed for, that the music doesn't work..."

Ozzie frowned, shaking his head. He raked his hair back. "I think it doesn't matter. Because we can't *get near* the original instruments, without bringing every cop in Cairo after us. And even if we *had* the instruments we don't have the original music. And *even if we had that*, and we had an ancient Egyptian music teacher too, it would take us *years* to learn how to play it just right. So we're not looking at a practical solution to the volcanoes here."

Freya felt herself smiling a little. *Go to the top of the class, Ozzie.* But she wanted to keep them all thinking together. They needed all the brilliance they could get.

"I think you are right." she said simply. "Then we are

all agreed? We need to look further. These ancient instruments are not the way to the music that we need."

**

The windows of the waiting room were dark by the time Seth and the policemen returned. Seth was stony-faced.

One policeman handed out the IDs to Ozzie and Freya, Norm and Alexis, while the other said, "We apologize for this mistake." He emphasized the final word, looking directly at Seth. "Slander is not a small crime here. For the future we advise that none of you indulge in it." He nodded curtly at Seth, dismissing him.

To the others he said, so Seth could hear it on his way out, "If you should wish to sue this young man, you have 45 days to enter a charge in the courts."

The assistant cop had papers for them all to sign: releases, holding the police and the museum innocent of slander or errors.

Once they had signed, the officer seemed to be relieved. He gave Freya his card with a charming smile.

**

Outside the museum the night air was cool and the bright lights of the city seemed cheerful to Ozzie. Sitting so long in the museum office just made him think of how he'd rather be working on the robot. It was a relief to leave the place. *And it was good to score one on Seth.*

The pools in the statuary garden reflected bits of moonlight in the spaces between floating lotuses and bunches of decorative grass. Beyond, traffic horns blared, pushing spears of light and rushing noises down the broad street they called al-Tahrir.

They were hungry. Alexis begged a moment to sit on a concrete bench and adjust her shoes for the walk back to the hostel. No one objected. Benches framed pools or bits of statuary sitting in circles or squares of grass. They all found their own seats near hers.

Freya dabbled her hand in the water behind her, looking up at a statue opposite. Norm checked holomail.

Ozzie watched Freya, forgetful of his own hunger and the delicious cooking smells that hung in the air. Were they coming all the way from the bazaar? He turned to test the water in the pool behind him, as she was doing, with his hand: it felt cool and clean. It seemed to wash away part of his lingering distaste for the latest incident with Seth. He wished he could dive in and get rid of it all.

"Weird that he hates us so much," he mused.

"Who — Seth?" she said the name as if it tasted bad. "I think it's because he's terrified. He's afraid of strong people."

When he saw that he was a shoulder-width away from the legs and feet of a seated statue, he reached out to lay his palm on one large stone calf. "It buzzed!" he said, jerking his hand away. "Electricity," he added to Freya.

She walked over and put her hand on the statue's other calf. "I don't feel anything," she said.

"Um. Wet your hand again and try."

She did, and jumped as the jolt hit her.

They all had to try it out on a few statues. Some were electric, some not.

A guard came down the front steps of the building with a bar of e-keys. He scowled at Freya. "Museum has closed. Gardens will be locked. You should be out! What are you doing?" When she shook his hand and told him about their final research notes here in the garden, he melted. He offered his services in the future and showed them out pleasantly, lulled by Freya's persuasion. Ozzie smiled a little, watching. But then the guy recalled himself again; he shut the gate with a clang and locked it.

**

The distance to the hostel was ten or twelve long blocks, but Ozzie said who knew when the next airbus was coming? So they went on foot instead, hunting for a restaurant along the way.

As they walked next to the din of traffic, Freya considered Ozzie's ability to look at things. It made her hopeful: he didn't have an ordinary way of seeing everything. "Those electric statues were odd," Freya mused as they stopped before a row of cafes.

"Oddness noted," Norm said. "But look at this." As she turned toward what he seemed to be interested in, a sign on a cafe door, the edge of her vision caught a dim figure gliding from behind them into the alleyway they had just passed.

CHAPTER TWENTY-TWO

NORM POINTED. They stood before a little restaurant called the Kasr al Nile Cafe whose menu, taped on the door, listed prices they could afford. She peered through the window; no one she could see inside looked like a tourist. "That's probably good," Ozzie said. "It must be decent food if the neighbors eat here."

While they found a table, many of the seated patrons eyed them curiously. *We must seem like an odd assortment to them*, Freya thought: an Asian with two lighter-haired types, and Norm with his exotic features, all four young and on their own. Freya saw someone enter from the street and sit in a far corner alone — another pair of curious eyes resting on her, like all the others, until she looked at him. Every time she glanced toward him, it seemed that he had just stopped looking her way.

Alexis looked up enough Egyptian words on her

phone to translate the menu and ask the waitress, awkwardly, what was good. Her choices were beyond good: something she called "pocket bread" and spicy meatballs, pickled vegetables, savory soup; they ate mostly with their hands, sharing it all and wiping up the juices with the bread, as they saw the people at the next table doing, until nothing was left.

They were too hungry to talk much till the food was gone. But they lingered over their Egyptian tea, sweet and mint-laced.

"Do you have a lot of relatives in Iceland?" Ozzie asked her, out of the blue.

"No." and she told him how the last of the relatives had moved to Denmark and Sweden for safety.

Did she think of doing that sometimes? He asked. He seemed to want to understand. She explained that her mother was having trouble keeping the family house up because there were so few people wanting to rent, but no one would buy it, and how could they leave it anyway? It was the only place where they belonged, and all they owned, really.

It wasn't a happy subject. Freya checked her phone and found a text from Arni, asking how she was. "Thanks for the message! I'm learning. How are you?" she answered. Then she sipped, feeling happier suddenly than she had felt all day.

"Well, the museum *was* interesting," Alexis was lecturing Norm.

"Yeah, I guess... All that gold," he said. "That death-mask that weighed 11 kilograms? And that was just a little bit of all that was there. You could buy some great toys, aircars and electronics, with that much gold."

Alexis said, "Hey, this is going to completely show what a nerd I am, but I loved that Senet game, the ebony and ivory one. I wanted to take it home and learn how to play that right now."

"Nerd-alert," Norm nodded. She giggled.

Ozzie said, "Did you notice? Some of the sculptures of people had heads that stuck out a long way at the back. Like those daughters of Akhenaton and Nefertiti."

Norm opened his mouth to say something humorous so Ozzie added quickly, "You could say it was the artist's imagination, but in the display it said Akhenaton himself decreed that all images had to be strictly realistic. So where did they get those weird heads?"

"I know: mutants," Norm said. "You're too serious, Freya," he added as she wrote down more notes.

She rolled her eyes. *What a clown.* But he had reminded her of something she noticed in the museum: that the flat, yoke-like golden collars on the royal statues, glittering richly with rows of lapis and turquoise, looked a lot like the woven ones on the wedding couple in her dream. *Could I really be dreaming the dreams of an Egyptian from long ago?* Her breath caught at the next thought: *Are the weird dreams related to Osiris?*

She would think about it later. Instead, she said, "Tomorrow we go to Giza..."

She was interrupted by something brushing the back of her chair. When she looked over her shoulder the man who had just passed behind her walked through a smudged and ravaged door into the restroom. He was the one who had been watching from the corner.

"Remind me not to use the restrooms here," Norm said.

Ozzie asked, "About Seth. Anyone think we should press charges?"

Alexis looked doubtful. Norm shrugged.

"I don't," Freya said. "We have better things to do. Not that he doesn't deserve it. But he's just been reduced to nothing in the eyes of the Cairo police. The disgrace should be enough to shut him up."

Norm and Ozzie exchanged a look. They didn't seem convinced.

Ozzie changed the subject. He got Norm to tell the story of one of his runaway pizzas at Dingo's in California. About how the spinning sheet of dough got away from him and wrapped around his head like a turban. When he got to the part where he left it on his head and went out to the booths to take orders, Norm's imitation of himself was so ridiculous that Freya chuckled helplessly in spite of herself.

She had forgotten how good it felt to laugh.

When they rose to go, Freya swept the room with her

eyes: the man who had watched them from the corner was gone. They were removing his dishes and washing the table.

"Aasif, Aasfa." *Excuse me.* The waitress apologized as she met them at their table, holding out Freya's daypack. She motioned to show that someone over there — and she waved at the other side of the room — had found it on the floor and didn't know whose it was, then gave it to her. She looked at each of them, her face asking "yours?"

"Mine," Freya nodded and pointed to herself. How sloppy of her to hang it on the back of her chair. This wasn't Iceland, and who knew these days, even there... It was stuffed full and when she rummaged, everything seemed to be in it: her wallet and keys, thermal jacket, even the protein bars and an empty water bottle.

"Shukran gazilan." She thanked the woman, seeing Ozzie's prompting eyes. Then on impulse she asked, "which man?" and gestured around the room. But the woman only pointed at the door through which he had left.

CHAPTER TWENTY-THREE

Y EAH, ALEXIS, LET'S STAY SAFE by keeping our packs connected to our bodies, even in a restaurant," Ozzie said softly as they climbed the dim stairway of the hostel. Their knives were in their hands. "Are you three making sure you're armed whenever you leave our room?" They nodded.

As he took the lead and turned the old-fashioned key, he could see an approving gleam in Freya's eyes. He breathed deep, as if to make room for some unexpected happiness somewhere in his chest, and put one foot over the threshold.

Wait, something is in here. Something large. He backed hastily out of the room, pushing the other three backward into the hall too. Reluctantly he pulled his gun from the holster in his jacket and hit the ancient switch, lighting the room as he swung the door open again slowly. His heart was thudding.

No one's here.

[Not exactly no one.] A cat was sitting before the open window on the sill.

The creature was gunmetal gray and seemed hairless. Its ears were very large. It was shaped as exactly as a statue, with its tail wrapped in a perfect curve around its feet.

[Greetings.] Ozzie thought at it, relaxing. [I just thought something big was in here.]

[I AM big. Looks are deceiving.]

[Something we can do for you?]

[Yes.] But the creature didn't give details.

Ozzie stepped aside to let the others in after him. "Our visitor is a cat," he said. He didn't have time to say more.

"Shoo!" Norm flapped his arms comically, charging at the visitor. "Get out! Leave or pay rent!"

The room dissolved in darkness. Alexis yelped like a small startled dog. The cat hissed, a noise as loud as if the creature were twenty times its size and they were inside its mouth. Norm yelled in pain. Then the light went back on again.

Norm was backing away from the window. As he turned toward them Ozzie saw that the front of his turtleneck was slit in four parallel lines, each slit soaking up blood at the edges from underneath. Taken together, the slits looked an awful lot like a big cat's scratch-mark, nearly a foot wide.

"Owww," Norm moaned. He looked badly stunned.

Alexis and Freya's faces froze in horror.

"Idiot," Ozzie muttered. *Showing off for Alexis.*

Alexis and Freya scrambled for wipes and water. The cat sat just as it had before. It spoke: [Looks are deceiving, as I said. He's lucky I didn't scratch hard.]

**

Freya heard that. She stopped and gazed at the cat; who was it talking to? When she looked at Ozzie's face, she knew, with amazement, then relief: *it's Ozzie.* Her respect for him went up another notch.

But Norm: horrifying. She turned to help Alexis cut off Norm's shredded and bloody shirt, and Alexis' face must have mirrored hers as they used the shirt to sop up the sickening red that was running from deep furrows in his chest. It would take more paper or cloth than this to stop the bleeding. Freya scanned the room without success for something that could be torn. When Alexis stopped dabbing for a second, Freya could see how hard those small hands were shaking. Sopping away with a piece of Tshirt in her own blood-smeared hands, she glanced at Norm's gray face, then..."Alexis!" she said.

The wounds were disappearing. Before their eyes the gashes lightened, then melted away like a holo-fade, leaving unscarred skin. The blood disappeared from the pile of wipes, from the bits of torn shirt, till there was no sign of any left.

Alexis looked at her clean hands, then at Freya's, then

at Norm — who blinked, coming back out of shock. He stared at the frightened tears on Alexis' face.

[How did you do that?] Freya heard Ozzie demand of the cat.

[I can do many things,] the cat said. [One of them is to protect you a little. I *will* be spending the night here tonight.] The cat gazed at Norm. With disapproval, Freya would have sworn it.

Freya looked at Ozzie, and he nodded.

[You are welcome here,] Freya said silently to the cat, inclining her head politely to show respect.

"What? What is it?" Norm was saying. He and Alexis turned from Ozzie to Freya, blinking.

So they had to begin the tale of the talking cats. After a minute or two they sat on the floor. After an hour, as the night air grew chilly, Norm remembered to put on a new shirt and got out some protein bars because by then they were all hungry again. Ozzie told about the cat-talking lesson from a gypsy named Malo, with side-trips for Norm's entertainment about gypsy swearing and other things. Freya ended, hours later, by repeating the cat dialogue from earlier tonight.

The cat sat on the sill without moving. It didn't seem to mind being discussed, either.

Finally, when they were all getting hopelessly vacant and sleepy, Norm yawned. "Nobody will believe this," he said. "*I* don't even believe it."

Alexis giggled and yawned. "I think I'm gonna listen a

little and see what I can pick up from cats in my vicinity."

**

It was long after midnight, and somewhere in Cairo an early rooster was crowing, when Ozzie fell asleep.

It may have been only moments later that he woke to hear a hiss, a yowl, a sound like something falling heavily outside their window. But then sleep pulled him under again.

CHAPTER TWENTY-FOUR

O H NO!" FREYA SAID. Over near the door, she saw Ozzie sit up abruptly on his platform, alert and groping for something under his sleepsack — his knife, probably. The sun was high. "We slept long. We're late!" Ozzie relaxed and rubbed his face, squinting in the light from the windows.

Giza. She sighed. They were definitely too late for what they had planned: an early start to avoid traffic. At this season the arteries to Giza would be clogged all day, according to the worldweb tourist lore.

Alexis rose to an elbow, her eyes only partly open. "I had a weird dream," she announced. No one asked, but she went ahead: "About a cat I took somewhere in an egg."

"Ha!" Norm scoffed sleepily.

She scowled at him. "I never dream things like that. It was weird because it seemed very businesslike, not dreamy at all, and I had this cat in an egg and I got into some kind of aircar? with it and we took off." She shook her head again.

"That's all?" Norm joked. "Didn't the cat drive the aircar or something?"

Ozzie chuckled and shook his head.

Always clowning, Freya thought irritably. She checked her phone. There was a text from Arni. Just wanted to know how she was. "It's going pretty well," she texted back.

"Maybe the museum inspired your dream, Alexis," Ozzie said. "Did you notice all the cat statues there?"

One thought led to the next: They all turned to look at the cat on the sill. It was gone.

Ozzie's phone made noises. He reached to pull it off the charger. "Missed call, No Caller ID," he muttered. "How does someone do that? IDs are just part of what your phone sends."

"That cat sure cost us an early start," Freya said. "I'm not certain he protected us from anything, really." Something nagged at her memory, then: a dream? Something while they slept? Nothing she could recall exactly.

**

They took her on a fast march to the Khan Al Kalili bazaar to show it to her and get some food. Maybe they could catch a bus to Giza in a traffic lull, she hoped, so they'd better get food now. As they passed one stall,

167

Ozzie said, "Hey, Freya. Let's make a fast trade and get your mother her scarf." And when she hesitated, he added, "There may not be another chance."

He seemed to know what she was thinking. She agreed, then, and he smiled as if he were anticipating some fun.

He sidled up to a pole hung so thickly with drooping clipped-on silk and satin scarves that it looked like a big flower. He fingered one or two of them, then moved away.

"Just one Egyptian pound," the seller was suddenly at his side. The man wore a dark blue fez above his western shirt and pants. Ozzie greeted him politely, backed up and fingered another scarf, then shrugged.

"Three U.S. dollars. Today exchange is four dollars to the pound," the vendor began again. Ozzie shook his head, shrugged and moved as if to leave. "Two," the seller urged.

Ozzie replied by holding up his index finger: *"One."*

The seller groaned and scowled as if he were about to threaten Ozzie. He poured out a long string of Arabic words with gestures that told his rage and frustration at this impossible offer.

Freya thought it was odd that Ozzie, who was so big on being polite, ignored the fuss the man was making. Ozzie looked around idly till his eyes rested on a clear tekryl hyperball below him on the vendor's table. He picked it up, with a nod for the man's permission. It had rainbow colors inside. He tossed it a little, experimentally. The impact, when he caught it, made the thing sparkle electronically. More impact, more sparkle. He tossed it up again and again.

Kind of fascinating, Freya thought. They were all watching the ball, including the vendor. Then Ozzie caught and held it, looking expectantly at the man.

The vendor seemed to know his cue. He said, "Scarf and ball, two U.S."

Ozzie shrugged and gestured to Freya to choose her scarf. When the vendor couldn't see, he gave her a little victorious smile that said: "Good game, we won."

She picked a silk one that she knew Mamma would like. The vendor didn't look sad either, Freya noticed. So maybe he thought he won too?

**

As they were pooling coins to pay for the scarf — Norm surprised them all with the idea — Ozzie's phone signalled. "No-ID caller. Again!" he said. He dropped his coins in Norm's hand and caught the call fast, without holo, while Norm bargained for a scarf for Mrs. Garcia, too.

The voice was one Ozzie struggled to recognize. *"Mom?"*

It was like falling through a paper backdrop into another world.

As if in a dream, he asked how she was, something

dumb. And answered that he was OK too, yes.

She said, "I've almost called you many times, but I decided not to because it wouldn't have made any difference."

No difference? In six years? He was so struck by the difference it would have made that he said nothing.

"Maybe this seems sudden to you, but there are some things I want to tell you and something I need to ask you. Can you talk for a little while now?"

Everything had gone away except her voice on the line. But now Ozzie was aware that Alexis had taken his arm and was walking him forward through the market, behind Freya and Norm. He was aware briefly of being glad that Freya was keeping an eye on Norm. There were minarets, and car horns, and food smells.

"OK," he said.

"These are things that are no easier to tell you now than when you were ten," she began, "but maybe you'll understand better because you're older now."

When he was ten. She must mean the day that was still vivid in his memory because of mingled gain and loss. More happiness and more sadness, put together, than in his whole life up till then.

Ms. Carmen had asked him over to her house down the road to help her with something. In her fragrant kitchen there was someone new, a nice-looking dark-haired woman whose eyes were full of warmth for him. She said she was his mother.

He had struggled and failed to recall her. He only remembered Dad saying she had been gone since he was five. She asked him grownup questions: about school and the relatives and his hobbies. She said his eyes were like hers. In a rush of ten-year-old affection, he had thrown his arms around her and hugged her a long time.

When she withdrew, her eyes were wet. She asked him, why didn't he go to the Space Academy? A bright boy like him could get a scholarship. She told him she would be in touch, gave him a gold ring as a keepsake, and made him promise not to tell his father anything about this.

And she left him again. He never knew where she was. He waited, always ready, but she never got in touch.

Now she was saying, "I had to leave when you were five. I was ruining your father. He abandoned his music when you were born. He was...in pain, and beginning to make some bad choices.

"We loved each other a lot, Ozzie. But our dreams fell apart and we did too. It was my fault."

"I decided to leave you and your father alone so you two could make a new life. Maybe I should have taken you with me. I couldn't, at first. I had nowhere to take you to. I went and stayed with Malo— "

"—Really? You and Malo?"

"No no, not like that. Malo is *very old*, Ozzie, older than you think." Ozzie thought of Malo's dark hair and so-alive eyes. "He was kind. They let me stay there a little while till I could get a place, go to school, get a degree. I kept thinking I was almost ready to come get you.

"After I finished studying I got a job in one of the big Space Valley companies out here: Asteroid Aeronautics. You've heard of them."

Asteroid. *Holy smoke.* "You're right near Las Cruces?" Ozzie was astonished.

"I always have been," she said. "Keeping an eye on you."

Someone had ordered food and Alexis, Freya and Norm were sitting with him at a little table near the food stalls. There were buzzing people, calling voices, ancient car-horns going. His friends were chewing and watching him gravely. He realized that his eyes were leaking onto his face a little, so embarrassing…

He brushed impatiently with his fingers to dry them and moved the phone back to his ear.

"I have another company now. Maybe I can tour you around someday…"

"Why don't you come live with Dad?" It was out: the dream of every kid with separated parents. Ozzie felt like a holovid cliché, and right there in front of his friends, too.

"He doesn't love the person I am now, Ozzie. We're different.

"We'll talk more. Right now I need to ask you something. That ring I gave you? It has something in it that I need to get. Do you have it?" Her voice sounded anxious.

"Not with me," Ozzie said. *And not anywhere I know of.* "I'm...doing a robotics project in California for the JPL robotics competition in December and I..."

"Good!"

"...and I'm not at home in Las Cruces," he said lamely. "But when I get back home in December ..."

"OK, I'll call you when you're home again," she said. "And how *is* your father? Oh! Carter, I'll be right there. I'm sorry, late for a meeting, Ozzie. I'll call you, OK?"

And she was gone.

His vision gradually focused on his friends. Alexis' raisin-dark eyes were soft with sympathy.

"Got you some falafel," Norm said.

He nodded and picked up one of the cold lumps with his fingers. Egypt was fascinating, but he was ready to leave right now, go find the ring, and see her again. How could there be something in the ring? *And where is it, anyway?*

**

"I didn't know you had a mother, Ozzie." Freya said softly. She watched him, sipping her tea cautiously, but she felt some of her own reserve melting.

"I *didn't* have one, really," Ozzie mused and shrugged, eyes on the sad face of a passing woman wearing a headscarf. He offered nothing further.

In the presence of this mystery no one spoke till

Norm licked his fingers, brushed some crumbs off the front of his blue turtleneck, and said, "By the way, Ozzie, what was that trick you were doing in the market a few days ago, about those stuffed dates? I forgot to ask."

Ozzie roused himself. "Something I learned in Advanced Trading: called Create a Distraction. What you do when things get too serious too fast."

Then Alexis made Norm tell Freya the tale of their first adventures in Egypt. "He almost got us killed," Alexis said. Norm acted out the heart-stopping moments from his viewpoint, and from that view they were more funny than fearsome, Freya thought. Alexis pulled out her pulp-book and did the last Advanced Level number puzzle while she helped Norm tell his elaborate version of the story, finishing the puzzle absent-mindedly and pushing it aside.

"So Ozzie saved Norm," she concluded for him. "Saved me, too." She fanned herself theatrically with her hand and bugged her eyes at Freya.

"Well, you should have seen how brave Alexis was," Ozzie said, anxious to fend off some of the praise. "She walked right up to that first vendor and got Norm out of there."

Norm yawned noisily.

"Brave of you both!" Freya said. "And that was pretty clever, Ozzie." She was still trying to be professional. But she couldn't keep the admiration out of her eyes.

Ozzie had surprising talents: A trader. A quick-thinking diplomat. *And he talks to cats.* She smiled to herself at the idea.

CHAPTER TWENTY-FIVE

FREYA TOLD THEM, "We need a vote. It's too late to start today unless we want to spend four hours breathing fumes on the bus. We might do better to get an early start tomorrow, and use the extra night that Alexis booked us here at the hostel. But that puts us here for the rest of today and I don't have anything further we need to see in Cairo. I could do more research on the worldweb—"

"Then we need to go play," Norm said. Alexis giggled at him. Ozzie looked doubtful, and Freya thought she knew how he felt: all the way here, with their project waiting at home, and they had nothing they could do today to get back home faster? *He's very purposeful, like me.*

As she considered, she pulled a pulp-map of Cairo from her daypack and spread it out on the table before them.

Norm was drawn in by the names and symbols.

"Hmmm, this is where we are now. And there's the hostel. We walked all this way? Hunger will do that for you."

"The Nile..." Alexis put her finger on the map where the broad blue river that ran north and south. "It's huge. Cairo is like London: built on a river."

"I guess Las Cruces is too," Ozzie said. "But that one's not such a big one." He was coming back to life, getting interested in the map, but he still hadn't returned from wherever that phone call had taken him.

Looking at Ozzie, Freya's years of experience at keeping her mother from coming unglued made her offer a plan: "Want to go see the waterfront?" she asked. "Maybe they have those triangular boats there."

"Yeah, we could go for a dip," Norm said.

Freya chuckled and rolled her eyes.

They were all fed, they had their walking shoes on. Even Ozzie seemed to brighten up at the prospect of something active.

It took about an hour for them to walk from the bazaar through dense downtown Cairo to the waterfront. It was cooler here on the pavement beside the river, but the sun threw sparks off the water and made it boil with light. Ozzie and Norm, who had both led fairly landlocked lives, chatted and pointed and ran out on catwalks to get the best views of the boats, including the ones with those flimsy-looking triangular sails. Alexis took holos of them with her phone.

Freya watched, brooding a little in the business-day quiet of the waterfront. On the way here Alexis had asked, "Why don't we use scientific methods in this research?" Such a bright-sounding question, but so dumb. Did she think Freya was here just to play scientist? She was here for answers. Sometimes Alexis and Norm didn't seem to understand. And Norm didn't seem like he'd be much help in a tough spot.

Alexis had just treated everyone to iced "Cairo coffee" from a vendor with a cart when one of the sailboat owners asked Norm if they wanted a ride, in English. "Thank you," Norm said in Egyptian, then *"Bititkallim Ingilizi?"*

The man nodded, yes, yes. Freya was surprised to see Norm the Clown remember his manners and his language lessons.

"About the boat," Norm said, "We'd like to but we have little money."

Maybe it was a slow day for boat hires. The man offered a ride for "little." Ozzie lit up with interest and entered the bargaining, a deal was struck, and they teetered aboard, iced coffees and all.

Once they had found seats it was surprising how quickly the boatman had the boat out on the water, flying across the ancient river.

Ozzie offered his almost-untouched drink to the boatman in exchange for the right to work the tiller while their captain supervised and managed the sail.

Glancing sideways, Freya watched Ozzie. His eyes — they seemed gray-green now, but weren't they blue before? — were sparkling at the challenge of maneuvering the boat. The wind blew his hair back and his tanned arms seemed to quickly learn the way to balance between water and wind. The water that was as natural as life to her seemed almost that familiar to him already.

The motion of the boat became so smooth they all relaxed and watched Cairo sliding by on the banks of the river. Freya sat with her eyes half-closed, enjoying the speed and the breeze.

But Ozzie's easy success made him and the boatman less watchful. Ozzie gave the tiller a sharper turn just as the sail shifted. The boat dipped crazily. Alexis, in the prow laughing at Norm, was suddenly overboard with the boat skimming past her.

Freya leaped up, ready to go in after her, but Norm was in the way. He stared, then turned, his eyes searching. When his eyes caught on a life buoy he snatched it and tossed it past Alexis with one hand while his other held the rope. It hit the water with a slap, behind the boat now, and as the boat moved forward it whacked her head. "Grab it!" he yelled at her.

She flopped her arms at it in ungraceful panic, but she didn't need to be told twice. Once her hands touched it she groped fast and held on fiercely while Freya gripped the back end of the rope for insurance and Norm hauled Alexis toward the side of the boat. Ozzie angled the tiller to hold the boat to a small circular orbit around her. She was soaking wet, spluttering and gagging. "Cold!" she yelped, followed by a loud string of Chinese words.

The boatman looked disgusted. He was already furling their sail to slow the boat. Then he issued orders: Ozzie with him to Freya's side of the boat, to balance the weight while Norm pulled Alexis back aboard on the other side. It was an awkward process, but after a couple of misfires Norm figured out how to do it — without rocking the boat too wildly — by getting Alexis to lie on her stomach, hug the lifebuoy, and float with her legs behind her. He lifted one, then the other, over the side of the boat and then levered her in by her waist.

"Norm, that lifebuoy throw! I've never seen you do anything so fast!" Ozzie crowed in admiration. Ozzie spoke for Freya, too — she would never have guessed Norm could react that quickly. He was always so much in nerd-world somewhere.

Norm smiled faintly, panting a little. He crouched by Alexis, who sat in the bottom of the boat dripping and shivering. She gave Ozzie a grouchy look. "Sorry, Alexis," Ozzie said. His face was getting red.

Alexis' phone rang. She got it out of the pack fast enough to see the ID. "My mother! Not taking it." Freya helped the boatman wrap Alexis in a very used blanket that he pulled out of a locker at the stern.

He seemed relieved when he could let them all off again at the wharf.

Once they and their packs were back on land, Norm sniffed at Alexis' sopping hair. "Mmmm. You smell like swamp water," he said, smiling at her pleasantly. Alexis giggled, then scolded, "I need to dry off!" Ozzie watched them with a strange intensity. To Freya he looked envious.

**

Walking back toward the hostel, Freya checked her phone: another text from Arni, asking how she was doing there. "All's well," she texted back.

She looked up and saw Ozzie, who walked beside her, watching her. The sun caught his face at an angle that lit gold flecks in his eyes. "Boyfriend?" he asked. She shrugged and turned away, suppressing a flash of anger. *Not your business.*

His eyes clouded and he turned them to the minarets and the traffic.

Then she was sorry to have shut him out. And she realized: *I feel guilty to be interested in two guys at once.*

**

"Time for my weekly parent call," Alexis said as they arrived at the hostel after dinner. "Keeps them from worrying."

"Good idea," Ozzie said, thinking again of his mother

and realizing that even if he were in New Mexico now, he couldn't find her. *How did I let her get away again, with no ID, no way to reach her?* "I'd better call my Dad too."

**

Among their combined voices, as they entered their hostel room, Freya heard another voice say Alexis' name. Alexis looked around her to see where it had come from. Ozzie and Norm chatted on together, dropped their things and headed back into the hall to find places to make their calls.

When they left the room was silent. *Guess it was no one,* Freya thought.

[No one?] It was the cat on the windowsill again. Alexis' head whirled to look. The cat returned her gaze without blinking for a few seconds. Then it jumped down from the sill and walked to her sleeping platform. There he made himself at home above her pillow and began licking one long back leg vigorously, holding it horizontally, chewing carefully between the toes.

Alexis heard that cat, Freya thought. *What next?*

**

Ozzie tossed and caught the hyperball as they talked. *Glad we're going to Giza at last tomorrow. A chance to see the pyramids! And another chance to get Freya's question answered so we can go home.*

Alexis seemed to be trying to brush her teeth in front

182

of everyone without looking disgusting. She went and spat out the extra toothpaste, then returned, still brushing. "Thanks again for saving me, Norm," she said around the brush. She smiled at him. Norm continued to check his phone so she went and spat again.

Ozzie pulled his phone off the charger and checked for messages too, then. He was startled to see that a text was in from No-ID:

Ozzie, that ring was your grandfather's. My father's. Maybe you don't know: he was a research scientist for Grand Galactic — one of the first. Developed precursor of modern drives. More later. Mom.

"What?!" His world shifted so fast it tore; questions began to pour through cracks in the landscape and pile up in his mind. *Wasn't her father a farmer too, like Grandpa Reed? Never heard her other name; what was it?* The others went silent, watching him. He looked up at Alexis, Norm, Freya. He felt a little dizzy. "Don't mind me, guys."

"If you say so, Ozzie." Norm grinned.

"We must start early tomorrow to miss the traffic," Freya said. "Can we all get up at 5?"

Norm groaned.

It was already October-dark outside the windows, and shadowy in the room. "We could just go to sleep early," she said. She walked to the raised window, reaching up as if to shut it for the night. She drew a loud breath in. "Ozzie, look!"

All three crowded around the window. Ozzie saw the blood on the broad wooden sill, dried smears of it, and deep gashes as if a knife point had struck several times. Nothing was visible down below but the dirty, trash-strewn alley.

Ozzie turned to the cat. It sat at the head of Alexis' bed, looking at them.

Freya shut and locked the window.

CHAPTER TWENTY-SIX

THEIR PACKS WERE HEAVY but the pre-dawn air was cool as they walked to the bus stop for Giza, near the museum.

The voices ahead of Ozzie and Norm rose to a higher volume. Ozzie heard Alexis say, "It's just that you don't seem to approach this with much scientific methodology."

Ozzie admired Freya's graceful walk. "I'm as scientific as I need to be, Alexis. I don't have time to test everything for months! I'm dying to know more about *all* these things, but we just don't have the time right now."

That's right! Ozzie thought. There was another exchange of irritable remarks that Ozzie missed, then silence for a while from the female department up ahead.

Ozzie said softly to Norm, "Well, you seem to like her."

"Who?"

"Alexis."

"Yeah. — You mean as a girlfriend? Nah, I'm too busy for a girlfriend! Also females seem dumb to me. Except for the robotics females, but most of them are disappointing as girls. It's a problem I haven't solved," he said.

Ozzie nodded, understanding. He couldn't claim to be an expert either.

"Anyone want a protein bar?" Norm called, grinning, and took the silence as permission to eat the last one in his pack himself.

Quiet followed, if the horns and rush of the traffic could be called that. Ozzie's thoughts went where they had not been for at least a day: to the problem he went to California to solve. He needed to qualify for the Captain's Apprentice spot. But when he did, he would be there on that first trading flight to Mars.

At the bus stop, he lowered his pack and began to tap a query into his phone; while they waited, he could look some things up about his mother and grandfather. Searching for Asteroid Aero personnel history, he got someone with her first name, Rachel, but with another last name and no other info. When he searched on "Who's Who in Space Valley," he found the same name, now part owner of I.R.E. Incorporated. Must be her.

The bus came then and interrupted him.

**

Freya was worried and edgy. *Alexis is right, in a way; there isn't a clear path for this research.*

As the public airbus crossed the bridge they stood a minute for a better view out the side windows at the Nile. Sunrise, over the city to their right, brightened the sky and lighted the faces of buildings there on the west side of the river. From the east side, European-style hotels and palms threw long shadows across the water. Those boats with the triangular sails skimmed like birds, in and out of the shadows.

"How long till we get to the hostel?" Ozzie asked Freya.

"It's not far — just 18 km (or 11 miles for you and Norm) west to the Giza Necropolis, the City of the Dead, where the Great Pyramid is. But see how slowly traffic moves, even now," she said. "It may be an hour or two."

They sat in facing seats at the back of the bus, looking at the buildings of Giza now inching past above each others' shoulders. "Giza looks just like Cairo," Norm said, and yawned.

Alexis opened the front zipper of her pack and extracted the pocket bread and tahini that she had ordered last night at supper and saved, wrapped in restaurant napkins. "Breakfast." She handed them out.

"Dry but delicious, my dear," Norm batted his eyelashes at Alexis. She gave him a minimal smile.

"Thanks, Alexis. Good idea," Freya said, to bury their quarrel. She was hungry and it was good. She was grateful that Alexis had taken over as food planner. Freya didn't want the job.

"So we're going to the Giza Necropolis to check out the music-making potential, right?" Norm said with his mouth full.

"Right. As I was saying last night, today we know these three pyramids were never tombs, because no mummy has ever been found in them, or wall paintings or other things like in the real tombs. The blocks they are made of, the tunnels inside them, and the maze of tunnels beneath them, were machined, never cut with primitive tools — you can tell by the precise fit, the exactness of the grooves and slots. They must have been made for technical uses — probably much longer ago than our histories think — by people with advanced technology.

"Some theories say they were beacons. Some say that they were developed as resonators: to make sound. I have thought their sound could be our answer. I still hope so! But I found something just a few days ago on the worldweb: an ancient oral tradition in this area is that they were great big generators that used the resonance of the chambers in the pyramid to break water — the water running through the tunnels below them — into hydrogen and oxygen to create a supply of power."

"Seems wild but it makes some sense," Norm said, "Technically possible, isn't it, Ozzie."

Ozzie nodded. "So...probably the Nile was further to the west in those days."

Yes, Freya thought. *He's right. How many millennia would it have taken for the Nile's bed to change by 18 kilometers? Could another local legend be right, that the Giza pyramids really date from before the Great Flood?* She saw something about it on the worldweb last night. But that wasn't important. Something to read about sometime when the volcanoes were fixed…

"So: we'll be looking for ways that the resonance of the pyramids can be used to tame volcanoes," Alexis said with the air of a student reciting a lesson.

"Yes." Then Freya sighed. "As I research, the more I learn the more I wonder if they could be the source we need. They were never meant for music, it seems. So could they be the music that Osiris used?

"But maybe I'm not thinking about this as they did. We will have to open our eyes and look. Please keep your minds open for anything that you think might help us with an idea."

Knowing that her hasty, messy method was being questioned by Alexis — maybe all of them — didn't make her feel any more brilliant. But somewhere in all the wrong answers, she had to find the right one. Fast.

**

To Freya, Ozzie seemed unconcerned. He was looking out the window at the slow procession of storefronts and mosques, palm trees and vendor carts as they passed. He seemed to love how different this place was from anywhere else he had been. He would make a good trader.

Then he turned to his phone again, and when he thought no one was looking, flipped some icons into the air, seemingly lost in thought.

She checked her phone: another text from Arni. How was she? "All fine," she texted back.

She and Ozzie had separated parents. Norm and Alexis had parents who were still together. She saw in memory the throne of Tutankhamon that was sitting in a glass case in the Egyptian Museum. The wood was completely overlaid with gold, silver and gems, and the back-rest was a sort of portrait of the young king and his wife. The image kept returning to her mind: those two with the lapis headdresses, gazing pleasantly at each other, her hand reaching to touch his arm. Thousands of years had gone by, and they were still there together.

**

"Hey," Alexis said. "I just remembered! I had another *weird* dream last night."

"Ooo boy," Norm said, and she scowled at him, then giggled.

"Really. I dreamed I was building a robot—"

"What a surprise!" Norm interrupted again. Ozzie elbowed him.

"The dream was full of technology like the last one. It was utterly real, only... not. I was building a robot that I had designed for livestock. Um, a sort of incubator or barn — at least twice as big as your garage, Norm, only low and portable, with windows and solar — that held animals, and fed them and cleaned up after them and regulated their environment robotically. It was for rabbits and mice I think, something furry. And chickens, and fish in a tank, and some lizards and things...It was fascinating. It was like an automated cattle barn only littler and for various animals and even some plants...There were lettuce and maybe basil and—"

"We *get* it!" Norm said.

She scowled — sincerely scowled, that time.

"Uncle Norm is grouchy. Up too early," Ozzie said to her.

"When did you dream it?" Freya asked. "I have had weird dreams too, but not since I came here."

"Um. Just before I woke up this morning." Alexis looked out the window for a minute. "By the way, you know what else? I found that cat on my pillow, right by my head, when I woke. Can you believe he hung out so close to me like that while I slept? After Norm's...incident, I was afraid to move him away so I covered my head with the blanket to protect my eyes. But then the alarm went off anyway and he moved."

How familiar: the weird dream, the cat on the pillow. *Are these dreams coming **from** the cats?* Freya wondered again. She had rejected the idea before, but maybe they were. OK, suppose they were. Why?

She had seen their hairless visitor melting out the open window as they were helping each other get their packs on this morning. Now she saw the cat again her mind's eye, leaping effortlessly to the sill. Unmarked gray, slender and shadowlike. And then gone.

**

Norm was right: Giza looked like Cairo. In fact, as Norm read from his phone, although the city of 4.5 million had its own government, it was part of greater Cairo, swallowed up by the bigger city.

But here is one big difference, Freya thought. As they rode through Giza, the pyramids began to rise above the surrounding buildings, first as distant symbols, then as huge, fascinating stone things, and finally as these enormous, surreal, almost live presences that dominated everything else. This close, there was nothing there at all for her but the pyramids and their magnetism.

Norm called out in a singsong, like one of the tour guides at the Egyptian Museum, "Giza! Home of the City of the Dead, the Great Pyramid of Khufu, the Sphinx, and the pyramids of Khafra and Menkaura. This is our stop, ladies and gentlemen, please watch your step."

**

"Ugh, bunk beds," Alexis said as they entered their

room. "I forgot to ask when I made the reservation. Boys' bunks there, girls' bunks here," she pointed, and took occupancy of the lower right-hand one by tossing her hat onto it.

Their new hostel was another rundown former hotel, covered with some kind of gray stucco, within sight of the Great Pyramid. A little courtyard out front was shaded by some palms. Check-in was quick because Alexis had arranged it all ahead of time. *Alexis is great to have on this team,* Freya thought.

"At least there's a shower in our room! Hot, not a shared cold-water bath down the hall, like in the other place." Alexis' announcement inspired them to pick their turns for the bathroom immediately.

Ozzie and Norm had already shucked their packs and were tearing them apart for bodywash and towels. Tossing hers up onto the top bunk, Freya opened it and pulled out the small daypack for today's trip to the pyramids. It was still loaded from their long museum day, and surprisingly heavy. While Alexis showered she lightened it by removing things she wouldn't need.

**

The hot water was delicious in spite of the squealing and groaning of the old pipes. Freya was rinsing the shampoo from her hair when she heard the last piece of Alexis' dream drop out of the air. Alexis was wrapped in a towel and brushing her teeth at the sink. She stopped and said, "It was cats, not mice! Mice, how silly. There was a pair of cats in the robot greenhouse."

CHAPTER TWENTY-SEVEN

T HEY BOUGHT some falafel and non-alcoholic beer and ate looking across the road at the pyramids. Ozzie couldn't believe they could sit at eye-level with the tops of those huge things, eating and drinking like ordinary mortals. "Well, the beer tastes authentic. Like it came from a tomb," Norm joked.

Alexis grew her lopsided smile and wagged her head at him indulgently. "You are absurd." Freya chuckled, eyes on the newsfeed on her phone.

A local shuttle took them up to the dusty plateau that overlooked Giza, where the pyramids called Khufu, Khafra, and Menkaura towered far above the colossal Sphinx. At the feet of these huge things were many low ruined structures huddled like villages, and what looked like several archeological digs in progress. The swarms of tourists, the camels and horses, buses and souvenir vendors, all seemed to be afterthoughts: small ground-creatures in a place designed for giants.

When the four of them stepped down off the open sides of the shuttle and shouldered their day daypacks, Ozzie's attention went to a man standing nearby who had left the shuttle just before them. His dark hair and eyes, brown skin, and western clothes marked him as a fairly typical local Egyptian. But as a tourist he wasn't ordinary: he was alone, without pack or camera or companions. He wore a shirt whose oddly long sleeves half-covered his hands. And as the shuttle passengers dispersed, he lingered, his eyes turned toward the four of them. When Ozzie looked at him he looked away.

Freya was already leading the way to the Sphinx, nearest of the enormous structures. Norm and Alexis chatted together just behind her. Ozzie followed them for about twenty yards, then turned in a slow circle with his binoculars at his eyes. The man's face looked alarmingly close in the glasses as they passed over him, but Ozzie memorized it before the man turned away again, just in case: moustache, heavy brow, cut scar on his right jaw, eyes yellow with jaundice, and a wound, just starting to scab over, on his nose.

The others were safely merged with a crowd of tourists now. They were resting their palms against one huge paw of the Sphinx. Even the forepaw of the reclining cat-man — or was the Sphinx a woman? — was higher than their heads. They each wet a hand with water from their bottles, and touched again. Ozzie joined them and did the same, feeling the little buzz of electricity. "Strange," Freya said, and made a note on her tablet.

When Ozzie turned, the face of the man from the shuttle was just disappearing behind the Sphinx's other paw.

He warned the others and they found a shadowy niche to loosen the knife-sheaths on their legs. They circled warily around the Sphinx, then joined the crowd on a raised observation platform.

"The head seems so small compared to the rest," Alexis mused. "Just as it does in the photos."

"Below the head it's rough. It looks like the water-worn rock layers in New Mexico," Ozzie said. "To me it looks like it was sitting up to its neck in fast-moving water for a few years."

"I think so too," Freya said. "Maybe the Great Flood?"

"Hey," Norm added. "Maybe someone did a new head after the Great Flood wore the old one away. You know, chipped away the worn parts to make a new head, only smaller."

And even if it was more recent, the Sphinx's current head had been damaged also. Looking at holos of the broken face, Ozzie had wondered why someone would damage it. Now, the birds roosting in the deep hollows above the curved cheekbones replaced the Sphinx's missing eyes with dark, flickering motion as if the eyes were alive.

**

There was a bus-crowded third of a mile of very worn road from the Sphinx to the pyramid of Khufu, but they decided to save bus fare and walk. Norm took holovids of Khufu and the other pyramids with his phone as they approached. While he did he kept up a running commentary. It was sometimes funny, sometimes not.

At Khufu, school children were sitting on the tops of the lowest blocks. Norm clasped his hands to make a step for Alexis to get up there and sit, too. Ozzie watched this with interest. He turned to Freya with a look that said, "Can you believe that?"

Then Ozzie offered her his hands too, with courtly gestures. He looked so irresistible that she laughed and accepted. *Points for charming,* she thought.

Ozzie and Norm followed. They jumped and boosted themselves up the huge blocks. As she watched, Freya thought of the charming looks men directed at her mother, and how useless they all were, and she dismissed the whole idea of charm. *Not worth much, I guess.*

They all sat drinking from their water bottles, craning their necks upward and sideward at the enormous stairway that climbed from the step on which they rested. Only then did one of them think of the water test. "This thing is buzzing," Alexis said. "Try it!"

They did, and it was. But there was more than that, as

Ozzie discovered. When he sat back against the next higher stone and his head touched it, he announced that his ears were ringing. He said, "It feels like one of those tuning forks has been set off on my head."

The others tried it. Freya pulled her head away quickly, astonished at the impact of the vibration. It was sound, but to her it felt as intense as a shock. "Hey, let's go see how electric the other two pyramids are," she said.

**

"We want a skilled guide for tomorrow morning, to take us through the Great Pyramid," Freya told the turbaned man with the donkey. The brilliant sun now painted shadows for miles across the plateau. Ozzie saw that it had also turned the man's face as leathery and wrinkled as a sun-dried fig. The guide's gaze was penetrating; it lingered on each of them before he relaxed and almost smiled.

They had found him by asking at each pyramid for a guide who was local and spoke English as well. Many generations of his family had lived at the Giza plateau, he said, and he knew the old stories.

Ozzie slipped to Freya's side to help with bargaining. He was already tired of today's round of nerdy data-collection and happy for some live action. It seemed like Freya had more tolerance for the kind of random research they were doing than he or Norm or Alexis did.

But the other two must have decided to treat the whole experience as the Help-Freya Tour of Egypt: all fun for a little while, if Freya was happy. Because he had heard more about her research than the others, Ozzie worried about how this would all result in what she wanted.

"Do you know why the pyramids ring with sound?" Freya tested their prospective guide.

Something kindled in his eyes. "Sometimes they do, sometimes not. I can tell you, yes," he said. "Tomorrow."

It seemed like a bargaining move to Ozzie. He asked, "How much for four of us, into the most resonating of the three pyramids?" The white-robed man turned and looked steadily at him. He seemed like Malo, or like a cat, so Ozzie looked back, waiting. Finally the old man said, "Four pears from the market. Be at Khufu tomorrow, soon after the gates open." He bowed slightly and was leading the donkey away before anyone could ask anything more.

"Four pears?" Alexis said as they watched the figures of man and donkey diminishing, casting long shadows ahead of themselves. "That's not much."

Ozzie started toward the gate. He said, "We'll have to see if anyone in the market even *has* pears at this time of year." What an odd form of payment. What if it were some kind of riddle or trick?

Well, at worst case, if the guy turned out to be a disappointment, they would just have to find a new guide.

"I guess the price is right," Norm said. "Especially since we're going to have to pay the admission fee to the pyramid, too."

Ozzie looked around again for the Stalker, as he had been doing all day. The man hadn't shown up again. No sign of him now, either. *Maybe a thief, thinking we were easy victims, and he changed his mind.*

"It will be dark soon," he said. "Let's find the market and the pears."

CHAPTER TWENTY-EIGHT

THE WOMAN SHOOK HER HEAD as she bent heavily to put some unsold cabbages into baskets. *We're all starving and this pear-shopping trip is taking a long time,* Freya thought. This was the third vendor who had turned them away. They had checked on the worldweb to get the word for "pear." No *kumetra.*

"Men fadlek?" (Please?) Freya asked politely, holding up her hand to stop the woman. She spread her palms and looked around, then back to the woman. *"Kumetra.* Where?"

The woman sighed and straightened for a moment, thinking. Then she used signs to tell them: that way two streets, then turn that way, then go three streets, and that way three (or maybe more) doors. There might be two lights. *"Kumetra,"* she nodded.

They showered her with thanks. Then, on impulse, Freya pulled out her wallet, held up a small silver Icelandic coin and pointed at the dates the woman was repacking. The woman brightened, took the money, and rewarded them with four fat stuffed dates each.

As they walked off, Freya had the impulse to turn and look back. When she did she was startled. The woman stood scowling blackly after them.

It was only when they were a block away, chewing on the sweet fruit, that Freya realized what she hadn't seen in her wallet. "My ID," she said, and looked again. It's gone!" They all stopped while she went through the things in her daypack. She began to empty the chambers of her backpack onto the curb.

Ozzie said, "Freya, it's nearly dark. This is a bad place to do that."

He was right. It was also a good thing he had remembered the directions, because by that time she was so distracted she wasn't sure whether it was three blocks that way, then turn left, or two and go right, or any part of what came after.

Ozzie got them to the right street. *He's not bad as a navigator, either,* Freya thought.

A nearly–full moon was rising between two tall buildings ahead of them. But when they turned left into the side street that should have been correct, it was very dark.

"Better arm," Ozzie said. They all followed his example, boosting their pant-legs and slipping knives into their hands. Ozzie looked a little worried, but he took the lead.

"No fooling around, now, Alexis," Norm whispered. She made a fist at him.

Ozzie led them down the center of the alley, looking right and left as he went. The dark doorways and dusty windows seemed to say that the places along there were abandoned, but Freya felt certain that they were not. She took the end of their column, walking backwards slowly to watch behind them. The missing ID unnerved her.

"No sign of any market here," Ozzie said disgustedly. But he said it softly. He turned to lead them out.

Norm yawned. "Some people just don't give good directions."

They moved quickly back toward the open end of the alley. Stepping into the light from the main street, they nearly ran into 5 or 6 ragged young guys who appeared from around the corner, muttering to each other in Egyptian.

"Come on!" Ozzie ordered. The four took a fast left and pelted down the street toward the rising moon, looking for shelter or a place they could defend. Ozzie must have been as blinded by the light as she was, because he led them down another dark little street, only to find that it had a dead end too. Freya heard him groan softly as they turned to meet their pursuers.

"Ozzie, can you shoot?" It was Norm's whisper.

But the foremost pursuer grabbed Freya's knife-arm just as she halted and turned. He pointed a gaunt, greasy finger at her and exclaimed something. Then two of them pulled her knife away and one held it at her.

She saw Norm put Alexis behind him and pull out his flashlight.

Freya cried, *"Láttu mig vera!"* (Leave me alone!) in Icelandic. Her unfamiliar speech stopped the Egyptians cold, but only for a moment. They wrestled her forward, slashing at Ozzie with her knife to keep him at bay as they dragged her out of the alley and moved down the street with her, knocking into crates and cartons on the sidewalk, struggling into and out of a stinking gutter.

Her heart was pounding. Ozzie was still with her at least. The two of them did all they could to interfere with the gang and turn the clot of foul-smelling bodies around. Where were the others? Freya could feel Norm and Alexis moving somewhere nearby in the shadows. All they had were knives, and it was too close for a knife-fight or a gunshot. What were they trying to do?

She did the only thing she could; she braced her feet to set her weight against the motion of the ragged bodies.

She heard something heavy club two heads. Cries. Shuffling. Then Norm yelling, "Sergeant Norman, Cairo Special Agent POLICE!" and two lights flicked on directly in the eyes of the ragged gangsters.

As they staggered back, blinded, Ozzie stuck the muzzle of his gun into the ribs of the one holding Freya, who spat out a word and released his grip on Freya's arm. She twisted away.

The gang scuffled and clawed at each other in their confusion. Then they ran.

The moonlight sent tall shadows fleeing ahead of them as they went.

Norm and Alexis turned off their laserlights. The four travelers stood and panted. Alexis hugged each one of them. "Thank you, all of you," Freya gasped. "Scary." Then, "Damn. They took my knife."

Ozzie put his into her hand. "We need to get back to the hostel," he panted. "Before..."

"Let's skip the pears. There's no sign of any market on the geo app," Norm said.

"Hey," Alexis whispered. "See the two lights down there? Maybe this is the right street?"

They stood before another alleyway, also clearly a dead end. The alley had a pair of lighted lamps halfway down it casting yellow pools on the ground — enough light to show that no one waited in ambush there.

Ozzie shrugged. "I'll go check. You stay," he said. The noises of the surrounding city became muffled as he walked inward, gun in hand. At a noise right behind him, he whirled and scowled to see them following.

"Watch how you point that thing," Norm said. "We're coming too. Scared without you." he smirked.

They reached the lamp-pools and stopped. Ozzie stepped up to the door, which was open just enough to paint a streak of light across the threshold and his foot. A dusty window beside it reflected the outside lamps dully.

Before they could decide what to do next, the door swept open to reveal a bent old man wearing a fez.

When his eyes met Ozzie's gun he gasped and let fly a string of Arabic with gestures. He scolded them for the weapons, pointed to himself, waved his hands in the air.

"Ahlan wa sahlan. Aasif. maAlish." Ozzie hastily gave the greeting and an apology, bowed and said, *"Kumetra,"* then gestured toward themselves, thinking he'd better explain their errand fast. The girls nodded politely. *"Ahlan wa sahlan. Bititkallim Ingilizi?"* Norm added. The man shook his head, still unhappy. No, he didn't speak English.

While they followed Ozzie's lead in putting their weapons away, Freya absorbed the dimly-lit room behind the man. It was a little store, more like a store room right now because it was stacked with baskets of dried things and the surfaces of a few old tables were piled with platters and bowls of citrus and other fruits, greens and roots. Even from here she could smell cinnamon and ripe fruit. Probably most of those goods spent their days spread out on the walkway for local people to buy.

The old man watched them soberly, then nodded when all the knives were sheathed. Only then did he reply to their greeting and step back to let them enter. He gestured at a wooden platter sitting in the shadows on a carved sideboard, heaped with pears. He watched as they each chose one, then a second one. The second was Alexis' idea: extras to be sure they had excellent ones for the guide and a pear for each of them for lunch tomorrow.

The price wasn't high. They thanked him politely and wished him goodbye, relieved to be going. Could they be blamed for thinking his location was a little creepy in the dark?

They were about to turn when he stopped them with an Arabic word, raising a finger.

A cat had entered the silence from somewhere behind him, a spotted, beautiful thing. Without hesitating he picked it up and walked to Freya, extending it for her to take in her arms.

She was puzzled. "We don't... need a cat. We have no place for a cat..." she began, looking around at her friends. No one else looked any less baffled. She shook her head a little, trying to understand. Then abruptly the whole thing became all right. She handed her pears to Alexis and accepted the cat. The cat formed itself to her arms and closed its eyes. *"Shukran gazilan,"* she said to the old man, smiling. The depths of his eyes lit.

The others stared.

He raised his hand, then, and said something to them in Arabic. She didn't understand the words, but they immediately created a picture in Freya's mind that was more vivid than the worn wooden doorway as they left, or the dark street with light pooled in the dust: In her mind it was evening, and the Old Harbor sparkled with lighted boats while music played from the pier. Her mother was there on the arm of a real gentleman. Mamma had just sung to the celebrating crowd. Freya walked behind her in a summer dress with someone's hand clasping hers.

**

They had lost their way; they would have to geo-locate their way back to the hostel. Norm and Ozzie led, navigating together. Norm tossed over his shoulder, "Hey, Freya. Why the cat?"

Ozzie looked back at her worried face. He guessed that she was considering how she could manage without her ID for the rest of this journey. She said, "I don't know the reason for the cat, but there probably is one."

Norm wagged his head and chortled.

Alexis shifted her knife to the other sleeve of her sweater and said, "What did that guy say to us before we left? When he held his hand up. Anybody know? Gave me the chills."

"Don't know," Ozzie said. They neared a main artery. The lights and noise were swelling.

"It's funny, Freya, but when he said that, I got the idea of..." Alexis walked on a little and then she began again, dreamily: "I saw my mother and father sitting in a garden — it was mine I guess — near the flowers, watching my little kids playing with a puppy while I picked some things for dinner. It was summertime.

Everything was green and growing."

Norm squinted at the Geological Positioning System data on the holo sheet, reading off directions.

As Ozzie looked for the next street sign, he saw again, as real as life, what the old man's words had conjured up for him: It was after Thanksgiving dinner at Uncle Lou and Aunt Rena's, the little kids running around and Dad playing the guitar and singing after the pie was gone. A woman beaming at Dad — was it Ozzie's mother? And then, with a million stars bright in the desert sky, all of them sending Ozzie and someone else off at the spaceport to fly his next Earth-Moon-Mars run.

**

Out again on the broad, brightly-lit thoroughfare, Alexis checked the worldweb while they waited at a traffic light. "That's strange," she said. "I memorized what that gang-guy said when he pointed at Freya, and I've just looked it up on the worldweb. He said 'There she is!'"

CHAPTER TWENTY-NINE

OZZIE AND ALEXIS GASPED. Norm groaned as he nudged into the doorway beside them, knife in hand, and saw. Still, they scanned the hostel room before they stepped in further and let Freya enter with the cat in her arms.

Their clothing, bedding, and equipment were thrown everywhere. *The whole room has been churned!* Freya scowled.

Norm and Alexis checked under the beds and in the bathroom for anyone hiding.

Ozzie found the window open, and below it an unnoticed fire escape. "The window lock was messed with," he said disgustedly.

The cat in Freya's arms raised its head to look, then closed its eyes again.

"Why would someone ransack the place?" Norm asked. Ozzie shrugged.

"Eww, my underwear all over. They put their dirty

paws on my underwear," Alexis said, snatching it from various improper locations.

Freya tugged with one hand to smooth the blanket on her bed and make a place to set down the cat. The blanket snagged. When she pulled it back, it was her turn to gasp.

On top of a piece of paper bearing a scrawled message in Arabic, a frog the size of her hand had been stabbed and nearly halved. The blood that oozed over the paper and onto her sheets was fresh and red.

**

Even after Freya had cleaned up the bed, the cat preferred the wide windowsill as a location. As they filled daypacks and laid out clothes for the pyramids tour tomorrow, Ozzie said, "Let's don't report the incident to the hostel management. They may be involved. We should keep our own watch and learn more first."

They agreed.

Freya hoped no one here in Giza would check IDs.

Alexis counted up their trip cash. "We're doing OK," she decided. "We can cover the big fat pyramid fees but let's spend less for the next day or two." Norm and Alexis went for takeouts, just rice and vegetables, from the café facing the entrance to the hostel.

They ate sitting on the floor in a circle, trying to help Freya think where her ID could have been left. "You had it at the museum," Norm said. "Was it in your wallet at the Kasr al Nile restaurant?"

While Freya tried to recall, Alexis looked up from her takeout box. "I just thought of something: What if we hadn't gone looking for pears, and we were here when whoever-it-was broke in?"

**

That night Ozzie attempted to brace the window shut with a toilet-bowl plunger from the bathroom. The cat objected: it dug its claws politely into Ozzie's hands each time he tried.

"Think he's as good a fighter as the other one was?" Norm grimaced.

[Of course I am,] the cat said, levelling his gaze at Norm.

Norm froze.

He heard it, Ozzie thought.

**

Instead of a book, tonight Ozzie was enjoying the nerdy pleasure of research. The really interesting kind, though. Guessing that the name his mom now seemed to use, Tersey, was also his Grandfather's name, he searched "drives" and the name. Bingo: there was lots of stuff about this guy who must be the person his mother meant. His grandfather, the scientist.

When Ozzie shut off, plugged in to the charger, and

turned the light off, he was the last one awake. The others were breathing softly. The cat sat on the sill, gazing into the room. The pears rested on a little table wrapped in leftover restaurant napkins. He lay back, thinking of tomorrow and volcanoes, drives and the robotics contest.

**

The next thing Ozzie knew was that he seemed to have a mustache that tickled, but then the moustache was a cat's tail, and it was persistently batting him below the nose. "Pfffff," he muttered, brushing it away. It returned.

He sat up and nudged the cat politely off his pillow. Across from him on the other upper bunk, Freya was already awake. She sat looking at the moonlight that the window frame had sliced and laid in cool rectangles on the wooden floor.

He looked at her wild curls, flying around her head and down her back. The way she sat hugging her knees, with her chin resting on them like a kid, seemed vulnerable and sweet.

The cat moved to sit at the foot of Ozzie's bed. It licked one paw carefully for half a minute. When Freya turned to look at last, it said, [The moon is full. Go to the sphinx now.] And it looked at each of them.

"Did you hear that?" Ozzie whispered. She nodded.

"Want to go?"

"Of course."

**

At 2:00 a.m. there would be no shuttle. They walked silently on side streets, then crossed the main thoroughfare quickly and hiked up the long roadway to the plateau. The moonlight was bright on the hem of Giza, but when they reached the sandy plateau, it was twice that: the light came from the earth and sky at the same time. The sand was like a mirror made of billions of grains of glass.

Now that they were away from the city they could talk, but they still said little. Ozzie whispered, awed. "I've never seen the moon like this," he said.

"It's dazzling." Freya's hair was struck and haloed, turned to silver wool, her face in shadow and light like a silver statue's face. She raised her arms and turned in a circle with her eyes closed as if she were a tiny ballerina in the middle of the huge plateau.

They had been working together like robotics partners, doing what they had to do. But there she was again just as Freya, that person in the holo. *There really is something about her...*

Nearing the Sphinx, they looked up at it, then stopped and looked again. Then stared at each other. "There are *cats* on the Sphinx?" she whispered. He nodded, mouth open.

Not just cats, though. Hundreds of cats, thousands of

cats. And they seemed to be arriving just now: they swarmed up and around the rough, rock-layer sides of the gigantic crouching cat-statue. Looking down from its head. Sitting in its eyes, on its cheekbones, crowding onto its paws. They may have been many colors, but the moonlight whitewashed and silvered them all.

Ozzie couldn't recall, later, how long they stood watching the cats swarming up the Sphinx from somewhere —where were they all coming from? — and taking places on its surface.

Eventually, the movement stopped. The Sphinx now wore a mantle of silver fur. Ozzie's heart skipped a beat when all the heads turned toward them; he could suddenly see thousands of eyes lit by the moon like tiny pairs of liquid crystal bulbs. Pale golden ones, the colors of tourmaline, topaz, and opal. And pale green, pale blue.

"Jewels," Freya breathed.

She was right: the Sphinx looked like it was covered with jewels. It seemed to Ozzie that only now was the Sphinx shown with the correct degree of splendor.

Was he really here? Was he dreaming? He dug the nails of one hand into the back of the other hard enough to know it really hurt.

A voice spoke, huge enough to fill the plateau with sound. Ozzie was startled; would the people of Giza be wakened by it and come find them here?

[Look,] it commanded again.

At what? He turned his head toward Freya. She was

looking up at the jeweled face of the Sphinx, her eyes full of wonder. The cool breeze stirred the wisps of hair that framed her face. Her features were noble and perfect, sweet and strong, and he had never seen anyone so beautiful.

She turned to him, her eyes flashing cool sparks. Her eyes went wide, her mouth opened a little. She looked at him as he must be looking at her: entranced.

"You are so beautiful," she whispered finally. Her eyes softened, then, and bathed him in warmth.

Later, Ozzie wondered how long it was that they stood there, moonstruck and transformed, as if they were in love with each other.

However long, it wasn't long enough. When the glamour had faded from them both they stood there again as the usual Ozzie and Freya, shivering a little in the night wind that swept the plateau.

[What did you do to us?] Ozzie asked the voice. The source of the voice resolved into a cat that looked down at them from the rock layer on the Sphinx's chest, where a collarbone would be on a human. The cat sat upright. It was white or at least white-looking, and nearly hairless, with very large ears. It was a hundred feet away, yet it was somehow right in front of them.

[What did I do? I let you see each other,] the cat said.

[But not as we are really.]

The cat looked, unblinking, at Ozzie for many seconds. It seemed to be studying a riddle.

[Yes, as you are, really.]

Freya and Ozzie looked at each other again. He raked his fingers through his hair.

This was the Gathering of the Nile cats, their host let them know. They had private business to discuss tonight, but before they sent Ozzie and Freya home to rest, the cat said, he had advice for them to aid in their search.

[You are looking at the surface of things,] the cat said. [Not everything is resolved by using the visible world. Listen more and look deeper — not just longer and wider — and you will find it.]

**

They walked down the curving road from the plateau. Freya was shaking. *She must be cold.* Ozzie took her hand. Touching it made his own hand tingle.

"Something is wrong," she said after a little while.

"What's wrong? Tonight seems perfect to me."

"It is. It was. I don't know why but now I have a bad feeling."

CHAPTER THIRTY

T HIS IS DAY SEVEN of our trip," Norm said on the shuttlebus to the plateau the next morning. "Day 11 if you count the four days of prep time." He looked at Ozzie. Ozzie nodded. Freya knew he was thinking about their robotics work in California. They probably all were now. *Damn, Norm. Why did you have to bring it up?*

Freya's eyes kept wandering to Ozzie's face as she checked the newsfeed on her phone, remembering last night. He's a nice-looking guy even though he is so fierce when he scowls. She suppressed a smile. But last night: So magic. Like a dream.

She and Ozzie had agreed not to mention it to the others. Till later, or maybe never. Never, if it was her choice. She wanted to leave it untouched by others, so it would never change for her.

In spite of last night there was no rest from the bad news. She shook her head. "Another volcano," she said grimly. One in the Philippines had begun to leak lava.

Alexis chewed her lip. Norm gazed up at the tops of the pyramids, rising above the plateau's edge as they rode upward. "Time for us to find you the answer, Freya," he said.

He was right: it was time.

**

Freya was awed as they followed their guide into Khufu, the Great Pyramid. She could feel the massiveness around her, imagining its ancient beginning not just millennia but maybe eons ago. She imagined she could feel the weight of that number of years.

"Look deeper," the cat had said. She was trying.

They spent the morning walking uphill and downhill through all the known passages inside Khufu. They talked, breathed and sang in the Queen's Chamber, testing the resonance in all rooms with notes from the recorder, laughing at the effects their voices made. Freya took flat-photos inside Khufu to remind her of each location.

Their guide watched all this silently. Was it her imagination, or was he amused?

They found group from a yoga retreat in Switzerland saying "ommmm" together in one chamber, letting it resonate until it was like sitting inside a bell. She could feel the *om* vibrating in her bones.

She told the old guide that they had touch-tested the

outsides of the pyramids yesterday and all of them resonated — that water increased the vibration. Could he explain? He said it was because of the layers of water-rock that extend deep below the pyramids. "The pyramids have their feet in water," he said, "and water magnifies sound." The pyramids were made to concentrate sound, he told them, and even now they do.

Why did some statues at the Egyptian Museum garden resonate? Some are made of water-rock, he said, and they vibrate in kinship with similar rock in this region. He used his arms to show circles expanding outward. Yes, even from as far away as here. "The vibration creates electricity, like lightning, a shock," he said. "But it begins with sound."

Freya knew there was another question she should ask, but she couldn't think of it yet.

**

They sat on tumbled stones at the bottom of one corner of Khufu, eating lunch. For the guide, lunch turned out to be the four pears, which he ate happily.

Freya was finished with her lunch. She was writing something in a small pulp-book, not the same book as in the pyramid, and Ozzie found he was curious. "Research notes?"

"No," she said. Then she looked at him squarely and said, "It's poetry." Poetry. *Didn't know she did that.* He had always thought his life was simple and obvious, and

221

other people's too. Now it seemed that his wasn't simple, and look: no one else's was either.

"Freya has won prizes for her poems and stories," Alexis bragged loyally. "She was asked to read her long poem in Paris."

"Wow," he said. There was so much to know. Like what happened to her father? He would ask sometime.

"This is really cool," Norm said, cleaning his glasses on his T-shirt. "The pyramids resonate, they make energy. And they once had the power to resonate much more than they do now..."

Freya asked the guide, "Is there any way you know of to make them resonate as they did long ago?"

The old man looked out at Giza and shook his head regretfully. "Sorry, no one yet remembers how. I have never heard how and I have asked. I know no way."

The others looked disappointed. Worse, they looked resigned. She feared that they were giving up. Freya leaned forward as one more question, the real question, came to her: "Do you know if these pyramids were used to make the music of Osiris?"

Their guide stopped in the middle of his fourth pear and looked at her. His eyes were shrewd, then soft. It was the look her physics teacher used to wear when you were beginning to really understand something. "It's a good question," he began.

Four uniformed figures appeared abruptly behind him, coming around the corner of Khufu with drawn guns. "Who is Freya?" one said in English. The guide turned to look behind him, then back at them. "Giza police," he whispered to them as Ozzie's and Norm's hands moved toward their knives. "Careful."

**

Ozzie saw another figure round the corner, behind the cops: Seth. Ozzie swore to himself fiercely and Alexis hissed softly. Freya's eyes narrowed at Seth, who was pointing at her.

Stinking Seth. Now what.

The four of them stood to make a semicircle facing the police.

"I am Freya Ilsesdottir. Do you want to ask me something?" She said it from that height of hers, the mountain peak.

"My apology. We need to search your things, ma'am. A theft has been reported. This man," indicating pale, spiky Seth, whose eyes were unusually poisonous today, "believes he saw you take something from the Egyptian Museum."

"I did not, so he could not have seen it." she said.

"She didn't," Ozzie said. "We were with her the whole time there." He groaned inside. More delays. And they were just about to hear something interesting from the guide.

"I'm sorry, we must search because something was reported as missing from the restoration room of the

Egyptian Museum in Cairo. You understand that we do not want treasures to leave the country, I'm sure."

"Of course," she said coldly. She held her head high. She gestured at her pack, which was near the officer's feet. As he began to unzip and work through it, she turned to Seth. "You have been busy, Seth," she spat. "Don't you have anything important to do anywhere?"

His eyes seethed as if they were made of tiny dark snakes. If any two people ever instantly and totally hated each other, Ozzie thought, these two did. Of course, that seemed to be easy when it came to Seth.

An outburst in Arabic to his companions. The officer was pulling a roll of cloth out of the expansion space in the bottom of Freya's pack.

"My shirt," Freya said, meaning, "What did you expect?"

"Very heavy shirt," he eyed her. And unfurled it into his other hand, which caught — *Oh no.*

Ozzie saw Seth sneering broadly at Freya, the officer holding up a small stone figurine, like a miniature King Tut in gray with forearms crossed on its chest, its bottom half chiseled with hieroglyphs. He saw their guide shake his head unhappily. All of it was like a bad dream. Even the guide thought they were thieves now.

"A *shabti!* Just like the one missing from the museum," he said at Freya, adding an "I've got you now" look.

Freya was ashen. The huge lie seemed to have struck

her like a slap, and Ozzie could feel her shock. Frozen, he watched the cop ask for her ID, then saw this second hit register on her face. Without it, she couldn't even prove who she was.

"Alexis, it's too bad you're hanging out with losers," Seth said. "Why don't you come back with me to California now? You and I have work to do."

She turned her downcast eyes up toward him, then down again.

The guide rose to go. Ozzie urgently wished for him not to leave them, but why would he want to be here for this? Maybe he would even get into trouble if he stayed. "You will not need me further, I think," he said sadly. Then: "You will find the answers to your questions in Memphis, in the old city."

He moved toward Ozzie as he left them, and as he passed close by he breathed, "At the Sphinx tonight — you alone."

The guy wasn't abandoning them totally. A little ray of hope. Ozzie gazed after him: with the white robe billowing like an Egyptian sail, his bent figure moved slowly across the bright sand toward the road.

**

Freya was explaining their situation to the officers, giving her name and her profession while Seth inspected his nails with a sarcastic look on his face. Norm and Alexis displayed their IDs with as much dignity as possible. Ozzie dug his out too. Under the pressure of the moment, a thought came, and Ozzie spoke as fast as he thought: about their dinner at the restaurant, the pack being removed from Freya's chair, the man who left the restaurant before them and turned the pack over to the waitress.

The Giza police looked unimpressed. "Students, hah?" their spokesman said, turning each ID card over and over as if he were looking for a new side besides the two that were there. "You should stick to studying, not stealing. And this unidentified young woman..."

"We're sure that Freya did not do it. This is a trick. It's slander." Ozzie said. He was silenced by a dark look.

**

The Giza police station was only a little less run-down than their hostel, Freya thought. Through the outer door they had entered a room with two nicked desks, some chairs for waiting in, and a row of cells along one wall. The rough plaster walls wore thick, shiny greenish paint that was chipped in a lot of places.

Their weapons had been laid aside on a table. A desk clerk was writing in a pulp-book as the English-speaking officer "told him the nature of the crime," dictating in Arabic. Not being able to understand the crime made Freya very worried. Seth had made his statement and left his hotel address before exiting with their disgust sticking like darts in his back.

When the "nature of the crime" was translated, it turned out that Freya was charged with theft and the rest of them might be charged as accomplices of some sort.

So far the officers had ignored Freya's request: she asked them to call her firefighting company to confirm her identity. Instead, they eagerly called the Egyptian Museum — in fact, right now two were talking into an ancient land phone together, telling some tale in Arabic. They were clearly receiving congratulations from whoever they were talking to.

When the officers finished their triumphant telephone call, Ozzie asked to make one. Instead, the officer on duty, who didn't seem to speak English, ignored Ozzie and locked the four of them into a cell without their packs.

**

Freya paced slowly, trying to ignore the bars and the panicky feeling they gave her. She was afraid for all of them. Norm said nothing for a change. Alexis looked pale — sick, in fact. Freya knew exactly how Alexis felt, because she could feel it coming from her in waves as strong as a bellyache.

Alexis' phone rang across the room, from her pack. "My parents," she said, in a kind of groan that told where she hurt. Every time one of them spoke, even in a whisper, the officer looked up warily. Their speech seemed to make him nervous. So they went silent.

Freya glanced sideways at Ozzie as she walked back and forth, back and forth. He stood near the bars and seemed to be searching for something. He put his hands in his pockets, absently. He felt for something at his throat and then, as if he noticed that it wasn't there, took his hand away. Finally, he sat and patted his cargo-pants, all the pockets, as the police had already done. Everything had been removed, so he shouldn't be surprised that there was nothing there. His eyes landed on the magazine that the on-duty officer was reading at his desk.

"Please," he said in Egyptian Arabic to the officer. The man looked up from the magazine. "Please," Ozzie repeated, pantomimed a drink of water, then indicated his friends and himself. The officer rose. Freya noticed that the gun in his holster was an old-fashioned one like Ozzie's.

"*Shukran gazilan,*" Ozzie said, with a meaningful look at the others. Freya strode forward. Norm and Alexis rose. "*Shukran gazilan,*" they said and nodded politely, accepting disposable cups of lukewarm water through the bars.

The officer waited to collect the cups. As Ozzie passed them back, Freya saw the folded-up copy of Rolling Stone Magazine under the man's arm. It was in English.

"Can I borrow that magazine?" Ozzie asked.

"No, I am still reading —" The officer stopped.

Gotcha! Freya thought. He does speak English.

But Ozzie's face didn't change at all. Smooth. He said in English, then, "Of course. You should finish it first. Instead, will you help us get some things from our packs to read or do? We have nothing to do in here but worry."

There was a brief confusion behind the officer's eyes, but he nodded. There was no rule against it, he said. He would need to go through the packs himself, though, and they could request something from the contents.

For four caged people, this was something to do at least: a sort of entertaining parade of items was removed by the officer, one by one, from the first pack, belonging to Alexis: Moisturizer. Suntan lotion. Hairbrush. Folded holophone in plastic sleeve. Protein bar. "I want that," she said. He considered, then set it aside.

A pack of gum. A small zippered bag, which he unzipped to remove feminine hygiene products. At those he blinked and flinched. He stuffed them in and re-zipped hastily. "I'm sorry," he said.

Alexis said that it was OK, and he looked relieved. Norm didn't grin or snicker, which must have taken real self-control.

The parade of Alexis' stuff continued: vintage flat-photos in a little folder. A sweater and rain-cape. Pulp puzzle book, a new one. (She wanted that, and the pen, please.) Alexis thanked him warmly for the puzzle book and pen. Seemingly pleased by her perfect manners and sweet voice, he handed her the protein bar too, and she offered him some gum from the pack as he put it all away again.

Ozzie's pack was easy to empty: a jacket and phone, two protein bars, a water bottle, the hyperball. He acknowledged the hyperball with warm thanks in both English and Arabic, then tossed and bounced the thing to show the guard how it sparkled. The guy smiled, enjoying that. He asked if Ozzie wanted one of the protein snacks to eat.

Freya's was up next. They all stood at the steel bars watching as if there couldn't be a better show. *It's the only show we have.* Was this part of some plan for Ozzie?

Freya's was her firefighter pack, like the ones for hiking and camping, so it had many pockets to unzip. The young officer seemed to find the pack itself interesting. It was like opening gift packages or one of those calendars with something behind the door for each day. They were all enjoying being surprised by what was in each part of the pack. One pocket at a time he opened and found:

Her book, the one she read from each night, turned off and zipped into a side pocket along with a little pulp-book of Icelandic poetry. A Swiss Army knife in a little side pocket of its own. In a medium-sized outer pocket, moisturizer and lip balm, vitamins. In another, a folded pulp-map of the Giza Plateau. And a little zippered bag.

About to unzip the bag, he stopped and looked warily at Freya. She nodded and play-acted embarrassment, covering her face with her hand. Norm didn't resist chortling this time. Their guard felt the contents through the bag with his fingers and, looking uncomfortable, put it aside.

There was a little flat pocket on top of another pocket. He unzipped it, put two fingers in, curious, and began to draw out several cards. Ozzie elbowed Freya gently. *What's he trying to tell me?* She almost could remember what the cards were, but not quite. "I'll need those," she said, without understanding. Then, part of a light went on in her mind. She said, "And the feminine hygiene products."

The guard looked distressed. Probably wondering how to let her take something into the bathroom without a female cop around for security. In his embarrassment, he looked only briefly at the business cards. They were less difficult to deal with. He handed the cards to her, hefting the zippered bag. "I will have to ask..." he said.

"That's OK," she said, and thanked him with a sisterly smile. "And I forgot to say: the book?"

He would let her have the poetry only, he said.

When the show was over and they all had their playthings, Freya glanced privately at each of the cards.

Of course. Ozzie was right.

"What do you think we should do, Ozzie?" Alexis said, still pale and not looking very entertained by her puzzle-book. He stood with the ice-like hyperball in his hand, flicking it upward, snapping it out of the air, flicking it upward, snapping it with his other hand, each snap rewarded by a quick sparkle of the internal lights. He scowled as he tossed, concentrating.

Now and then their jailer looked up from *The Rolling Stone* and watched the rainbow lights for a half-minute, then returned to his magazine. Finally: "Want to try it?" Ozzie offered.

The man smiled a little, then smiled broadly, and came to take the ball extended through the bars.

They all watched him play with it. "Hey, good one," Norm drawled, as he flipped it high enough to sparkle off the ceiling.

"Wooo," Alexis clapped when he did a billiards shot off two walls and the ceiling, then back. Freya joined her at the cell bars to watch. Pleased, the officer tried another one: floor, wall, ceiling, and home to him.

"Holy smoke!" Ozzie's admiration had to be genuine, but they all clapped too, to make it theatrical. The guy must be a good pool player, or soccer player, or something, Freya thought.

When the guard handed back the ball, he offered Ozzie *The Rolling Stone* to read too. "Thanks, nice of you," Ozzie said, and their eyes exchanged a good-buddy look — but he held up his hand to stop the man. "You finish it first." Suddenly Freya knew what was next:

Ozzie said, "Right now we need to make our phone

calls. Will you give us our phones?"

The guard hesitated. He knew that it was an International Human Rights violation not to permit "one completed call out" for any person incarcerated for a crime. But the call could be delayed endlessly. And an unscrupulous official could delay it forever if no one was watching.

"May I call first?" Freya had already had time to think this through, thanks to Ozzie and the ball.

"Sure," Norm said, as if it were all up to him.

Alexis got it and went with the flow. "I don't mind," she agreed politely.

"Fine with me," Ozzie said, and they all smiled expectantly at their jailer. "Freya can be first," he said.

The fella was caught on the moment like an insect with a pin through it; then the moment carried him onward. He sent three of them to the back corner of the jail to "enjoy themselves," and handed Freya's phone through the bars to her. "Call here," he pointed at the cell floor to show where she should locate herself, directly in front of him. She did, nodding and smiling obediently as he sat on the desk behind him to watch her. He swung his legs a little.

She pulled out the phone and spread the sheet on her right palm, flicking icons up and keying in the number from one of the cards with her left fingers: Lieutenant Abdel Naguib, Cairo Police Department. The one who had given them waivers to sign at the Egyptian Museum.

Her holoID was showing so he'd recognize her.

"Lieutenant Naguib," she said, when he came onto the line. Their jailer froze. She talked fast. "Freya Ilsesdottir here. You very kindly investigated the false charge by Seth Raker against my research assistants and me a few days ago," she began. Their jailer was tensed, ready to rise, but he stopped when he heard Seth's name.

"Yes, that's right," Freya smiled and nodded reassuringly at the officer sitting on the desk, as if to say, "Don't worry. I have at last reached my old friend in the Cairo police, and he will help you."

"And what can I do for you today?" Lieutenant Naguib asked, a little wary. *Maybe he thinks we are going to press charges.* Another small light went on for her.

"We are doing very well with our research, thanks to your help, and we are nearly finished — just a few more days...But, sorry to say, we may have to press charges. The same Seth Raker has followed us to Giza and is now accusing me of stealing something from the Egyptian Museum.

"My identification was taken from my wallet — do you remember my card that shows I am a corporal in the Icelandic Firefighters? You called Iceland to confirm it — yes, that's it. It was taken and someone placed a stolen *shabti* in my pack. We think we know when this was planted, at a time when my pack was taken from me in a restaurant. We can prove nothing because we are incarcerated in Giza as thieves. And again, our accuser is the *same* Seth Raker.

"Yes. We are located in the— "

She raised her eyebrows at the Sergeant, who fidgeted and didn't answer. "—the police station near the Giza Necropolis. Sergeant al-Attar? is here with me," she added, reading as best she could off his name tag. He squirmed. "He has been most kind to us," she smiled her sisterly smile again at the Sergeant, "but we do need to continue our research to get back on time. Can you help us?"

"He would like to speak to you, Sergeant," she said, extending the holophone toward him through the bars.

CHAPTER THIRTY-ONE

OZZIE'S HAND still buzzed a little with electricity. Three of them sat in the first floor of the restaurant that faced the pyramids, eating a gloomy supper and staring through the window as the pink faded from the western sky. Ozzie, Norm, and Alexis were out of jail, but not Freya.

Once the Giza Police had heard from Lieutenant Naguib in Cairo they were more interested in taking full statements from all four of them, including the part about the break-in at their hostel and the pack at the restaurant. When Freya asked, "How could I possibly have gained access to the shabti, when you say it was in a secured restoration room?" the Giza police decided that they really should investigate further. Maybe ask a few more questions of Seth. They had a search going for Seth — who had not answered their call.

So Freya was in jail for the night while the Giza police hunted for Seth and Cairo police questioned the museum staff.

The three of them had been ordered to go and return in the morning, but it was hard to leave Freya alone there.

"Can't we bring her some food?" Alexis had urged the officer.

"She will be fed," their young guard said, but he accepted a jacket from Alexis and a protein bar from Ozzie for her, and one for himself. Ozzie shook the man's hand. When Ozzie took Freya's hand also, comfortingly, she slipped Lieutenant Naguib's card to him. That made Ozzie think of asking the Sergeant for his card, too.

He stopped eating, now, and looked at his hand curiously. Touching her seemed to make his skin take on a load of electricity. Ozzie took a long drink of the café ice tea while he looked out at the traffic on the darkening street. He and Norm were polishing off the last of what their waiter had brought them: baskets of hummus and bread, bowls of sauces and greens. "I think we'll get Freya out OK, now," Ozzie said. "But how long will it take?"

"Right. No fun for Freya, but also we're into our second week here and no end in sight," Norm said. "Two weeks is all we had as fudge room for this trip. And it took us four days to get ready before we left. I was hoping we'd be back by one week from then, really. By now."

"Yeah," Ozzie worried. "We have about six weeks of

work to do on the robot, I figure. Right, Norm? So even if we're home a week from today the December 15 deadline is too close — doesn't give us any extra room at all."

Alexis became glum as she listened, and Ozzie realized: *She doesn't even have a partner now — not one she wants to work with anyway.* Alexis needed to get back there and get reassigned to a new contest partner to make her trip to California work out.

One worry made room for another: Ozzie checked the newsfeed. Another sign of a volcano going live, this time in Australia. An ancient one. Ozzie yawned. He knew it wasn't that he was tired. He was yawning because it was all just too much.

"Let's get to the hostel and relax a little," he said.

But when they walked out into the dusk and Khufu towered above them, it came back to him: he had a meeting with the guide at the Sphinx.

**

They'll just have to get each other to the room safely, Ozzie thought as he hiked up the road to the plateau again with his knife in his sweatshirt sleeve. He didn't like letting Norm and Alexis travel alone. He hoped they would feed the cat.

Tonight couldn't be any more unlike last night. Was it really last night that the sky was like a picture book painting of the moon and Milky Way and the sand was like a mirror?

He saw Freya again as she was last night. He shook his head a little in wonder. And she called him beautiful.

Tonight, there were heavy clouds that covered the rising moon. The Sphinx was bare, shadowy and dead-looking. Ozzie shivered in the chill wind.

Up here the horns and engine noises of Giza were lost in the steady wind and the muffling sand. He crept around the Sphinx in a full circle, scouting to make sure it was safe. Then he walked deep between the beast's huge paws, climbed up a little behind the heavily-carved tablet stone, and sat against her gigantic chest, feeling protected.

He didn't think he would, but he fell asleep.

**

It was dark in the cell. Freya lay on the hard bench trying to sleep because there was nothing else to do. There was a small light on the desk of the night officer, who was reading. She wished she could read but he had refused to turn on the room lights.

She wondered what the others were doing right now. *Clever of Ozzie to do that trick to get them out.* She needed for him to get her out too. They wouldn't abandon her in Egypt and go home, would they? Fright made her shudder.

But I trust him more. I'm counting on him more every day as a companion and a friend.

In her mind she saw him at the Sphinx, half-smiling at her in the moonlight. Even now she was wonder-struck, recalling it.

Now she also recalled his stubborn, skeptical look and realized she had begun to like that, too. *I do like him.* It made her happy to think about that.

**

Ozzie's eyes opened. The moon was sailing high above him and the clouds were trailing away from it so it looked like a boat coming out of the weeds at the edge of a midnight lake, shaking off the last dark shreds and moving into the open water. Whiteness washed the Sphinx's paws above Ozzie and beside him.

It must be after twelve if the moon was so high. He groaned. *Maybe the guide has come and gone.*

He heard a soft scratching sound like footsteps in the sand. Was that what had wakened him? He silently gathered his feet under him and rose.

The scratching was coming around the tablet stone. His heart thudded. If it was someone he didn't want to meet, he was trapped by the giant paws. He let himself down onto the sand and froze with his knife out.

It was a cat.

A cat?

A big one, white in the moonlight and nearly hairless, with large ears. A lot like the one who spoke last night, but who could tell?

Ozzie was baffled. Still, he remembered to be polite.

[Greetings,] he thought at the cat. [I was expecting the old guide.]

[Yes,] the cat said.

[Is he coming?] Ozzie asked, trying to be patient.

[I have a message for you from him.]

Another cat-messenger. *You'd never know how busy these guys were if you weren't listening,* Ozzie thought.

[Yes,] the cat said.

Turning red made Ozzie feel dumb, but he figured that a cat wouldn't notice or care much about that. Then he shut off his thoughts before he really got into trouble, and just listened.

The cat continued: [You must go to Memphis soon, to the old city. But if you visit the stones there you will learn nothing of value. Go instead to this place in Mit Rahina:]

A picture bloomed in Ozzie's mind, startling him: a rundown building, a sort of apartment house with palm trees around it, broken paving-stones before it, and a large silvery hieroglyph of a bird clearly marked on the black front door.

[There the living reside with the dead. Stay and eat, rest there for the night. You will learn what you need to know.]

[Thank you,] Ozzie said politely. *The living with the dead?*

Thinking fast, he added, [But one of us is in jail. Can

241

you help with that?]

[No,] the cat said. [You must find a way. Be sure you go there soon.]

[Why soon?] But it crouched and leapt easily above Ozzie's head, to the top of one of the Sphinx's glistening moon-painted paws. Ozzie could see just the tips of its long ears. Then it disappeared.

**

It would be a long walk back.

He found himself trying to recall the bird hieroglyph exactly. He wasn't sure he could. What if every door in Mit-whatever-it-was had some kind of bird on it?

Outside the safety of the Sphinx's paws he stopped short: there was something like a large drawing in the sand ahead. He walked closer. Maybe some joke, sand-graffiti left by a tourist. He hadn't noticed it on the way in. As he neared it the moonlight made it as clear as a hieroglyph carved in white stone. It was the figure the cat had shown him: a six-foot rectangle with rounded corners, framing the outline of a bird with a long, wickedly curved beak.

**

"Wait till you see this, Ozzie."

He couldn't believe Norm and Alexis were still awake. When he opened the door quietly he found the hostel room lighted, and the two of them still in street clothes. They showed Ozzie: The window had been broken. Their elegant spotted loaner cat sat on the sill before the broken pane, licking its paws thoroughly.

Before him there was a pool of dried blood on the floor. Ozzie looked closer: there was also dried blood on the toothlike edges of broken glass remaining in the window. Who would enter that way?

Wait: what if whoever-it-was had broken the window on the way *out*?

"Keep going," Norm said. Ozzie stuck his head between the two sets of glass teeth and looked out on the fire escape: another pool of blood dried there, and smear-marks going off the edge.

"Ugh," Ozzie grimaced. The floor of the alley was lost in darkness.

"We took pictures," Alexis said.

"And we didn't touch because of fingerprints," Norm said proudly.

"Good idea." Ozzie withdrew his head cautiously. "Did you look down below?"

No. They had waited for him.

"Good. Take my gun," Ozzie handed it to Norm, "In case. *Don't shoot me.* I'll go below." He took his laserlight down the rickety hostel steps and out the front door, turning to follow the narrow alleyway back under the window.

He wasn't really surprised to find a body there. He nudged it with his foot. No motion. His knife ready, he

243

put his foot under the near shoulder and levered it over. It was stiff and heavy. Really dead. Ozzie had never been near a dead body before.

He turned on the light, ready to be tough about it. Still he gasped.

Four long slashes ran down the front of the man, from throat to groin, together about a foot wide. One slash slit his jugular vein. The blood smeared down to his ankles made it look like he had been dragged, or he had belly-crawled.

Ozzie put a hand cautiously near the face to feel whether it was warm. It was a chilly night, but no warmth radiated toward his cool hand. The face was twisted in fright.

He tried hard not to, but he threw up against the wall of the hostel, all over a pile of rubbish. *If I ever have to kill someone I don't know how I'll do it.*

When he had thrown up everything in his stomach he threw up again, till nothing came out but long strings of drool. With a shaking hand he wiped his face with a café napkin from his pocket.

Taking a deep breath, he shined the laserlight a little more directly and saw the face clearly for the first time. He was startled: it was the Stalker from Giza. There were the marks Ozzie had memorized — the cut scar on his right jaw and the scabbed-over wound on his nose.

"What is it?" Norm's text showed up on his phone when Ozzie opened it. "Body," he texted back. "Stay there a minute."

Ozzie pulled out the Giza sergeant's card and in the laserlight called the police station. It took a while to connect because of the technical differences between a holophone and the ancient landline, but the connection happened. A new officer was on duty.

"Sergeant, I think I have your suspect here," Ozzie said, feeling like he was in a bad holovid.

Then he took a bunch of pictures with his phone and went back up to the room.

**

While the police were on their way, Ozzie worried wearily that he and Norm and Alexis might be dragged back into the station themselves as suspects in the Stalker's death. But lucky for them, the two officers brought a specialist cop who did some fast tests that proved the Stalker had died during the time when they were locked in jail.

After the police took statements and left with the body, the horrified hostel manager gave them a new room with more bunk beds. This room had no fire escape, so it seemed safer. They moved tiredly in, with the cat.

The cat had already placed himself on the sill, looking out, when they turned off the lights at 4:00 a.m.

CHAPTER THIRTY-TWO

FREYA WOKE LATE. Her head ached and she was terribly thirsty. She asked for a drink.

There had been a commotion in the middle of the night about Ozzie catching the suspect or something. She was wildly impressed. After which Seth had arrived. Seth and Freya were in different cells — *lucky for him.*

The two officers who were talking ignored her. It was their voices that must have awakened her, she thought — they were reading the official death report in English. For Seth's benefit, she guessed. *Why couldn't they have done things in English for us?* she scowled. The report said that the guy Ozzie found had died around 4:00 p.m., when they all were in custody (Freya rolled her eyes with relief. They didn't need another crime pinned on them.) The body lay amid the rubbish in the dim, narrow alley for hours. It was a gang killing, "done with some kind of hook," the report explained. And the terrified man had attempted to escape through the window, off the fire escape platform.

"Will you show me the holos?" Freya asked. One of the officers brought some water, then took Seth into another room for questioning. Seth was extra-pale and kept his eyes on the ground. *Good. OK with me that you are worried, Herfilegur Seth — Disgusting Seth. What did Alexis call him? Scumbag.*

The guard who remained finally showed her a couple of holoprints through the bars. She recoiled from the distorted, blood-smeared images but the structure of his face and body were familiar. So was the giant cat scratch. It came to her. "The one who was watching us in the restaurant!" she said. "The one who brushed by my chair." *And probably took my pack.*

Also probably the same guy who threw our things around, who killed the toad on my bed.

Her head still ached, and a photo of someone dead wasn't cheery, but things looked a lot brighter. She thought of their own search: before her robot-making friends lost heart, they needed to go find the answer, go to Memphis. It was the next destination on her plan, so it was a good sign that their guide also said to go there.

"Look deeper" was the cat's advice. The tools they had brought, and the testing, her research, all their notes and gathering of information had helped, but only in one way: it told them where the answer wasn't.

Now her head was pounding.

I'm trying so hard. There had to be a way to "look

deeper" in Memphis. But it was hard to imagine how. The worldweb and the pretty travel folders made it seem like the place was just more statues and more ruins.

How odd: I'm not having any of those dreams here, in spite of all the cats around us. She made a face, thinking of Alexis' dreams. *Maybe now it's everyone else's turn to get dreams.*

She sat back on the cell bench with her head against the cool wall and closed her eyes, wishing the others would arrive. Wondering what was next.

The street door opened. In walked a middle-aged man in a suit and tie, followed by a small group of reporters.

The police officer ordered, then pushed, the reporters back outside.

"I got here as fast as I could," the man said. I'm Representative Raker, United States." When the on-duty guard looked puzzled, he added, "Seth is my son."

Freya was watching from the shadows of her cell.

"I see, sir. They told me when I came on duty that his father was called by Seth Raker late last night.

"You will want to know: We received a report early this morning from the Cairo police that involves your son in criminal activity. The Egyptian museum staff was questioned last night. The police got a confession from a young cleaning woman with night security clearance. Someone paid her to steal the *shabti* and give it to her boyfriend."

Freya bit her lip to keep from making an angry noise. "And someone paid the boyfriend to harass and scare a young woman and her student friends. Also to put the *shabti* in a young woman's belongings to make her seem to be a thief."

Freya was furious and jubilant at once.

Representative Raker mopped his forehead, took off his suit jacket, and sat heavily on the edge of one of the waiting-area chairs. "What are the charges?" he asked.

"Robbery, theft of government property, destruction of property... And perjury."

Perfect. Freya sat in the dark corner, silent but fierce.

"I need to speak with my son. He should not be questioned without a lawyer."

"We do things differently here, sir."

The antique phone rang. The officer refused to confirm any rumors. It must be a news service calling. No he could not give information. He hung up. The officer consulted some papers, received another call.

Raker was just opening his phone himself, when the officer stood and showed him through the door to the questioning-room. *What fast service he gets,* Freya thought.

Freya had no comb in the cell. She pulled the tangles out of her hair with her fingers and tied it up into a new bun at the back of her head. She wished for more water to wash with, but she opened the poetry book instead, half-heartedly.

249

A group of odd characters entered through the street door. A young guy with a moustache and a retro fedora, a girl wearing a cheesy blond wig and very heavy makeup, a local-looking young guy with a fez...

"May I help you?" the officer looked up at them, surprised. Freya almost laughed out loud. She pressed the pulp-book to her face to prevent that. It was Ozzie, Norm and Alexis in disguise.

"We came to visit our friend Freya," Ozzie-with-fedora said.

Today's officer was easy-going and bored, although he looked curiously at their costumes. He accepted two bottles of water and two protein bars and passed one of each in to Freya. They turned three of the waiting-area chairs to face Freya, who worked hard to keep a straight face.

"You aren't going to fool anyone much with those disguises," she whispered. "They look like Halloween." She stifled a laugh with her knuckles.

"We got them from the party boxes at the hostel," Ozzie shrugged.

"We got the newsfeed leak about Rep. Raker," Norm whispered back. "That's why we're in disguise: media mongrels outside, don't want holos going back home to London..." Alexis mugged comic terror.

Now, following Norm's lead, they casually removed hats, wig, and moustache and tossed them into Alexis' cloth bag. They rearranged themselves to look more ordinary. Her eyes and throat felt like sand was in them, but the comedy did Freya good.

She whispered to them about the cleaning-woman's confession. And told them that Seth and his father were in the room behind them talking with police.

Alexis said, "You must have heard. That guy dead, and blood everywhere, Freya. It was awful. Did you see holos?"

"Yes. Ugly."

The door opened on the other side of the station office, and Freya's guests turned in their chairs toward Seth and his father. Seth avoided their eyes.

"...and I will take care of any damages to the hostel," Representative Raker was saying, as if he was showing special generosity. "I assume these young people will not be pressing charges," he said. They regarded him silently.

"I am Congressman Raker of California," he said to them. They stood to face him silently, gazing at Seth with dislike that included his father.

Raker filled the silence: "I understand you four are doing research regarding the increased volcanic activity in Iceland. You need to know that people who think hydraulic fracturing or electronic waves are causing disruption of the earth's crust are absolutely wrong. They are just paranoid. Conspiracy theorists."

"Who said anything about either one?" Norm muttered.

Freya shook her head. *Raker did, that's who. And maybe he should know.* She guessed that *Herfilegur* Seth must have passed on what he overheard of the statements she gave to the police.

Alexis was talking now. It was surprising to hear her voice raised so boldly, "...Conspiracy theory, Mr. Raker? That's what they said before the Great Crop Uprising in China 15 years ago. They said that genetically engineered plants were a safe and cheap way to plentiful food, till infant deaths went to 75 percent in the Chinese cities where that was all you could buy. Then, we had a Chinese version of the Boston Tea Party: rioting people destroying the food warehouses."

Her face was flushed. "After that the backlash was terrible," she whispered to her friends, staring at the floor.

"Good shot, Alexis," Norm whispered sideways at her.

"You all should know that these issues are nothing for you to worry about," Rep. Raker said. "They're being researched and considered by skilled scientists. Our government is seeing to that. You should leave these matters to the experts."

Freya's eyes narrowed.

Seth looked at his father, then at Freya, and then a small smile arranged itself on his face. "You'll have to tell me more about that, *Dad*," Seth said.

Representative Raker seemed pleased. He took a deep breath and started in on it right away.

"The earth is a self-healing mechanism. We don't have to do anything to fix it."

"Not even stop doing what's making it sick?" Freya said. Her eyes felt hot, she was so angry.

"What you young people don't know, because you have not studied enough on this subject, is that there is a whole body of knowledge... several very important papers and books have been written..."

"And that's why the volcanoes get worse each month?"

"Young lady, if you had studied these things as I have..."

Then I would be unable to think straight either, Freya thought.

Seth said: "My father is right. People like you should stay home and be farmers or run stores." He smiled a nasty smile. "Alexis. When are you going to leave these losers and come finish building the winning entry with me?"

Her eyes were fortresses.

Raker left the police station with Seth in tow. The reporters and photographers were waiting for them on the sidewalk.

**

Walking beside Freya, Ozzie saw her blink hard and shake her head. She seemed to be a little dizzy. He supposed it was because of the bright light out here on the street after twenty-four hours in a dim cell. He offered his hand to support her. To his surprise, she took it and even leaned on him a little. He tried to ignore the way his hand and arm felt electric, resting against her skin.

Seth's confession had freed Freya. And she had her ID back, too. It had been found in the Stalker's pocket.

"But I can't believe Seth got off," Ozzie said.

"Probably his father bought him off," Norm grumbled, making a face. "They've been taking our bribes, so they probably would take his, too."

They entered the cool dimness of the café and found a table.

Ozzie watched out of the corner of his eye as Freya checked her phone for the last day's worth of messages: one after another from that Arni-somebody in Iceland. *Looks like the guy was worried. Well, we all were.* "Received" was all she sent back.

Once they had ordered, Norm didn't waste any time: "Let's go home," he pleaded. "To California."

Alexis was already on his side: "The timing isn't working out right, Freya."

"This is not a tourist trip, exactly, that I can make the timing perfect," Freya answered wearily.

"But looking at our itinerary, we are only halfway through it after 8 days. If we figure another 8 days, that means we miss our scheduled return..."

"There's no need to go to Edfu anymore," Freya said.

Ozzi remembered from the bus conversation: Edfu, Egypt, located quite a way south along the Nile, held a monument called the Edfu temple, where there was a particular ancient carving of a cat... In her earlier research she had named it as an important site to look into. "We have learned a lot more about cats already than I ever thought we would," she said. Norm grinned. "And we know they aren't what we need to find out about anymore."

"They just give us advice." Ozzie mused. "Who knows why."

Norm said, "The problem is the contest, Freya. You know that for Ozzie and Alexis and me, it's a big deal and we're running out of time. I've been looking at contest updates and there are some amazing contenders who have leaked some things about what they're doing. We need to get on it fast..."

Alexis said, "Freya, don't you have a deadline too? You have to get back, right?"

"It was ten days. After that they take me off the firefighting team." They all eyed her soberly.

"Today is Day 8," Norm said. "Just enough time to get back, isn't it?"

Alexis added, "With all the trouble we've gotten into... What if there's more? Don't we want to quit before more goes wrong?"

"I have to see this through," Freya said.

Norm asked, "Who says *you* are the one who has to

do this?"

"We. Who is going to do it if we don't?"

Norm looked at her.

"Do you see someone doing it?" she asked again.

"What about Dear Old Congressman Raker and those people he's talking about?"

She just looked at him while whole seconds went by. Ten seconds. She looked like one of the cats, Ozzie thought. Finally she said, "Does Raker seem like the kind of person who actually knows what to do about it?"

No, Ozzie thought. *If it came to actual knowledge, I'd bet on Malo first. Or Freya.*

"Well, since you put it that way..." Norm pretended to consider it carefully. "No."

At least he didn't crack a joke, Ozzie thought. Freya looked miserable. Her eyes turned to him, pleading. Her face was flushed.

Ozzie sighed. He felt torn. Then he remembered: "Hey. I didn't tell you all what happened at the Sphinx last night."

**

The waiter was clearing their table around them. Freya smiled a little and her eyes had a faraway look. "An ibis on the door," she repeated.

Something was wrong with her. He reached over to feel her head. He felt the buzz of electricity from her skin, and she flinched. "Cold hand!" she said. Alexis reached across the table and put several fingers on Freya's forehead.

"You're cold too, Alexis!"

"No, *you are on fire*. Let's go back to the hostel."

Ozzie took Freya's daypack and his. Alexis hugged her upper arm to help support her. "You'll be OK, Frey. We'll get you better. At least Seth has gone home now."

**

The spotted cat wasn't there. Their new room was full of late sun; no one had skimped on the windows for this one. Ozzie wondered what it had looked like in its glory days. The cracked walls almost looked glamourous, coated with pink light that even made their dumb standard hostel beds look interesting.

Alexis was doctoring Freya, who lay on a lower bunk with her eyes closed.

Ozzie watched every few minutes when Alexis wet and wrung and placed a newly cooled cloth on her forehead. He tossed the hyperball quietly, catching parts of a tourist holovid with the sound off — it was in Egyptian anyway — about the ancient city of Memphis.

Norm sat checking the Jet Propulsion Lab contest sites for more of the latest news.

Freya must have fallen asleep because now she stirred and moaned in her dream: "the children — the fires—"

Alexis rose abruptly. Ozzie was startled to see how

257

bad she looked, too, as she took up the bowl and went into the bathroom for more water. White even for Alexis. Norm glanced, then did a double-take as she passed him, probably seeing the same thing. When she returned he stood, hesitated, and walked over to her. She put the fresh dish of water down on a little stand.

"Need a hug, buddy?" he said, and didn't wait for an answer; he folded her in his arms. Ozzie watched, riveted. When she got over being startled, Alexis leaned against Norm with her head on his chest and her eyes closed.

He must have learned that from having little sisters. Minutes later, it seemed to Ozzie, Alexis decided the hug was over and stepped back out of it.

Norm said, "Hey, after you're done being nurse for the moment, how bout a puzzle on holo? I found one I'm *sure* you can't do." He grinned annoyingly.

A small lopsided smile crept upward on her face.

**

It was completely dark now, and Freya was sleeping again after eating a bowl of soup from the cafe. They sat and ate their own dinners quietly, sitting on the floor a distance away from her so they wouldn't disturb her.

"OK, so you're saying a couple more days, right?" Norm said.

"Yes, that's what I figure it will take. You checked the transportation, right, Alexis?"

She had. "Just about a 22 kilometer bus ride — thirteen or fourteen miles, fellas," she said.

Then they couldn't help sliding down into the familiar funnel-shaped conversation. They began talking in whispers about the robotics contest again: the days, the work to be done, the odds, the unknowns. Norm reported his findings from the contest sites: scary. And Norm had received a text-mail from the scholarship fund that made the whole thing a little too serious. He read it to the others: "Congratulations on your entry in the Jet Propulsion Lab annual robotics competition. If you place in the JPL competition, we can assure you a scholarship..."

If. That made them all think. Finally Ozzie swallowed his last bite and said, "I think we can do it. We said we would help her with this mission. I'm in."

Norm sighed. "That's true. We came to help Freya. We said we would. Dammit, let's do it."

"You're right, Norm. Ta hell with danger, and all that," Alexis said. "We'll make things work out anyway."

Ozzie hoped they weren't crazy. Actually, he knew they were.

A floorboard creaked. Freya was up, tottering toward the bathroom. "Memphis is our final stop, right, Freya?" Ozzie said.

"Right." She looked awful, but better.

"We're all in, then: we agree to travel to Memphis as our final stop."

She nodded, smiled faintly, and disappeared behind the closed door. They heard her filling the bathtub with water.

CHAPTER THIRTY-THREE

ALEXIS STAYED UP ALL NIGHT nursing Freya. She refused to sleep, although Freya insisted that the fever was a small thing. Alexis seemed frightened by Freya's sickness. She had to do battle with it. Only in the morning when Freya was clearly much better did she smile her lopsided smile at Ozzie and Norm and relax enough to joke: "I'm just a Chinese doctor at heart. It's a hobby of mine."

Not a hobby, Ozzie thought. *She's afraid of death. But maybe not for herself, like some people. She's afraid of it happening to people around her.*

**

It turned out that there was no bus going to Memphis at all. All that was left of the ancient capital city, the worldweb said, was assorted ruins at a place called Mit Rahina — the place the cat had named. It was possible to take a bus to Mit Rahina, of course.

So they climbed onto an ugly old gas-bus that crawled through the crowded, noisy streets southward from Giza. Horns blasted, pedestrians and donkey carts wove among the gas-cars, and the rare aircars dodged in and out of side streets to try to get ahead of the choking traffic and the toxic air.

Norm and Alexis shared a seat. She slept with her head against his shoulder. Something new, Ozzie thought. Lucky Norm.

Freya lay near Ozzie on the long seat at the side of the bus, sleeping too. He sat by her head on the seat beside it, to catch her if she started to roll off. He looked at her upside-down face, wondering at all that had happened to bring him to this moment: here he was, in legendary Egypt sitting guard duty over an Icelandic sleeping beauty on a mission, instead of making a robot in Pasadena California, where he had gone to save his future career in Space Valley, New Mexico. *How did all this happen so fast? Am I crazy?*

Looking at her, he did feel a little crazy. Something that was solid seemed to be dissolving inside him. He wished she were his sister or something because that would make it safer, but he couldn't help admitting to himself that he loved her.

He sighed and tossed more icons into the air, looking for more info that would help them find the house with the ibis door quickly. The worldweb article that had the best maps said:

The ruins of the ancient Egyptian capital of Inbu-Hedj, later called Menfe and altered to Memphis by the Greeks, is just twelve miles south of Cairo. In ancient times it was the Egyptian center of industry and commerce and in it craftsmen abounded, blessed by Ptah, god of creators and craftsmen. Ruins are all that remain. Today the ruins are mingled with the modern structures of Mit Rahina, and residents there live among the ghosts of the past.

Isn't that what the cat said? The living with the dead?

After half an hour of chugging the bus entered greener, more open country where industrial parks and clustered apartments gave way to neat farmed fields and large estates. And then they were in Mit Rahina.

When they had asked to get off the bus near the ancient city, they didn't know that the nearest stop would be directly across the street from a sign that said "Memphis Open Air Museum."

**

The driver assured them that this really was Mit Rahina, so they hefted their full packs and stepped down off the bus into the bright sun. "That thing makes The Heap look magnificent," Norm muttered, watching the bus drive away. Freya paused a minute, blinking to wake herself more and gazing across the street into the shaded gardens of the museum. The inviting shade would not be their destination today.

Ozzie was already leading the others up the street, past four- and five-story buildings with ground-floor storefronts. As in Giza, these seemed to face the ruins casually, like old neighbors. Ozzie would be taking them on a trek that might be long, or short, till they found the house that the cat at the Sphinx had shown him. She walked quickly to catch up.

She had closed the gap to a few yards when a pair of arms grabbed her pack and jerked her sideways toward the darkness of a narrow alley.

She shouted, and Ozzie whirled. She used what she knew from firefighter defense training, kicking so hard that the arms released her and she pitched sideways into the gravel and dust on the edge of the road. The man leaped onto her, swinging at her face. His jeans and white shirt were a blur. She jerked her head frantically away from his fists.

She heard Ozzie. "Guard the stuff, Alexis. Norm!" Bystanders were appearing as if from nowhere. Freya was struggling, against the weight of her pack, to fight her attacker off of her when Ozzie kicked, then swung a punch, then kicked twice, and the guy lay still on the ground. Ozzie pulled her up and took her pack off.

The small crowd around them was moving inward now, and it was clear that they were not just bystanders, and not friendly.

"Taxi!" Norm called.

Joker. Freya gasped for breath. It was an oxcart passing by, that was all. But Norm used the wheel as a springboard, leaped up onto the seat in the face of the startled driver, and waved a crumpled U.S. dollar at him. "Please?" he asked in English and Arabic. The driver quickly took the scene in, including the payment, and nodded. By that time, Alexis already had two of four packs thrown into the high-sided cart and was on her way up too.

The driver grabbed a hay rake with gusto, following Norm's lead, and together they used the stout handles of his tools to keep the attacker's friends away from the sides of the cart. It gave Alexis time to catch the other two packs and give a hand each to Ozzie and Freya as they scrambled up.

The farmer got the oxen into motion. With four passengers using tool handles and booted feet to detach their pursuers from the cart, they gradually left all of them behind, a little trail of them, picking themselves up off the street.

Norm joined the driver on the seat. The others sprawled in the empty bed of the cart. "Amazing work, guys," Alexis said.

Freya looked anxiously at each person, but no one seemed hurt much. She ran her fingers over her left cheek. It felt bruised. There was a welt blooming on Ozzie's forehead.

"Hey, Alexis, you're stronger than you look," Norm

called back. Alexis was flushed and smiling triumphantly.

Such quick thinking from Norm. Freya stared up at him. "Wow, Norm. Your idea saved us from a bad spot." *I thought this guy could hardly take care of himself, let alone save someone else.*

She was still panting. The fever had left her weaker. She turned toward Ozzie, who was getting his breath too. Both began at once: "How did you learn…" and Ozzie finished: "to fight like that?" Both shrugged.

"Anyway, thank you, Ozzie," she said.

His smile was a painkiller. She hoped everything in her mind didn't show in her eyes.

"Where?" the cart driver said in English. Norm said that they were house hunting (with a silly grin at the others) and let him know that he should drive through the neighborhoods around here, near the museum.

Ozzie stood looking over the sides of the cart while they creaked up and down a maze of little streets, doubling back and doubling again. He scrutinized each house and building they passed.

"I think we've lost those thugs," Norm said over his shoulder.

"Seems like Seth is still around, though, isn't he," Freya said. It wasn't just an idea. She could feel it.

She whispered to Norm, who told the driver. They went back to the street in front of the museum entrance, and all four hid in the cart as he drove them slowly along the boundary of the museum land. As they went they peered between the wooden slats that formed the wagon sides. Freya could squint, and using the wagon as sunglasses, see deep into the Open Air Museum's palm-shaded gardens and across the dusty ruins.

There. She saw him. Seth was skulking along, sticking to the shadows, heading toward the entrance. To catch a cab, probably, she thought with scorn. To his hotel, so he could plot his next trick.

"There he is!" Alexis hissed. Ozzie nodded glumly.

We need a way to get rid of him for good, Freya thought. Where Seth went, there was trouble. And delays. *And who knows what next?*

"How would he know we're in Memphis?" Norm asked.

"At Khufu, remember? The guide said go to Memphis," Alexis answered.

Their driver pulled onto a side street and paused. When Norm told the driver to go on, he held a work-worn hand out for more taxi fare. Ozzie said, "Wait a minute, Norm." He took paper and a pen from his pack, drew a hieroglyph of a bird with a long curved beak, and passed it forward. Norm nodded. He added another wrinkled bill from his pocket.

"Know where this is?" he asked the driver.

The man gaped. "You go *here*?" he said. When he saw that Norm really did mean it, he shook his head wonderingly, pocketed the bill, whistled and flicked the rumps of the oxen with his stick.

They circled through quiet lanes that smelled of cooking, garbage and dust, then creaked off southwest of the museum into another maze of streets. They had not gone very far before the cart stopped in front of a worn multi-dwelling building, more than a century old. Cracked pavement led from the street toward a door that was glossy black, and on it an ibis was outlined in silver.

Ozzie nodded. "This is it, no mistake." He shouldered his pack and climbed down from the cart. Freya followed the others down, looking around.

The driver said, "Not go in, bad place." But when they thanked him politely for saving them from the thugs, he flicked his stick sadly at the tails of his oxen. The cart creaked away.

**

Alexis grimaced. "It's spooky here," she said.

"So what else is new?" Norm shrugged.

The place really was decrepit and gloomy, shadowed by thick palm trees in front and behind. The windows were caked with dust.

"I guess spooky is what we are after," Freya said. "It's what we were told will be here: someone who can tell us what the local spirits know — maybe some history."

She loosened her knife, though. The others did the same. Ozzie stepped up beside her and she knocked.

CHAPTER THIRTY-FOUR

THE DOOR WAS OPENED by a plump woman in a headscarf and traditional dress. Her dark eyes shone. She greeted them by name. How could she know?

She turned and led the way down a dim corridor to a sort of parlor, seating them there. The floor was covered by worn Persian carpets. Freya sat at one end of an old two-seater sofa by a lamp whose base was a large ebony and ivory African elephant.

The woman left the room. Surprising that she knew their names. Was she a servant, gone to fetch the hostess? Freya barely had time to take in the dark wood trim, the dim paintings on the walls, before the woman returned with a tray loaded with a steaming teapot and dishes. To each of the four she handed a saucer carrying a cup of Egyptian tea. There were small mint leaves floating on the surface. It was refreshing just to smell them.

Freya would have said something, then, but the woman waved at them to begin so they sipped, watching her.

She lifted a little bowl that was ornately decorated. From it she took a folded cloth that had soaked up some liquid. She bent toward Freya to dab some of the stuff on her painful cheek, then on Ozzie's swollen forehead, then on Norm and Alexis' scraped and scabbing knuckles.

When the woman stepped back, Ozzie said, "Freya! Your bruise is gone."

"Your lump is gone, too! Alexis?"

"Wow." She stared at her knuckles.

The woman poured steaming tea for herself, then. She sat near them on a tapestried chair with spindly wooden legs, and sipped her tea calmly. A longhaired cat entered the room, wove itself around all their ankles in succession, and walked out.

The woman collected the cups again, placing them carefully on the tray. "You have to do a lot quickly," the woman said. "I won't delay you."

She led them down some very old stone stairs to put their packs in the basement, where there were two rooms with beds, "one room for the young ladies, and one for the young men."

Then they returned upstairs as she had instructed, for the midday meal. She waited to show them into a dim dining room, paneled from floor to ceiling with dark wood and decorated with an odd mix of wall art:

270

yellowed tomb rubbings of hieroglyphs, a yellowed papyrus with brilliantly colored designs, and a few Western-style paintings whose oils and varnishes had simmered in the heat of many summers till they were just murky glimpses of long-ago landscapes.

"You can call me Anai," she said. "This is my home." Their eyes went to the table, where a number of extra places had been set. "We have a guest today," she told the four. "Good day to you, Pentu." A turbaned and white-robed old man bowed to her as he entered the room. Freya gasped: It was their pyramid guide.

How odd, but not odd, that he was here.

And they had so much they needed to know, but a small, mystifying question came out as soon as he was seated, before she thought. "Why did you send us to that man for pears?"

"I sent you to no particular man; I sent you anywhere. I just like pears."

"But the cat he gave us..."

"His idea, I think."

"But it saved us!"

He looked at her a moment, then said, "If you are determined on a goal every road takes you there. Everyone helps you there."

She frowned. It didn't seem that way. "But—"

"Even those who try to stop you will find that they have only helped you toward your goal."

She sat considering this while Anai continued, "Some

of the other residents have joined us today: Betrest" — she indicated one of the empty places at the table — "Meriptah, good day to you sir," — she pointed at another of the places — "Herit, Ahmose..." Freya strained to see, and saw a shimmer at one place, then another. Ozzie seemed to be looking at something too, or trying to, nodding politely at each spot. As for Norm and Alexis, they were a bit wide-eyed about it all, watching Anai place a plate containing a little of everything on the table at each of the four empty-looking places. Serving the oldest guests first, Freya supposed.

The food had to have been Egyptian. They all remembered it as delicious, later. But Freya could never recall exactly what they ate.

"So Memphis is very close to you," Norm said. He pointed in the direction of the Open Air Museum.

Anai looked amused. "No, Memphis is *here*. We are in it. There is an ancient temple next door, and in this house is the gateway to the temple courtyard: what was once called 'the gateway of spirits'."

Freya considered that, watching Ozzie help himself to another ladle of soup. As he did, his eyes stopped on something beyond the soup tureen and he now seemed to be making out, as Freya did, the pale forms of the two people at the other end of the table. The spirits wore something vague — robes of some kind — but their eyes were very live. One wore a headdress like Nefertiti's.

Freya found that the spirit sitting on her left was

clearly visible now, although you could see through it to the dark wood of the sideboard. She asked it a polite question silently, with her thought, and heard its answer like the rustling of leaves, deep in her eyes and her bones. Norm, at her right, had his own eyes riveted on something across the table from him. Now he must see one of them there.

Of the four of them, only Alexis wasn't curious about the other visitors. She seemed gloomy and downcast whenever no one seemed to be looking.

Pentu prompted, so Freya told why they needed to know more about the music of Osiris. She told about the increasing volcanic activity, the danger that something huge like the Great Flood could happen again. Their hostess's eyebrows raised and she half-smiled at Pentu. The ghostly guests turned and looked meaningfully at each other. Norm must be able to see them now — he was staring at the far end of the table.

"I will be your guide again," Pentu said, "to help you find what you need to know. But I can only go with you so far. You will go through a false door. Do you know what that is?"

Alexis said, "It's a door that doesn't really open, so you can't just walk through it, but a spirit travels through it to the other side." She shivered a little.

"Exactly. I will help you all through it to another dimension. Then you must travel the path on which your questions lead you. There are dangers, not so much to your bodies, but... On this path, when things are not as you want, you must exercise your will and decide that the vision should change. And as much as you can will it to happen, the change will occur."

By the end of dinner, both Norm and Ozzie were able to see and converse with the bodiless guests. "It's like the cats. I mean, it just takes getting used to," Norm whispered proudly to Alexis.

Freya realized that she was no longer tired. She had no trace of weakness left from being sick, either. It was the food, maybe.

"Soon you will be flying back to America, all of you?" Anai asked.

"Yes," Ozzie began.

Alexis said, "But I will return to London, where I live."

"No!" Norm countered. "Really? —No, you need to come with us."

"Norm. I've lost my partner. I don't have a new one. My parents are upset — they think I'm hurting my future reputation in my field because I've lost my chance to be in the contest..." Alexis grimaced and looked down again. Norm looked at her. He was as close to being sad as Freya had ever seen.

So that's what is on her mind, Freya thought. *Another text from her parents.*

"Then we won't delay," Pentu said. "I will show you all where the false door is."

They rose from the table as he did, but the spirit-guests startled them by just fading away, leaving the savory food untouched on their plates.

**

As they entered the hallway a loud knock vibrated the front door. Anai opened it. That voice: Freya and the others hurried to stand behind the woman, as if to defend the house.

Seth had asked for Alexis.

"I want to talk to you about the contest," he told her boldly, when she stood in front of him.

She appeared to be startled, then seemed to make up her mind abruptly. "I'll walk with you and we'll talk," she said. They left immediately together, to Freya's amazement.

"Wonder how much he gave the cart driver to get the address," Norm said with disgust.

"Or how much he threatened the guy." Ozzie was still staring after them as they disappeared around some shrubbery. "Do you think she's going to go back to California with him?"

Norm's dismay was becoming horror. "I'm going after her," he said. "So he doesn't hurt her again."

"Damn, Norm. He's so nasty he's actually dangerous."

Norm hesitated, then decided. "Well, I'd better go protect her then, huh?"

Ozzie made Norm go armed, at least.

**

"We need to do something about Seth," Freya said to Pentu. "And the best defense is a good attack, right?" She had a plan, she said. Could their guide assist them with it? Could he get some of the ancient inhabitants to go after Seth? "A good scare would take care of him. He's such a coward."

Good idea, Ozzie thought.

Pentu smiled a crafty smile. Anai said, "I think my old friend can do even better than that."

"Let me tell you what you need to know," said Pentu. "The dimension you will visit contains everything that ever has been — all at once, so space does not behave the same as ordinary space. You can't orient on *things*. You have to orient on yourself and your own thought. And your friends.

"If you are confused while you are there, find yourself again and your own purpose for walking there. If you lose each other, find the other first. Finding another helps you find yourself."

Their guide linked arms with them, one on each side of him, and drew them to the wall.

"Final words: stay together. You will return to the parlor by deciding to be there, when you have found what you want to know. Remember who you are." And he walked them right smack into the carved stone face of the false door.

CHAPTER THIRTY-FIVE

OZZIE WINCED, expecting a knock on the head as they hit the wall. But they were someplace new. *We've gone through!*

Pentu sent them a thought: [I will show you what you need now.] In Ozzie's mind something opened up and a picture formed, just as it had at the Sphinx. He saw Alexis standing in the corner of a ruined wall that came to her shoulders. The bright afternoon sun shone on dusty ground and sparse tufts of grass growing at the base of the wall. She looked fierce but tears were running down her face. Seth stood facing her. His voice was ugly. The scene faded.

[Did you see that?] Ozzie asked Freya. [The wall...]

[And Seth bullying Alexis], Freya said grimly.

Their guide pointed down a dim hallway that flickered ahead of them. [That way, you will find them] he said. [You will scare him away.]

[Will the spirits help us?] Freya asked.

[No one else will be necessary.] He was gone.

**

Ozzie was doubtful about this, but they walked side by side down the hall. As they walked the walls became lighter. He could see, now, that they were covered with hieroglyphs and painted murals. Every few yards, small brass lamps burned in little niches above their heads.

And they themselves were transforming as they walked: now they wore beaded collars and sandals. Freya had a long black wig, bound with a golden headband, and a skin-tight bodysuit like overalls that hugged her figure from her ankles upward, barely covering her breasts. And wings. Her arms were wings now. She looked amazing. And a lot like — who was that goddess? — Isis. Ozzie looked down at the snug white suit that encased him, and reached up to touch a tall hat. He found that he had a crook in one hand and a flail in the other. He was going as Osiris for this masquerade.

The hallway opened into a square anteroom with an open doorway on the opposite side. They heard arguing in the next room, Norm's voice now pushing back at Seth's.

Their thought took them to the door and through it instantly. There was Alexis, standing in the corner where two ornately decorated walls met. Norm and Seth quarreled in front of her. Flame quivered in a lamp set in a niche just above her head.

Alexis' eyes went wide and her mouth made a little O. Norm turned to face them too. But it was Seth that they wanted.

Seth! Ozzie bellowed.

Seth turned. Sparks flew from Freya's eyes in a shower that enveloped all three of them. Norm grabbed Alexis and pulled her out of the firefall.

Seth! Ozzie's anger towered like a thundercloud.

Ozzie raised his crook and flail. He shouted with all his pent-up rage at this sicko who was trying to ruin everything for them, and the sound wave was a blow that knocked Seth over.

Ozzie roared again at him like the blast-jets on a rocket, and Freya poured enough sparks on him to make a hometown fireworks display.

He was lying still. *Maybe that was too much*, Ozzie wondered, impressed.

But Seth sat up and stared at them.

Seth! Leave and never come back! They poured it at him again, walking toward him now.

Seth howled in terror. He scrabbled past Norm and Alexis in his panic and leaped through the lamplit wall as if he were going over an invisible traffic barricade.

Ozzie was tempted to say something to Norm and Alexis, but really, it would have been hard to talk at such a moment. Together Ozzie and Freya seemed to be possessed by perfect showmanship. They roared after Seth one more time, and Freya pitched a fireball just because he deserved one. Then they decided to be gone, and they were.

**

The electricity was so strong that Freya's hair stood out from her head — it was like standing under the old high-tension lines at home, only ten times that. Ozzie felt his hair moving out from his head, too. He couldn't stand the current flowing through him much longer.

But they were in their jeans and T-shirts again, or seemed to be, in a place where there was no wall to tell them where they were and no path to tell them what was forward and what was back. His flesh felt like it was disintegrating, turning into nothing but electrons in motion. *What are we doing here?*

He looked at Freya but she had disappeared. Panic clawed at him. *Where is she?*

Looking for her made her reappear. She blinked at him, her tendrils of curly hair flying outward and upward around her head. Seeing him she seemed to recall herself, too. She breathed deeply and they walked onward in the direction that drew her.

As they walked he found that he had changed costumes again: now he wore a pleated linen loincloth and Freya was dressed in a snowy linen gown. She wore a tall slanted headdress like the ones the pharaohs wore, like Nefertiti's. He reached up and felt one on his head, too.

Another few steps forward and the floor began to rise and fall. The vision perfected itself:

They were on a boat that soared skyward and dived deep on enormous waves. The skies were dark with heavy clouds pouring rain, slashed with lightning. Somehow Ozzie knew these were the waters of the Great Flood. Off to starboard they saw the Great Sphinx with currents swirling around its paws, rising fast.

A monstrous wave pitched the large sail over their heads, and after it the bodies of the crew, their stores of food, their own Royal Selves. All went down in water churning with refuse and bodies, the eyes of the bodies staring in permanent surprise. Through the water they saw columns toppling and the outer crusts of the mighty pyramids tearing away like so much papyrus. They were drowning.

Freya looked around her frantically. Ozzie's lungs were burning for air. He grabbed her hand and pulled her toward the surface, turning her to look at him as they went. She saw him. They remembered, and decided. The whole scene disappeared.

Something new appeared. Below them, the waves rose steeply and fell steeply like those on an open ocean. They saw the earth turning quickly beneath them: the land heaving and rippling, the volcanoes pouring flaming lava into the sea, the lava making the seawater boil and rise as gargantuan clouds of steam. The hot seawater melting the ice caps, the water rising to swallow the masses of land. Clouds raining water in gusty sheets on pathetic boats that pitched and wallowed on the water, and sank.

The scene beneath them ceased whirling, then, and as they walked forward the new vision perfected. They stood on a mountaintop with flood waters swirling around it only a thousand feet below. They seemed to know things they could not know: they knew it was Mt Ararat, a peak that should rise many thousands of feet above the lands between the Black Sea and the Caspian. There was a volcano, a little way from them, that poured lava downward into the sea.

It was quieter now, in this place. And now in the quiet they heard singing. With wonder that opened their mouths — even though they were part of this vision — they heard and then saw something coming toward them just above the waves: it looked like a flying saucer — one of those unverified photos of a flying saucer that you saw among the space lore on the worldweb. Someone stood on the top with his arms outstretched as if for balance, like a surfer, and he was singing above the water. His voice was huge — was it just that the waves and clouds magnified it? Freya tugged Ozzie's hand and they found a rock to hide behind as the saucer-like ship landed nearby, leaving a skid trail down the half-hardened lava skin on top of Ararat.

The ship's circumference was about the same as the length of a small spacetrading vessel. Without delay, figures began to climb out: they were beautifully shaped and very human-looking, but their skin was the color of green olives and they had elongated, bulbous heads. Like the daughters of Ahkenaton. Was he making this up?

Most wore loincloths. Some wore robes. About 50 of them exited, some carrying jetpacks, some carrying tools. Some pulled small craft from the side compartments of the ship till there were a half-dozen lifeboats arrayed there. They all put on headgear that hid the unearthly shape of their skulls.

And they sang. Maybe they had been singing all along, but now Ozzie heard them. Some of the voices boomed, some were creating melodies, some seemed to harmonize with the others. The sounds braided together like a strange rope made of rare fibers, many kinds.

They sang while the sun rose and fell there on Mount Ararat twice, three times. Ozzie forgot Freya, forgot everything, till he noticed that the lava near them had stopped flowing. The hot crater pulsed and glowed like a coal in a dying fire.

Freya? Again he was momentarily frightened at the idea of losing her, or being lost. He searched for her. She appeared, blinking at him. Then she gazed below as if he had interrupted her; she had been busy with what was happening down there. He took possession of her hand.

The flood waters were receding below them. Land had emerged all the way to the horizon.

Without ceasing their song, the singers were

stepping into their crafts or shouldering jetpacks and taking off. One, who seemed to be the saucer-surfing leader, stayed and continued to sing, raising his hand in farewell and watching till the last one was airborne.

Ozzie and Freya looked at each other. What they wanted next came into both their minds, it seemed to Ozzie. They decided, and now they stood in their own craft sailing high in the air, watching the others land one by one: in places that Ozzie recognized as Israel, Egypt, Greece. The singers touched down and continued to sing.

As they moved they watched below: saw one singing in Ireland, where red-haired people had just been joined by dark people arriving on a shipwrecked barge from the Persian Gulf. They saw one singing from a mountaintop in Mexico. And one from a perch in China, and one in Nepal. Then they saw singers locate themselves in other areas as the land masses rose from the sea: Australia, North America, Southern Africa, France. There even were singers landing where there was little left but sad clusters of islands, the newly drowned mountains of the Pacific.

The water rushed up at Ozzie and Freya. They had forgotten to pilot their craft! They were about to hit the water, hard. [Ozzie!] Freya yanked at Ozzie's hand, looked in his eyes, and they decided. The scene disappeared.

But they wanted to see more. The new decision hung them in the air miles above Egypt without a vessel, hearing the fifty voices sing from their scattered locations as the earth turned through night and day, again and again. It was like a speeded-motion holo: the waves settling, the land seeming to rise again from the sea, the pyramids showing above the flood waters in Egypt. Ozzie suddenly worried about time passing. Were they really living through forty days and forty nights, as the Great Flood story said?

At last, as they hovered they saw that the water was in the oceans again, and the land was where it belonged — with a few changes.

But where was Osiris?

They looked at each other and they were gone to find him. They were getting good at this. Ozzie made sure he had her hand as they walked forward. The vision resolved: they walked to a small rise in the desert that overlooked the fertile Nile basin, green with planted fields.

In a field just below, one of the olive-colored people was teaching a ragged, cowed-looking group how to plant a crop. Somehow Ozzie knew that the green man had coaxed them out of lairs in the hills and convinced them to stop fighting each other, as they had probably been doing ever since the Flood, out of pure terror. He was showing them abundance and civilized life again, and something new: their own land, their right to make choices.

This was the one who had surfed on a saucer across

the waves from some mother ship to calm the waves enough for a landing. This olive-green man with the luminous eyes was singing again, or still. He sang as his students worked, and sang as he demonstrated tools to them. The singing was odd but entrancing. Some of them sang with him, mimicking clumsily.

Now Ozzie could almost understand the song: something about the wonders of the stars and moon, the thrill of flying through space, the joys of discovery and trading.

**

Freya heard it too: the excitement of building a renewed earth. About the magic of poetry and song, the joy of making beautiful things.

She strained, as she listened, to hold the music in her memory, or hold onto anything at all about the way the notes went...it all escaped from her, each moment of music yielding to the next, then gone.

But she knew that this was Osiris, even before one of the humans called him something that sounded like the name.

Ozzie tugged her hand a little. He meant: "Time to return?"

What have we learned? She tried hard to think.

That the "music of Osiris" didn't come from the pyramids or from instruments. That it came along with him, from some unearthly place... Hearing Ozzie's thought, she recalled the holos she had seen of the temple at Luxor, where there were hieroglyphs like spaceships.

They had seen Osiris use the music he brought with him to harmonize the self-destructing Earth, to make its rock and lava heal. Then, to civilize the people again. No wonder he was revered as a hero, and later as a god.

She was too awed to think any more. She felt full of answers; this must be what they needed.

She nodded to Ozzie. His eyes seemed to glow and shed fire. They decided to be in the parlor in the ibis house. An arm reached out to each of them, then, and pulled them through a wall.

**

They sat on the two-seater sofa, still holding hands, looking at the dissolving shreds and sparks of their final vision.

Pentu gave them water. "Your friends returned yesterday evening. You were very successful in making Seth go."

Yesterday evening?

He nodded. "You have been gone for about 30 hours." He motioned and they followed him to a sort of atrium in the middle of the building, open to the night sky. Ozzie breathed deeply and saw Freya do the same. Starlight and the cold desert air were pulling them into the here and now. Pentu nodded approval. "It's very hard, walking for so long through visions."

The three took seats together at a table. He gave them oranges, which they peeled and ate hungrily. And sweet dried figs.

They sat in silence looking up at the stars, until he said, "It is late for an old man." They rose as he left them.

Then they looked at each other. Suddenly the number of stars made him dizzy. Ozzie's face felt hot. He wanted to fall into Freya's eyes.

He was probably hungry or delirious or something. "Well, we'd better get some rest," he said, trying to sound cooler than he felt. "You should turn in." *I'd better leave before I kiss you and things get confusing: like maybe you hate me, or even worse, maybe you laugh at me.*

He turned to go. She caught his hand and tugged gently, pulling him back around to face her. She stood for a second with a look on her face that seemed to say "you are dumb but I like you." Then she stepped forward and kissed him warmly on the mouth. She smiled and left.

He stood there for three huge seconds like a dolt, watching her walk away, before he could recover enough mobility to leave. He had just stood there and let her go, like he was a little boy being kissed goodnight by his mama. What a dolt.

Why was he so happy, then?

He tranced his way down to the room, being kissed again and again by her, like in holo-replay. And the more he replayed it the less he cared whether it was a mom kiss or a sister kiss or a girlfriend kiss; it strengthened him and warmed him and life was good.

CHAPTER THIRTY-SIX

FREYA WOKE the next morning with terror in her stomach. And a terrible thought: She had missed something. Now they knew how the music had come to Egypt. They knew something of what it sounded like. *But I still don't know how to get hold of the music of Osiris. Where to find it? How to make it? How could I have overlooked that?*

Alexis was gone, already upstairs she supposed. They would all have a lot to tell each other today. *But how can I end this trip without knowing how to get the music?* The thought made her heavy. She ached.

Breakfast smelled just right, whatever it was. When she arrived at the table the others were already eating. One of the spirits — was it Betrest? — sat with a lightly filled plate in front of her, seemingly taking deep breaths of the food aromas. Maybe that was how spirits ate, Freya thought suddenly, seeming to remember it from somewhere.

Ozzie was looking at her with warm eyes, half-smiling. She must be a mess, funny to look at. She pushed back her curls. Then she remembered yesterday and last night. Involuntarily she smiled back and blushed. How odd that she felt suddenly shy.

She nodded politely to Anai, wishing her good morning in English, wondering how it was that everyone here, even the spirits, spoke English. Or did they?

She took a seat by Ozzie. Norm and Alexis were cheerful. They gave her bright smiles and continued chattering to each other.

She accepted the food Anai served her. While she chewed mechanically she worried. She didn't want to spoil the moment for the others, but the music: what were they going to do?

"Freya," someone said. Who? Her eyes traveled around the table. No one seemed to be paying attention to her — except Betrest. Betrest, whose filmy, almost-there dress and headgear marked her as a queen.

[Freya,] The voice was in her mind.[About the music: today, it still exists. A little.]

[Where?] Eagerly.

[On another planet. There is a Singer...] The sound of the singer's voice suddenly pealed in Freya's mind, as loud as real sound. She started at the noise, for a second wondering if everyone at the table could hear it. But no one turned their way.

The voice was rich and thick like chocolate, then

clear and sweet, then raw with power: a woman's voice, she thought, raging, crying, soothing. Enough like the music in the vision of Osiris to convince her, but also different. Freya's hope soared.

[Where is the Singer?] Freya thought to Betrest. Ozzie's eyes were on her face now. Could he see it in her eyes? Could he hear the voice?

[The planet of the Beginning.]

Another planet? [Where is that?]

Her filmy hand moved in a vague arc, pointing skyward. [I was here, near the Beginning. Ptah, the god of creation, came from the planet of the Beginning. Ptah, the god of creation and craftsmen, the god of Memphis, who brought the first cats.] *The first cats.* Freya remembered Ptah. Besides Osiris, he was the only other green-skinned god she had seen in the tomb murals.

[Where is it from here — the planet?]

Again the hand pointed skyward.

Freya sighed. She tried to eat and failed. Good news: The music was still there, somewhere. Bad news: Betrest didn't have a way to tell her where. The table had fallen silent. When she looked up, they were watching her.

She looked at Anai, who shrugged. "So much has been forgotten," the woman said.

"Pentu? Maybe he knows?"

"He has gone." She shook her head. Did that glimmer behind the woman's eyes mean that she knew a secret? The others just watched uncertainly.

**

There wasn't anything more anyone could think of to do or say, so they stowed their toothbrushes after breakfast and shouldered their packs. Anai accepted their grateful thanks, and embraced each of them, but her farewell was simple, as if she expected them to be gone for an hour or two. Maybe having so much time stacked up around you made you feel that way.

They walked the few blocks from the Ibis door toward the bus stop, stopping by the temple ruins so Alexis and Norm could point out the site of Seth's hasty departure. The dusty grass near the wall was trampled where he had fought his way out of the ruined room. Freya listened with delight to Norm's description.

She took a picture of the others in the corner as a souvenir, and then let Norm take one of her and Ozzie, too, standing together in front of the ruined wall. Every time she looked at it, Freya thought, she would see it as it was that night, when she was Isis and Ozzie was Osiris in the wildest costume party she had ever been to.

Alexis said, "Hey, maybe you won't believe this, but I decided to go with Seth, when he came to the door, to lead him out of your way. So you could do whatever-it-was without him interfering."

Ozzie nodded. Freya knew that she was telling the truth.

"But he didn't so much come to snoop this time. He

came to try to win me back as his contest partner."

"Didn't work," Norm said smugly.

"He was pretty sad and pathetic," Alexis nodded. "He did all he could to make me feel guilty and obligated. Promised me the moon, too. I felt sorry for him. He's kind of pathetic. But I didn't trust him. I knew that I was right, for sure, when he started to threaten me again, and just then Norm came, thank goodness. And then..."

"Then we had a visit from some friends." Norm did not grin.

**

They decided to make parent calls from a nearby part of the ruin because the place was so quiet, this weekday midmorning. Each one could take one of the ancient rooms for soundproofing.

Alexis quailed at the idea of calling her parents, though. "Their texts have been pretty harsh, all this week," she said.

Norm said, "We'll find you a partner, Alexis. We haven't even gotten started on that yet...Hey, look: if your parents are worried about *shame*, isn't there some reason why it would be more shameful for you to leave California than to stay?"

She hadn't thought of that angle. She considered. "Well, there's my scholarship...If I leave without being in the contest, I actually will be in violation of the terms of my scholarship..."

"Bingo," Norm said. He grinned at her expectantly.

The little smile moved up one side of her face. She shook her head at him. "OK, OK, I'll call them now. Quiet, everyone, please?"

**

As they walked on to the bus stop Alexis reported:

"You saved me again, Norm. They were like lambs when I told them that. They just agreed with me that I must of course stay through the contest. That buys me a little time to try to get a partner...No shame YET."

Norm's mom was a little worried about the delay but she was glad they'd be returning soon and wondered if they were eating OK. "By the way," he said, "what was all that stuff Anai fed us?"

No one could recall.

"My dad played in a cafe last weekend," Ozzie's eyes were wide. "He hasn't done that since before I was born."

Mamma's portrait was done, she had told Freya. And she was paid. But her new art patron complained that it wasn't as he thought it would be. Then he tried to seduce her. Freya wasn't surprised.

"Hey, look what I found on the worldweb while you guys were away in Dreamland," Norm grinned.

But then the Cairo bus pulled up to the stop, trailing toxic fumes.

**

"Tell us about what you saw on the other side of that spirit door," Alexis said. They stowed their packs on the racks in the half-empty bus and took the rear seats.

Ozzie and Freya did their best to describe the vision they had shared. They interrupted each other a lot, struggling to convey the epic scenes and the grandeur. Norm and Alexis listened in fascinated silence all the way to the end. With no jokes from Norm. Freya ended by saying, "It's so hopeful, that a Singer is still out there somewhere! We just don't know where, yet." She was trying bravely to stay positive.

"That reminds me..." Norm took out his phone again and spread the sheet on his knee, flicking through the icons with one finger to find the link.

Alexis sat beside Norm, and Freya was here on the seat with Ozzie, facing them. She was still worrying, he could tell. She was so close to him that he imagined wrapping her in his arms like Norm had hugged Alexis — what it would be like to hold her that close for that long. He was frozen by his own hesitation.

"What did you and Norm do while we were gone?" Freya asked Alexis.

"We played Senet! They had an old board there in the house."

"And she is one wicked Senet player," Norm added absently as he flipped icons.

Then they summarized their Senet standings and gossiped about meals at the ibis house, including who attended and how much they could see of the deceased ones.

Ozzie thought of the tale Norm had told him while they were in the basement packing up this morning: that in their absence he also had the opportunity to use Ozzie's trader training module, "Create a Distraction," to dodge a kiss from Alexis. Earlier, Ozzie would have been jealous. He shook his head, astonished even now. Only Norm would want to escape a kiss from Alexis. "The second and third times I didn't dodge, though," Norm had said.

Now, after flicking dozens of rejects off into the air, Norm pulled up the right holovid finally and tapped it to make it play in the center of the space, where they all could see.

It was a news story about something found recently on an asteroid where they were mining nickel. The holovid showed the mine, the miners, and the equipment moving around, then interviewed the men about what they had found, then showed it, finally: buried under a pile of rocks, preserved by the vacuum of space, a tightly-lidded metal box. They opened it and pulled out a small square of papyrus with hieroglyphs on it. It looked like written documents Ozzie had seen in the Egyptian Museum in Cairo. Then there was a background story about beads found in an Egyptian tomb, made of metal that could only have come from the asteroids.

"Cool, right? From what you said about your

experience in Dreamland," Norm said, "The Egyptians were not strangers to space travel. At least at one time. This just proves it."

Freya nodded, interested. Ozzie smiled a little. She was lightening up. *What would we do without Norm to create distractions?*

**

Freya checked the newsfeed as the bus labored northward. Remarkably, there were no new volcanoes in two days. And she checked her phone: from Arni, the news that she had been dismissed, sorry. Was she OK? "OK," she answered.

Ozzie was watching her. The news about firefighting school must show on her face. She looked up at him and shrugged it off. She said, "Norm, you seem more alert and you react faster now than when we first came here."

"Holo game withdrawal," he said, handing her a chocolate bar. He passed two more to the others. "This is to celebrate ditching Seth," he said, "Egyptian chocolate, secretly splurged by yours truly from the trip money — when Alexis wasn't guarding it. It's the kind with cinnamon and cloves, laced with ancient orange peel..." Freya chuckled dryly, liking him.

"This trip has been like boot camp," Norm said. "But fun."

Then all four of them were quiet for a mile or two. Freya knew that the three robotics contestants were resisting the temptation to talk about what they had to do after they left Egypt. After they left her and the volcanoes problem behind.

As the bus neared Cairo airport, she brought up what they had all been avoiding. "Guys, we are near the end of this research trip. We have been betting on a complete answer. A solution to the volcanic disruption. Thanks to you all, we have the data we wanted to get but we don't quite have the clear solution that I hoped for. We need to know more."

"Yes," Alexis lamented. "I'm sorry we couldn't find anything. We wanted to help you get a solution and we haven't yet, and here we are running home to cover our butts. I need to get a partner so I can help someone in the contest and not go home to London in shame — but go home I must, in a few weeks." Norm chewed his lip. She added, "I hope I can find a partner who thinks I'm good enough—"

"—And Ozzie and I need to salvage our chances of winning the contest," Norm said. "I wish we could get you the answer, Freya, but how can we?"

Ozzie said, "We've found out a lot about what it isn't."

"A lot about what it is, too!" When she nodded Freya's hair came loose from the knot and fell into a heap on her shoulders. "I mean, that the music was brought by Osiris and it had a magic sort of effect, and it's still out there somewhere..."

Ozzie looked torn. There was a lot he wasn't saying,

J.K. STEPHENS

Freya thought. He said only: "Well, we'll have to work hard now, to catch up on the contest. What about your training program and the Fire Company, Freya? Can you patch that up?" Something was showing in his eyes: longing. He hated to leave her.

Well, she hated to leave him, too. If the truth were known — and she wouldn't have the chance to say it. "They have told me no. The conditions were strict. I will think of something," she said. "I do need a job.

"But hey, I want you to win the contest and succeed at that. — Because you are my friends," she added, lamely. More than friends. She couldn't remember having such friends before.

**

They made it to Cairo airport just in time to get standby tickets for overnight flights. They parted hastily at the division between two concourses, each of them hugging Freya in turn — awkwardly because of their heavy packs. Ozzie knew his pack felt heavier because they had less optimism now. Freya looked a little sad. He heard their flight being called; it was a long way to the gate.

He wished she could have what she wanted. *Why do things have to be sad?* he thought suddenly, then he protested stubbornly: *Maybe they don't.* He decided. Before she could turn away, Ozzie took Freya by her shoulders and kissed her soundly. When he saw her eyes

300

brighten, he couldn't resist. He kissed her again, longer. He smiled in her eyes then, delighted with himself, and exited after his astonished fellow-nerds.

CHAPTER THIRTY-SEVEN

BEFORE THEY EVEN REACHED THE GATE for their flight, Ozzie, Alexis and Norm had launched a strategy meeting: what to do now, and when they arrived in California, and the next day. They made the list.

First priority: a partner for Alexis. At the gate Norm and Alexis got on both their phones, and while Norm researched the Jet Propulsion Lab Contest Comments and JPL Gossip sites for partner-less people — and as fast as he spit the addresses out — Alexis texted one after another offering her help. With little more than six weeks till the contest, it looked like there had been a few partner casualties: because of a ski accident, some weird contagious disease, a flood and a freak lava flow that took out telecommunications in Bali. No one mentioned an abusive, evil partner. "You were just lucky to get Seth, Alexis," Norm said, grinning. She was sure to get a good partner now, with all of them working on it.

Ozzie used his phone, which was slower, to research the updated contest rules: He confirmed that you really had to have a partner for the Freestyle competition. How late could you change partners? There seemed to be no limit. Could three be partners? A third could help as a "Contest Apprentice" but the apprentice couldn't get credit for actually participating in the contest. And so on.

Then they were on the plane, crowded together in one row with Alexis in the middle scribbling with a wand on her holosheet and sometimes with a pen on a pulp-pad that she pulled from her pack: Norm named the steps to complete execution of his robot design, then Alexis stretched them out on a timeline and counted the days it would take. When Alexis and Ozzie thought of more steps, she added them, redid the timeline and counted again.

Finally they had to stop. They all had headaches from trying to build a robot in their heads. They gave up, then, and slept while the plane droned on toward California.

As he was falling asleep Ozzie noticed that his lips were tingling. As if they had been touched by something that gave him a mild shock. It was Freya, he mused, already slipping into a dream. Electric Freya.

**

"Such a relief," Norm's mother said when she hugged him at Burbank Airport. "I wasn't sure how much longer I could write 'Norm is sick' excuses for you." The little brothers had tried to saw through the lock on the garden shed. When Norm and Ozzie checked the shed, they could see the hacksaw marks. And Norm had lost his key somewhere in Egypt, so Ozzie was glad he had the other one.

**

It was Saturday again, and the familiar garage smells of rubber tires and oil and musty wood were comforting. But they were getting stressed out from pushing so hard.

In spite of the headaches, maybe it had helped to preassemble the robot in their minds on the plane. Ozzie swore later that he dreamed the whole process as he slept through the second half of the flight from Cairo:

"Have you got the gear box assembled, Ozzie?"

Ozzie held it out, Norm took it without looking and began to attach it. Ozzie was at work on the mechanism that elevated and lowered the robot's arms, putting together small subassemblies that Norm could install. "Here's the other one, Norm," Alexis said as soon as he looked up. She mirrored Ozzie's work, only on the opposite side. They moved without a hitch, as if they had been trained for this...

Whatever the reason, their teamwork got the Creature put together pretty fast. Although its official name was the Hot Rod, "Creature" was Norm's nickname, short for The Creature from the Black Lagoon, and like a lot of his joke material, it seemed that this one came from 100-year-old flat-films.

They were still racing against the clock, with a week left before the contest deadline. But they had been at the top of their game when they began the programming yesterday. The robot looked great and performed its functions exactly. Ozzie could just taste the victory as they put it through its paces mechanically. Sweet. This idea would be a sensation.

Today they were doing — actually, Norm was doing — the fancier programming that permitted the robot to make decisions about which action to perform. This was the programming that Norm had expected to be simple: "icing on the cake."

Today's news was that it turned out to be difficult. Not simple at all.

Ozzie was now a wizard at reading design documents and assembling. He even understood the design principles involved. But he was no programmer. For the last hour he had looked over Norm's shoulder and chewed his lip, unable to be much help.

Alexis was looking over the program too, line by line, on the screen of the holo-monitor Norm had brought down from his room. Next to the screen a holo of their bot floated in the air, waiting for commands.

She had no new partner yet. Norm's mother had agreed to let her stay there so she could help Norm and Ozzie while she searched for one. Ozzie and Norm had each decided, without even discussing it, that it was safe to have her here. With so little time till the contest she couldn't take their idea to a competitor. Even if she wanted to.

She said her parents would have a fit if they found she was staying at a boy's house, but she was having fun being part of the living room dormitory, sleeping on an opened-flat lawn chair across the coffee table from Ozzie. Due to her influence, she and Ozzie now neatly folded and put away their bedding each morning.

"You have a lot more to do here, Norm," she was saying. "Days' worth...weeks even...This is complicated. What you're trying to get the Creature to observe, and decide, is complicated."

Norm's sisters brought in sandwiches. No one ate them.

Alexis' phone sounded, and she jumped up from her pages of programming notes to get it out of the case for holo. When she saw the holo ID, she said, "Another one of the partnerless people! Thank goodness. You'd think he would have called earlier." She opened up the line.

"Yes, it's Alexis," she said. "Hi Barrett. Yes, I did.

"But I didn't...

"But it wasn't like that...

"Barrett, this isn't fair..."

The call was over. She turned toward Ozzie and Norm. Her eyes welled. "Seth again," she said.

"The bastard," Ozzie snarled. His eyes burned with hatred for Seth. Twisted creep. Seth had qualified for a new partner on the grounds that Alexis "deserted" him. Not satisfied with that, he had destroyed her chances by telling everyone so. He seemed to have started a "Don't Work with Alexis" movement.

"Are there *any* more who haven't called?" he asked her. He could feel the fury turning to panic in his stomach. No time for this.

"No, that was the last one," she was weeping openly now. "My mother and father said…"

Ozzie knew. During her last parental phone call, with no partner in sight, he heard her parents worry and scold her again, telling her to leave before she was publicly embarrassed. She hadn't told them that she already *was* publicly embarrassed.

Norm was aghast. And you could see the stalled program frozen in his eyes.

"Let me help you," Alexis said, "while I think what to do." She sat down in front of the screen again, sniffling and blinking as she stared at the lines of the program and made notes on a pulp-pad. Norm's sisters ran by through the front yard squealing in the December sunshine.

We scared the crap out of him, but Seth has succeeded in costing us too much time, Ozzie thought. *With help from his interference, Freya's side trip has hurt us a lot.* He moaned inwardly. *It may have wrecked the chances that Norm and I can place in the JPL contest.*

But we have to win! My apprenticeship depends on it.

And Norm is depending on me... Why do we have to solve Alexis' problem and Freya's problem in the middle of our own problem?

His friends were impossible. Looking back, life before he had met them seemed so simple. He watched Norm's panicked face as he and Alexis went through the code. She made some more notes, still crying. It was hard to see so much misery on their faces. Added to his own it was intolerable.

On automatic, Ozzie pulled out the hyperball and began to toss it up, bounce it off the cement floor, toss it up, bounce it, watching the lights sparkle with each impact. He saw New Mexico in his mind's eye, the desert passing him as he ran. He saw the Grand Galactic bay where the assembly crew was making his ship ready for the first Martian trade flight.

"What do you think, Ozzie?" Norm demanded. Maybe he was annoyed by the thumping ball. Ozzie stopped thumping and scowled as he tossed and caught, tossed and caught, gazing at the sparkling lights. The truth was that he couldn't think at all. His wits were totally paralyzed. It was his worst nightmare: they were counting on him, he was counting on him too, and he had no idea what to do. Could this get any worse?

Yeah, it could. Seth could jeer at him and defeat him by taking away what he wanted most, his seat near the captain on the *Liberty*.

His phone signalled. Freya's ID again. Freya in

Iceland, out of a job and probably not allowed to return to firefighter school. Freya, digging out of her research pile every day to call and ask what he knew about recent exploration on the moon or the asteroids, and tell him about exploratory photos. Yesterday he wouldn't have minded, when everything was going perfectly. But today it was different. *Now what does she want? Doesn't she remember what this contest means to us?*

He took the call without holo, for speed. "Yeah, Freya?" He tried to be businesslike because that was the best he could do. He walked around the garage to the back yard as she talked.

She wondered about recent findings on Venus or Mars. What did he know about that? He told her what he knew as fast as he could. She sounded like she was taking notes.

"OK, I'll check that," she said. "Ozzie, have you looked at the newsfeeds?"

He hadn't.

"The volcanoes have ceased, everywhere but Iceland. Just stopped, and they're cooling. They don't know why — of course."

Some good news. "That's a relief. Maybe the volcanoes are really just — "

"Just the problem of those poor Icelanders?" she said bitterly. "That may be. Iceland is the place most vulnerable to volcanoes. So maybe.

"But I don't think so. This is temporary and we're

lucky. But not a time to stop."

We have to stop! For now, at least. I have to go win that contest.

"Ozzie?" There was something plaintive in her voice. He reached for the ring on the chain around his neck, found it gone again. He was suddenly homesick — for what? For anything like home. For his father, who wasn't answering his calls, why? because maybe he was struggling with something scary? For New Mexico, the long violet shadows on the desert sand? His mother, still out there somewhere? *What was his home?* He didn't know.

"Yeah?" he said cautiously.

"I guess I just — need your help," she said.

It felt like a smothering weight: Norm, needing him. Alexis, needing him. Freya, needing him. And what about Norm's family, who had passed the hat to get money for them all, because they thought it would get Norm and his friends a better future than their own? How could he repay them if he had wrecked Norm's chances by letting this Egypt thing happen? What about his spaceship, the merchant flight that belonged to him! Then, in exasperation, feeling like he was tearing in half, he gritted: "You said you wanted us to win!"

"I do. Why are you so wary of me?"

"Why shouldn't I be? You're trying to take me away from what I want."

"That's not true! I am taking you toward it!"

"Prove it!"

Silence. Like a vacuum, it pulled everything into it. His dream. His hopes. A torrent of anger. *What about me?*

Then it was breaking out, like a flash flood, and there was no stopping it:

"You have wrecked my chances for what I've always wanted. You have wrecked my life. My plan to win back my chance on the *Liberty* is ruined. I've lost my chance to fly for Grand Galactic. The robot can't be finished on time. We're missing our chance — because of that screwball trip to Egypt. This is your fault!"

A long silence, then:

"Ozzie, don't you believe in yourself?"

Ozzie was stunned into further silence. His chest heaved with fury. *What kind of riddle is that?*

"I don't have time for this!" he roared. He cut the connection.

**

As he dragged himself back into the garage, Alexis' ringtone sounded from the rusty folding chair near Ozzie. He picked her phone up, numbly. "Your parents, Alexis."

"Not taking it," she said. He put it down.

Alexis and Norm were still poring over the program on the screen. Alexis had stopped crying, though, and Norm looked a little less freaked out.

"Hey," she said. "Here's a small idea that could help with this part." She pointed at two lines of the program on the screen. "See, you could use this command, then alternate with this command…"

Norm sat back, stunned. "Brilliant," he said. "I think it'll work." They leaned toward the screen again, their heads close together. Norm began to type in some new lines.

Ozzie was almost struck blind with jealousy. She knew what he didn't. She was helping Norm when he had no power to. It was all so unfair. If it was possible to become a solid mass of pain, Ozzie had just become one. He felt, again, like he couldn't hold on any longer, he was tearing in two and he didn't know why. Was it Freya? Because if this was what they meant when they said someone's heart was breaking he was a live specimen.

Then things went into slow-mo for him: Alexis there, the pulp-pad with her notes on it. Her brightening face, Norm's hopeful one. He and Norm winning. Ozzie as Captain's Apprentice on the *Liberty*. The Grand Galactic memo about robotics. He and Norm losing. Norm's scholarship letter: "IF you place we can assure you…" Freya and the volcanoes. Freya and the visions. Osiris surfing on the saucer over the waves. Running on the desert. His father's wistful smile. Malo and the cats. Seth and Raker. Real enemies, real friends. His life.

"Don't you believe in yourself?" she said.

Of course I do! He bellowed internally.

He just didn't know enough things to understand all this. Hell, he didn't even understand half the things he did know! He had just hit a solid wall with no opening.

And then, just as suddenly, there was a door there and he walked right through. Suddenly he knew enough, and he understood enough.

"Ozzie?" Alexis said again. "Ozzie, look, see how we can do this?" Her face was lit by her amazing intelligence. She pointed at the screen. "We can just reprogram here, and change this..."

"Alexis, stop."

"But Ozzie. But Ozzie, I think we have it. Then we can..." He felt a gush of affection for these friends, both of them, just the way they were.

"*Yes. You can,*" he said. "Alexis! I have a partner for you."

"Really?" she halted, befuddled. Norm gaped. When Ozzie said nothing more for a few seconds, collecting his wits, the dawn broke for her too. "No no no," she said, standing to face him, "No, I'm happy to..."

The slow-mo became live motion, vividly. He said it as fast as it came to him: "Alexis and Norm, you will be partners. That's the only way Norm will win so late in the game. It means school and careers for two people instead of poor odds for Norm and a wild gamble for me."

Norm and Alexis stared at each other.

"But your place on the spacetrader, Ozzie!" Alexis'

face was crumpling and it looked like she was ready for another round of tears.

"I will be *fine*," Ozzie said. And at this moment he knew it was true. He realized, as if he were looking from a great distance, maybe from a mountaintop somewhere, that he could take care of himself. He knew he was going to be a merchant captain and nothing could stop him really. Nothing, nobody. "Maybe you can write me a letter of recommendation, Doctors Norm and Alexis." He gave them a smile that he hoped was reassuring.

Norm grinned back. Relief was spreading over his whole body.

Alexis quailed again. "Oh, Ozzie. But what if I let you down, Norm, and we fail?"

Norm looked at Ozzie, then at Alexis. He shrugged. "You won't," he said.

"You are brilliant, Alexis," Ozzie said, feeling again an impulse to care for her. He took her in his arms.

She emerged from the hug with new tears pouring down her face. She looked from Ozzie to Norm. "You guys," she scolded softly. "I don't know…"

The tears kept coming, and now she was actually sobbing. "I don't know if I can. I'm so afraid of messing things up for you, Norm."

It was nonsensical. Does Norm have a better choice than you? Ozzie thought, but he didn't say it. Maybe she needed to figure that out herself. Maybe all our fears are that silly, when you really see them as they are.

Norm's mother was standing in the doorway looking worried.

Alexis stopped sobbing. "Do you really…"

Norm nodded, emphatically, yes.

She took a deep breath. Nodded. Stared at nothing, nodded again. Stared a whole minute. Norm and Ozzie waited. "OK," she said. "I think I can do it. I think I know enough to help you win, Norm. I'll stay. I will help you win! And I will turn my shame into victory."

"I'll help you too, of course," Ozzie said. "I'm not going away. I'm going to help you beat Seth."

Alexis hadn't thought of that.

"Let's go!" he commanded. "Not much time, we have a lot to do. First, Alexis give me the printouts of your entry forms. I'll call and get you registered as Norm's new partner."

"Oh! I forgot that! They won't let you!" she wailed. "It's too late!"

"Just watch me," Ozzie said. He had read the rules.

**

Around midnight his phone went off and woke him. Stifling the noise quickly to keep it from waking Alexis too, Ozzie saw a text from Freya. "I'm proud of you" was all it said.

CHAPTER THIRTY-EIGHT

THE PASADENA ARENA parking lot was parked solid with cars — including The Heap, driven by Norm's Uncle Fred, which had carried Norm and Alexis, Ozzie and the Creature. Ozzie said, "We'd better stick to calling this bot the Hot Rod, Norm, or you'll have everyone confused by your fertile imagination."

Ozzie had been too excited to eat. Norm and Alexis looked pale but fortified by Mrs. Garcia's *huevos*. Alexis was developing a taste for Tex-Mex food — as well as American Chinese food, which was nothing like what she ate at home. The family aircar was parked next to The Heap. So was Uncle Chen's hovervan. A dozen assorted family members had managed to fit into those two vehicles, some sitting on laps.

The Arena holomarquees announced that this was the Jet Propulsion Lab Annual Freestyle Challenge for high school contestants.

Ozzie had entered himself as a "contest apprentice."

To get Alexis re-entered as Norm's partner, he had to tell the JPL Robotics Contest Committee about Seth's mistreatment. When they offered the opportunity to file a complaint, he made Alexis file a complete report with the Committee on Seth's behavior as a partner, including hitting her, for the contest records. Ozzie composed it for her so she could keep programming. During breakfast one day he got her to help him make it sound like her, then put her live holosignature on the final draft and sent it from her phone.

**

And now this was contest day, December 15th. While they were setting up the Hot Rod together, Ozzie looked up and saw Seth and Representative Raker in the center of a group of media people, talking into the mike and posing for holos. As if Seth had already won. *What is it about them, that the game always seems to be arranged in their favor?*

Their setup was almost finished when Seth came by to sneer.

One look at him and Alexis turned her back, her fishtail braid swinging. She found important things to do in the tool bag.

Norm was ready with the first shot: "Did something scare Sethie away from Egypt?"

Seth paled and his face hardened.

"She your little apprentice?" he waved a finger at

317

Alexis.

"No," Ozzie straightened up and faced Seth. "She is Norm's *partner*."

Seth was stricken. Ozzie knew he would be. These two together would be scary to any competitor here who knew their capabilities.

But Seth pretended quickly: "Looks like a losing combination to me."

"You *wish*, Seth."

"What about *you*, Ozzie—"

Seth was blocked by an offensive shot from Norm, who waved a polishing rag at the guy standing beside Seth: "Who did you get to be your fall guy this time?" It was one of Seth's two goons. Ozzie remembered his face.

A loud gong-like sound, then a deafening voice: "Five minutes to contest start. All robotic devices must be on the risers now. Contestants take your seats."

Seth said, "I finally found my ideal assistant." The goon looked dumbly at them. "He does exactly what I say."

"That's too bad," Norm chortled, clearly delighted at being handed such an opening.

Norm's family had disappeared somewhere up in the arena seating. Norm waved to them theatrically, to cut Seth off. "Let's go," he said. Ozzie ported the bag of tools. Norm and Alexis rolled the Hot Rod, seated in its picking dish, toward a perch on the stepped risers. The three lifted it.

Their change of partners so late in the contest period had won them the honor of being last in line for judging, among fifty-plus other entries. It would be a long day for everyone there, and the judges might be tired of it all by the time the Hot Rod's turn came up. The audience probably would be.

I sure hope they're impressed in spite of that, Ozzie thought. They put the Hot Rod at the end of the back tier of the risers, in the place marked "56" to match their contest envelope. An automated picking device would use the picking dish to lift one device at a time to the floor to perform.

For now, all the entered devices were displayed there on the risers so they could be viewed throughout the show. Attendees were already putting enoculars to their eyes to get detailed views of the devices. Some of the attendees, Ozzie had overheard, were corporate talent scouts, or university recruiters.

Metallic surfaces shone in the brilliant light from above. Some of the entries twinkled or blinked — their owners had clearly spent time on special effects. That was such clever marketing that it made Ozzie nervous. The Hot Rod sat quietly, looking well-polished but not glamourous.

Their seats were on the arena floor facing the risers. The autovoice system was already calling out show announcements when they got to the seats with their number on them: "...grateful thanks to the many fine sponsors who have helped us with their support..."

The list seemed endless. When the autovoice called "ParKay Flooring and Tile of Los Angeles, California" Ozzie nudged Norm. Ozzie had talked ParKay into delivering a twelve-foot-square slab of epoxy resin flooring — a hundred layers heat-sealed together — to the arena floor for the Hot Rod to show off on, in exchange for publicity shots of Alexis and Norm with the flooring and the robot after the show. "Wash your hair and wear something civilized," he had reminded Norm this morning.

ParKay must have bargained to be listed as a contest sponsor. But the company deserved it, Ozzie thought. ParKay had even delivered the slab to Norm's driveway and left it there till this morning for them to practice on. In fact, they had rush-tested the bot on the slab for the last three days — round the clock, in shifts.

Norm still thought it was pretty clever that Ozzie had made ParKay a sponsor. "Want to be our agent?" Norm grinned at him now.

"Sure. I may need the work," Ozzie joked. That made him think of the school store job that he had given away. And the months of school he would have to make up when he got back home. And then what, exactly?

No time for that now. The first entry was being lowered to the floor.

**

Some of the entries were a little dumb, Ozzie thought, like the one that would wash and detail your aircar for you. Because anyone who could afford a robot could afford a live servant who could do a lot more than wash a car. But most of them were pretty clever. Some of them were downright scary as competition. *What a great idea*, he thought, as one finished going through its routine. But not as great as theirs. He hoped so, anyway. All they needed was to be one of the top three, for Norm's scholarship. *And all Alexis needed was to have this day happen — and it already has.*

The judges were marking their electronic ballots. The autovoice call for the next device droned across his dulled ears, as the picking arm located the next one and grasped the picking dish by its four handles.

The voice gave a description for each device, telling what it was for, what it could do, and what was important about the idea. This one had a boring description — or maybe he just didn't understand it — but it blinked and played music as it moved. *Jeez*, Ozzie thought. *I hope the judges aren't as bored as I am. If they are, they'll give the prize to the one with the best visual effects.*

Seth's name was announced on the autovoice. Ozzie and Norm sat up for a look at what the picking arm was swinging downward to the floor. It looked ordinary, but the description said that this device was designed to perform an impressive list of research functions in space. Ozzie was alarmed. Had Alexis leaked Norm's idea to Seth? When he looked at her, she shrugged. Well, space research wasn't a surprising concept these days. But if Seth's bot could really do all those functions they were beaten.

He watched as Seth and his contest partner faced the robot and Seth began to control its functions with a remote. It raised a pair of arms that were temporarily linked to position a tool precisely. The positioning was correct. The second function, to place samples in a container: it worked perfectly. The third function, pretty routine but it went off perfectly. Ozzie's mouth was getting dry. Seth's bot took off up a little ramp and stopped without falling off at the end. So far no flaws. Now the fancy fifth function.

The robot whirred, froze and wouldn't go on. Tried again, froze, and wouldn't move. They could see Seth's whispered argument with his partner, the angry s-sounds hissing louder, and then Seth stalked off the floor, leaving his partner alone with the failed robot and the judges and the onlookers watching, as if this was all his fault.

I'm glad that's not Alexis, Ozzie thought. He found that she was looking at him, nodding. She knew what he was thinking. Norm patted her on the back. "Way to look 'em over, Alexis," he said. "As a partner, Seth was death."

At last the autovoice began to read the bit about "Device Number 56, by Norman Garcia and Alexis Wu, nicknamed the Hot Rod because of its unique land-hugging laser-heated rods..." Ozzie had written the thing himself. The autovoice bragged about their robot's features.

"This bot was designed for asteroid mining and exploration, where it will make rock sampling easier. And for use on Mars, with its reputation for crazy storms, because of its ability to anchor to the surface."

There was a small audience murmur. *They're impressed,* Ozzie thought. *Now we need to show that it works.*

Through a large bay door that was rising, an enormous forklift entered the arena, hefting a slab of flooring that was twelve feet by twelve feet by about three feet thick. There was more murmuring at this bit of showmanship. Both the forklift and the slab said, ParKay Flooring" on all sides in large letters. And the slab wasn't flat. It was sculpted on the upper surface so it looked like a real landscape. In fact, its surface was marked as a relief map would be, with lines of latitude and longitude.

The forklift lowered it to the arena floor and backed away as the picking arm set the Hot Rod beside it. The three rose from their seats, took it off its dish and lifted it to the rocky surface of their pretend planet. Norm and Alexis stood by with their remotes.

Somewhere far up in the arena seating a group of people began to whistle and cheer wildly. They were shushed by the announcer.

The judges looked at the "moves sheet" supplied by Norm as contestant. The moves were also displayed on a flat screen scoreboard high up on one wall.

Ozzie checked them off in his head. First move: Norm started the robot rolling across the ridiculously bumpy Martian surface from P to Q. It traveled uphill and down successfully, avoiding slopes that were beyond its ability to balance by choosing alternate routes, arriving at Q safely.

Second move: Alexis punched in coordinates for location z and hit the "go" button. Little jets fired and its small jetpack lifted it up and over, for a graceful little touchdown at the intersection of two lines, marked z.

And so on. Each new move, Ozzie's heart was in his throat as the Hot Rod began, but then... When it drilled a meter-long core sample diagonally into the surface and deposited it neatly in its rear basket, the crowd sighed happily. Even if the last trick didn't work or something, they sure had the crowd interested. The judges wore poker faces. He craned his neck to see the last move.

The Hot Rod was traveling again, obeying directions and rolling forward close to the edge of the slab. Norm walked over beside the Hot Rod and gave it a hard sideways shove, imitating a gust of wind interfering with its forward progress. Immediately foul-smelling smoke started to rise, as the robot drove its ultra-hot, special-design hollow rods down into the ParKay flooring to anchor it against the "winds of Mars." It brought a laugh when Alexis and Norm scrambled up onto the Martian surface in their sneakers and acted like wild Martian winds by leaning against the robot with all their weight, rocking and pushing against the anchored robot without success. The audience burst into applause. There was more whistling and howling from that group in the upper seats.

What really did it, though, was when Alexis and Norm jumped down off the slab and the robot noticed that the wind had stopped; it re-melted its rods, withdrew them from the surface, and resumed its stroll across the ParKay Martian landscape.

Ozzie was up out of his seat, whistling and clapping Space Academy style. Some of the audience were better bred, but some were not, so he had company.

**

It was a hit. While Norm and Alexis posed with the Hot Rod and the flooring for the ParKay publicity photos, Ozzie collected cards from the people who pressed around the photographers' barricade: college recruiters, recruiters from a corporation or two, a government agency, someone who wanted to write a grant proposal for them.

Media reporters, seeing the cameras going and thinking that Norm and Alexis must have won, rushed down from "media seating" and took photos too. Norm's delighted family plowed a noisy furrow through the growing crowd and they each insisted on hugging Ozzie because he was the only one they could get to. Then the family members were in the photos and the media were interviewing them, too.

In the din, the announcer's voice became sharp: "— please! Return to your seats! The judges are not finished conferring!" And realizing their mistake, the people on the floor hurried back to walls or seats, looking embarrassed. The media moved off. The ParKay photographers hastily folded up their cameras.

"Thank you to ParKay for the donation of its flooring," the voice hinted firmly. The picking crane hovered above the Hot Rod waiting to pick up the bot. ParKay's enormous forklift hurried forward to heft the chunky map. Norm, Alexis and Ozzie hastily got the bot off the slab and onto its picking dish.

About the time the picking crane had the Hot Rod returned to the risers, and the forklift had backed the ParKay flooring out of the arena, the judges nodded to the announcer that they had their decision.

OK. All we need to do is place, Ozzie thought.

Third place was announced, to enthusiastic applause. Then the second place winner, to wild cheering. Ozzie's stomach lurched. *Well, we wanted to be first. Now it's first or nothing,* Ozzie chewed his lip, looking at Norm and Alexis' pale faces. What if they hadn't even placed in the contest?

The arena was hushed. Ozzie noticed the reek of

electronics and ozone, as if that were the real smell of suspense. The announcing voice started up again. Ozzie was having trouble listening to it at all. The guy sure had a lot to say. Why didn't he get to the point?

The second the word "Norman" was out of the announcer's mouth, Ozzie stood and clapped blindly, and didn't stop till after everyone else did.

**

It was a victory for Ozzie too. He had not forgotten all the ways in which it was.

Norm's family couldn't thank him enough. He had never been so thoroughly hugged in his life.

That proofed him a little against the sting when Seth returned to the arena with his buddies to find Ozzie — who was left alone while the media people photographed and interviewed Norm and Alexis — to gloat over the only victory Seth had achieved: forcing Ozzie to forfeit the Captain's Apprentice spot. "It's a pleasure to see someone like you lose, farmer boy," Seth said. Following them to Egypt had probably cost Seth himself a trophy today, but he seemed satisfied with his triumph.

Seth's henchmen echoed his jeers. Ozzie's blood was pounding in his ears but he did his best to grin like a gypsy at them all.

Without warning, Raker appeared behind his son. "Seth, that gentleman over there wants to interview you about your plans for a Grand Galactic Captain's Apprentice post..."

He recognized Ozzie. "Mr. Reed," he said to Ozzie with naked dislike, "I'm glad to see that you no longer seem to be accompanying that Icelandic girl with her weird ideas. Promoting such ideas has not helped your success."

CHAPTER THIRTY-NINE

SOMETIME AFTER things died down, when they had all stopped at the Dairy Swirl for ice creams, Alexis thought to turn her phone back on and let Freya know. Well, Freya already knew — she had been watching for results on the worldweb. "She says she is proud of us all, the three of us," Alexis read from the text. Ozzie was looking at the same text on his own phone. And what she had added: "Especially you, Ozzie."

His eyes started to bother him then, and he didn't know why.

He pretended to clean ice cream drips off his cargoes so Norm's mother, who was watching him, wouldn't see.

**

At Norm's house Ozzie showed everyone the cards he had collected from the recruiters and all. That started a new landslide of talk. In the kitchen and the living room there was gabbling and beer-opening and excited predictions. "Norm could get a scholarship to MIT!" Uncle Mike thumped Norm's dad on the back. "Maybe one of these days he'll get you a speedboat, hah?"

His dad blinked a lot but otherwise he just smiled and shook his head various ways to show he was listening. Norm's mother cried happily as she and the aunts chopped onions for supper.

Norm's Uncle Lee handed out beers to Norm, Alexis, and Ozzie for a toast. The little sisters danced around, giddy, while the little brothers used up their adrenaline wrestling with each other. Norm's dad sent the four to play outside: "Go out now! Before you knock someone over."

It was turning into a party: more relatives arrived every few minutes, most of them with food in crocks and on platters. Ozzie saw Mrs. Garcia put the chopped onions in a jar in the refrigerator. She and the aunts filled plates from the arriving platters and crocks and joined the others.

Alexis somehow found a quiet room in which to call her parents. Ozzie saw her emerge with her pale cheeks rosy and her eyes sparkling. He walked over, high-fived her and handed her a bowl of snacky things. "They are planning to buy a bigger house when I'm rich," she said, the lopsided smile curving upward on her cheek.

Now there were about thirty people crowded into the little living room. Norm finished his story about their robot and left the circle of admiring aunts and uncles to walk over to Alexis. "Everyone, a toast to my brilliant partner, who saved my butt! Alexis!"

After the toast Norm put down his beer, took her hands, wrapped her in his arms, and hugged her hard. "I will kiss you later when no one is looking," he said in a loud whisper. She shook her head at him, then at his grinning family, and she giggled. She seemed giddy with relief.

Then she whispered to Norm, and he nodded, Of course! "To Ozzie, the world's best friend, who made this all happen for Alexis and me." A cheer, and they drank. The toast was an exaggeration, but Ozzie felt the warmth of the eyes turned toward him, knowing that he felt richer than he ever had before.

He smiled at them all. "Thanks," he managed.

He ate for the first time today, and then, before he could get too tipsy from the beer, gave a grateful toast to the Garcias, the uncles, and all the other friends and relatives who had chipped in money and food to support a think tank for the last few months. It was a toast whose time had come, and when Norm remembered to give his Dad the prize-money check "to pay all of you back for the research trip to Egypt," that brought down the house.

Ozzie thought of Freya, and the idea of toasting her, if she were here. What would they say? That she was the one who almost ruined their chances at the contest? But then, that wasn't her fault. It was his fault for taking her up on the Egypt thing. *Which, by the way, I would hate to have missed.* How confusing that was.

Would they say that she was the one who made things so complicated this contest looked easier by comparison?

He decided he was glad she wasn't here. Too complicated if she were here. As the beer made him mushy-headed, he entertained for a moment the pleasant memory of kissing her. Then he remembered yelling at her on the phone, and winced. He was still glad she wasn't here right now; too complicated.

And he would call Dad later, when it was quiet. There was a lot to explain.

**

It was dark and quiet except for the sounds of crickets and Alexis' soft breathing. If he had been asleep before, he was now wide awake, lying on Norm's couch with the smells of party food and beer still lingering in the air. Now he knew what the toast to Freya should have been: to Freya, who created this winning team, three of us so strong we could even win a losing battle.

But in the midst of all these happy endings, even after Freya's texted praise, he longed for the kind of completeness that Alexis and Norm had. His life was still pretty unresolved.

He was wide awake. He let himself out the front door and sat on the porch swing in the moonlight.

He would return home soon looking like a failure.

And it wasn't just the contest or the apprenticeship. His relationship with Freya was more important than he had been admitting to himself, and that wasn't what you'd call a success. Besides, her search wasn't finished, and now he realized what that meant: for him it wasn't really finished either.

He lay back on the length of the swing to let it rock him like a hammock. As soon as he did, the messenger cat landed with a soft thump on the porch and bounded to his stomach, stretching out there. *Looks like the Sphinx,* he thought drowsily.

His eyes were unfocused and crossed, so the moon looked double. Or were there really two moons now? Someone was singing to him, or two of them singing together, but he couldn't quite hear it; they were getting married, and you could hear the hum of flying lizards in the warm night air.

Sometime later the chill and damp of the night air woke him. He slipped back inside.

**

Next day, when Ozzie heard his friends hatching a plan for Alexis to linger at Norm's a few extra days, he saw his moment to exit and bought his train ticket back to New Mexico. Time to go face his own life.

CHAPTER FORTY

S O I TOLD HIM to get out this morning, Freya." Mamma was holding the hot teacup to her left cheekbone. "After the portrait was done he just wanted free rent and free—"

Freya nodded soberly. But in her mind, a crowd stood up in the bleachers and cheered loudly. "Good call, Mamma," she said.

Mamma looked puzzled.

I sound like Norm now, even in Icelandic, Freya thought. "I mean, I'm glad you saw what he was after and got rid of him."

Mamma smiled. She sipped. Behind her were the cheerful colors of the cupboards, the bright mugs on hooks, the teakettle on the stove. The kitchen smelled of cheese and fresh bread. Snow was falling against the rectangle of gray sky framed by the kitchen window. You could almost forget the steady vibration from the volcanoes.

"Good for you, too, Freya, that you... are doing what you think is right, whatever you think you should do." She didn't fully understand, but she was trying at least.

Freya knew her mother must be worried. They were near the end of the portrait money and Freya's saved money from the Firefighters. Freya had checked the jar when she returned home from Egypt, and each day since then, when Mamma wasn't looking.

Mamma took a deep breath. "Freya, while you were gone, I thought about some things, and also during these last few weeks while I was dealing with *him*. You won't always be with me, and I need to decide what's right for me to do too, not just lean on you and think of you and me together.

"I'm not so great as a portrait artist. I can teach art well enough, but what I've always done best is singing." The crowd was on its feet again, beating its hands, whistling. "So I think I will see if the three cafes that are still open might want an evening and weekend singer—"

"I'm *so* glad, Mamma!"

"—But Freya, you need to find your life as much as I do. I don't want to weigh on you. So. I have taken a new job to support my singing," she said this proudly, "teaching art at the lower schools in Reykjavik. —Did you hear? The old teacher has left for Denmark."

Freya was astonished. "Good for you, Mamma!" she said. "Then we will both work, you and me." *And brave the volcanoes, maybe till the last bitter ash.*

**

The December air was cold and sweet, like a drink of icy water. A pale sun cleared the treetops at the horizon as Ozzie ran along the trail, sprinting by the yucca and the shriveled beds of prickly pear. In his mind he saw them fatten again and bloom in the spring as they did every year, and would again this year. Everything was the same, but new in his eyes. So different here from California and Egypt. It wasn't so bad to be back here.

Running made him feel cleaned out, took the bitterness away.

He hadn't heard from Freya for a while.

He would be starting school again in January and go through the summer to graduate from the program. He'd have to go back to face all the questions and tell them he had failed to get the kind of experience he needed for the Captain's Apprentice post.

Of course I can make something work out for myself, he thought. But for now he had failed to achieve either Freya's way-out dream or his own very real one. He must look like a fool to anyone with any sense. He couldn't wait to hear his school friends give him crap. But he sure was a hero to Norm and Alexis — even to Freya, a little.

Not to Georgie, though. When Ozzie walked with Dad into the house for the first time in weeks Georgie hissed at him ferociously. "Don't you remember me, Georgie?"

he asked, kneeling to scratch her back. She hissed again, violently, and ran off.

But Dad was the one he had really worried about.

They had met at the train station Monday night. No chance to actually talk before that, because it turned out that Dad was playing an all-weekend gig at a local holiday fair, and that meant morning, noon and night for three days with short breaks. "I was sort of a hit," he said, cheerfully. "Show you some holos when we get home." Ozzie would have been happy to stop right there and finish the day living in the world of his father's success. How great was that?

But Dad asked, so Ozzie labored through his carefully rehearsed explanation of his failure: how he had ceased to be Norm's partner and how he didn't win the contest even though Norm won. Leaving out the part about Egypt, he struggled to say the right words to overcome his father's disappointment and make him see how it happened that, after all Dad's and Mr. Brunelli's help, he still wasn't eligible for the Captain's Apprentice post...

Dad stopped the car by the side of the road and looked at him. *Here it comes.* Ozzie sighed. "Sorry, Dad," he said. "I know you took on my chores for months so I could do this, and — sorry."

"I'm so proud of you," was all Dad said.

Ozzie's running shoes thwacked on the hard trail. His lungs took the dry air deeply.

Proud of me? Freya was proud of him for giving up

his dream to help her try to fix the volcanoes. His Dad
was proud of him for giving up his chance at Captain's
Apprentice to help Alexis and Norm. Well, not really
giving up, but still he wasn't sure what to make of it.
Were people proud of you when you sacrificed your
dreams for theirs? Why couldn't everyone win?

A possible answer came to him: Maybe his dream
had only expanded to include more people. So it might
take longer to get all the extra stuff done. He considered
this new idea as he ran.

On impulse, he turned the other way when he hit the
campground road and headed toward the gypsy camp.

**

"Malo, can you see the future?" It was sort of a dumb
question, but after all that had happened recently, Ozzie
could see no reason not to ask it. And Malo had
welcomed him back in a new way. It was as if they had
become relatives during Ozzie's absence. Something was
different now.

Ozzie was absorbing this difference as they sat in the
warmth of Malo's tent. Old tapestries, hung from an
inner frame, held in heat at the sides and the roof of the
place. In fact, Ozzie had been right when he imagined
what Malo's place might be like: besides the thick
carpets on the walls and floor there were round brass
lamps suspended from a diagonal wooden rod that
pinned the ceiling carpet into place. They cast a sort of

medieval light. The air in here was flavored with cloves and cinnamon, and below those two cookies-and-pie smells there were layers of spices that were deeper and more mysterious.

Malo was making tea on a little stove that also heated and lit the place. The stove was not an ancient thing at all; Ozzie had seen one like it in a very high-tech camping store. He wondered what Malo had traded for it.

Malo passed Ozzie a spiced mug and offered the small bottle filled with yellow cream.

"See the future? Sometimes," Malo said.

They drank their tea in silence. The white-chested black cat stepped out of the shadows to stand between them, looking at Ozzie. [Hello,] Ozzie thought politely. It shot back some polite greetings in return, mixed with opinions about mice, then moved on into some different shadows.

Malo pulled out a deck of Tarot cards, fanned it, and asked Ozzie to pick one. Ozzie had seen Tarot cards here and there before. These were worn fuzzy at the edges. But the images on the backs of the cards were unfaded by time and richly colored.

Ozzie pulled a card, flipping it over to show the picture on its face: a blindfolded guy in a tunic who was about to walk off the edge of a cliff, happily looking up in the air, holding a flower. "The Fool," Malo said.

Ozzie turned gloomy. "Well, I do feel like a fool pretty often, these days."

Malo shook his head, dismissing the idea. "Interesting. The Fool. Sometimes the one who looks foolish is wise, and the wise are foolish. The Fool predicts beginnings, journeys, a leap of faith."

He took the card back from Ozzie and shrugged as he put them away, as if to say, "Some people believe in these things, but we may choose not to."

He added, "By the way, I found a gold ring on a silver chain in the sand of the stream bed, a couple of months ago. Good thing I found it before the snows. The chain was broken at the catch. Yours?"

"Yes," Ozzie breathed, hugely relieved. "Thanks. Where is it?"

"You know by now that your mother and I are old friends, from the time when you were a little kid. True?"

True. His mother: another missing item for Ozzie. Silence from her again, since Egypt. At least now he wouldn't have to be embarrassed when she finally did call again to ask for the ring.

"She came by to visit a couple of weeks ago and recognized it on my clothes-cupboard there. She took a sealing-wax impression of what was engraved inside," he said. "She said you would be glad you didn't have to worry about getting it to her."

He pulled them from a drawer in the cupboard handed Ozzie the chain and ring. The catch had been repaired.

**

Every day Freya checked the newsfeed for the volcanic activity report. If the Icelandic volcanoes were a graph, it was flatlining: no new ones starting. And in other parts of the earth the volcanoes remained inactive and cooling.

Almost two weeks after the contest news from California, Freya hit a wall in her research. She just didn't know where to take it next.

Besides, she needed to get back to earning. What if she needed money to do more research, or Mamma got sick again? She went to the Icelandic Firefighting Technical School to ask for her job back. After the curt dismissal letter the Director had sent, it took courage to show up again and endure the stares of the men who had been on her team.

The Director said maybe, but not now. There was less volcanic activity, so there were fewer brush fires and less danger to the populated areas. They were hoping they could do without another firefighter. Her replacement on the training team was Jolina from France or somewhere.

She answered that she'd rather not have firefighting work ever again, if that was because the volcanoes were gone. But she knew, as she walked out, that it wasn't over yet.

Freya took a job bagging groceries because a clerk

had left. In two weeks she could be a checker *and* bagger, they said. She hoped she didn't see anyone she knew there.

Right now she was sick of struggling. She longed to be free of the volcanoes as a worry, a study, a life.

"You should have some fun, Freya," her mother advised.

It was a rare thing for her to take her mother's advice. She accepted Arni's latest offer to escort her somewhere: an invitation to the New Year's Ball to support the firefighters, thrown by the Icelandia Association. The ball was funded by people who had left Iceland and hoped to return someday when the danger of volcanoes was over.

Arni was happy to be out with her. He was handsome and good-natured, not as hot-headed as Ozzie. *Not as hot-headed as me, either.* She wore a dress of her mother's, a retro strapless, floor-length white satin thing with a pattern of polished snowflakes woven into the fabric. He admired her and smiled brightly at her. She felt like a lady for a change.

They spent the evening talking about fighting fires. And about the volcanoes. And worst of all, everything just reminded her of Ozzie.

**

Alexis called Ozzie, live-holo, one late afternoon early in the new year. A thin snowfall had collected on the porch and the railings outside, and he was building a fire in the fireplace.

This was the first word from her or Norm since the day Ozzie had left. Not that Ozzie minded much. He knew they were busy catching up on schoolwork and fielding college recruiter calls. And before that, they were busy with each other, happy to loaf a little in sunny California.

She was in London again, now. It was gray and nasty, she said.

"Hey, Alexis. I never remembered to ask you: If you got your info about the robotics contest from Freya, why did you call Norm in the first place — when Freya told you that he was already my contest partner?"

"Yeah, I knew he was. Didn't you both guess why I called him? I thought it was *way* too obvious: he was good-looking and it was an excuse to meet him." There was that lopsided smile.

That's all it was? And she thought it was obvious? Guess I still don't know much about girls, Ozzie thought, helplessly.

"Hey, Norm wrote a detailed report on all you did to help him win the robotics competition."

"*Norm*? Wrote a *report?*"

"Well, I helped him." Her funny smile again. Ozzie missed her. Liking her was simple, not so complicated as the way he felt about Freya. "We filed it with the JPL Committee, with the Space Academy, and with Grand Galactic."

"You're kidding."

"Nope."

Ozzie laughed. Well, at least Mr. B would hear most of the story before he got back to school. It would save Ozzie the trouble.

**

One late afternoon after school, in February, his mother called. Dad wasn't around — he had taken one of the horses to do his daily ride-through at the campground. It was startling to hear from her again. Maybe it always would be.

"I need your number, Mom." *I'm not letting you go off again without giving it to me.* After she recited it he said, "What do you want?" He knew that didn't sound friendly.

"I think I know how you feel, Ozzie. Life changes so fast sometimes." She told a story he had never heard: about how she ran away with Dad, crazy in love, and didn't see her father again till near the end of his life. How hurt he was. Ozzie wasn't sure he was getting it all straight, but he caught a glimpse, for the first time, of how her life might be complicated, too.

He was silent. *Crazy in love. Wonder if I'll ever be.* Maybe that was how you knew the real thing? But it didn't last long, did it. So maybe not.

"Ozzie, thank you for the ring."

"Well, maybe you should thank Malo. He found it for me. — But I haven't been careless with it. I've kept it safe for years…"

"I know."

He had begged some sealing-wax from Malo to take his own impression of the letters and symbols inside, but they made no sense to him. "What's the engraving mean?"

"Have a few minutes?" she asked.

Are you kidding me? She must be used to people who are in a hurry. "Sure."

"Last September I found an old letter in which he said a formula was engraved inside the band of his ring for safekeeping. That was the ring I gave you! He gave it to me shortly before he died, back in '51 — a year or two after you were born. I wore it for years as a keepsake but I never noticed any engraving. Did you?"

"No."

"Well, when I read the letter I wanted to see the formula. My company is researching enhanced drive speeds so I was eager to find out what it means — but it doesn't seem to be about that, and after so many years I'm afraid it's useless technology, you know?"

Drive speeds. I'll have to ask her… But then she wanted to know about the robotics competition, so Ozzie had to tell her about the preparation and the outcome. Omitting Egypt, of course.

"Well, Ozzie. You lost but you gained. That's often the way it is." There was a sort of motherly smile in her voice. He hadn't thought of that. Maybe it was true. "And you're right! No one can stop you. We need to meet and talk…" An interruption forced her to sign off quickly.

But now he could call her himself, if she didn't call soon.

**

It was dark and bitter cold when Ozzie came in from his chores to the welcome of lights and warmth inside, and the smell of Dad's-turn-for-dinner cooking. Dad was sitting at the computer in the living room. He didn't use the computer often but he had been at it a lot during the last few days.

"What are you doing?" Ozzie was very curious.

"Researching," Dad said, gazing at the screen. As Ozzie washed up at the kitchen sink he craned his neck so he could see through the doorway. There was some kind of list that displayed holos when Dad tapped the items. Dad pulled himself out of concentration and added, "Looking for a singing partner. I figure if you can get a robotics partner this way, I can find a singer."

**

Georgie was in his bedroom when Ozzie headed for bed later with some sci-fi loaded up to read. He opened the door wider so she could hiss at him and run away as usual, but she sat quietly, eyeing him from the nightstand.

The absence of hissing reminded him of his cat

manners.

[Hello, Georgie,] he thought at her, politely.

She gazed for half a minute. Then, [That's better.] she said.

He walked toward the bed. Her eyes were locked on him. [Thanks for sending me messages to help us,] Ozzie remembered to say, while he was at it. California seemed like so long ago. He sat on the edge of the bed, just far enough away to be out of reach of her claws.

[Thanks for finally listening.] She hissed, but it mostly sounded like escaping irritation. She inspected one paw, extended the claws slowly, and began to lick very deliberately between them without taking her eyes off Ozzie.

[Sorry I was so dumb,] he said.

She stopped licking abruptly and sheathed her claws. Then she leapt onto the bed beside him and began to purr.

**

Sometime in the night, Ozzie dreamed:

Their happiness was huge; it seemed that it could never end.

She sang to him and he sang back to her. There were others all around them, but she was all he saw. The night was dark and warm, and the lighted lizards were flying. The place was draped with flowering vines. Small lamps hung from curving poles. This was the Ceremony of the Moons, and it made their lifetime friendship sacred: they would live together and be a pair for the rest of their lives.

Life was for two, the saying went. His voice harmonized with hers. She held a glowing phosphor flower and an ankh in her hands.

The twin moons were shining on them, Daimis and Febos, the symbols of love and union...

Ozzie woke, startled. Georgie was purring beside his head on the pillow.

What a wild dream: People with skin that was green as unripe olives and large, beautiful eyes, and elongated heads like the daughers of Akhenaton. He felt the intense singing, full of emotion, but he couldn't really hear the notes. The moons: one large, one small, and they called them Daimis and Febos...

Wait. *They must be the moons of Mars.* The two moons that the Greeks called Deimos and Phobos. Two moons... Now he remembered a dream on Norm's porch, a vague one, similar.

He sat, turned on the light, and squinting in the blinding brightness, scrabbled in the side-table drawer for a pulp-pad, an old pen. He wrote the dream down, wrote some more, all he could remember.

Then he read it to make sure it was all there. He nodded. It had to be Mars that he was dreaming about.

He turned off the light and lay down again. Now he

would remember all of it in the morning. He would call Freya about it tomorrow. She might treat him coldly, but what was there to lose now?

He felt homesick. — Here in New Mexico, at home? It came to him abruptly that Freya had begun to seem like home to him. He missed her a lot: her messy morning hair and her chuckle when someone could get her to laugh. Also her fiery eyes and the graceful way she walked. It was a little lonely, too, here. So different after weeks of living with friends, as close every day as a litter of puppies. It might be nice to talk a little with her, if she wanted to.

If he got the chance he might tell her how beautiful she was. He never had told her that.

But he wasn't sleeping. Or had he slept? There was a sound: *Maybe I was asleep again and that was what woke me?*

And here it was again: a sort of call for help. Spooky. Georgie purred beside him. Dad? It wasn't Dad's voice. There was really no sound in the house, when he listened. He listened hard in Georgie's direction, too, but the cat said nothing.

He took a deep breath, relaxed, and just waited.

It's Freya.

But how could he be sure it was her? Or that she wanted him, not...someone else? Well, if he had learned anything in recent months, it was to entertain weird communications.

He pulled his phone off the charger and called.

"Ozzie?" She sounded surprised.

"I've just had a dream," he said. "I thought maybe you would want to hear about it..."

And he told her about the girl with skin the color of green olives, the elongated head, the moons called Daimis and Febos—

"The answer!" A gust of relief. "Your dream was the same as mine except I didn't see the twin moons — and I didn't hear their names!" There was no holo, but he could just see the delighted sparks coming out of her peridot eyes. "Then Ozzie, Mars must be the place the spirit called the Planet of Beginning, and the Singer must be there on Mars somewhere — I don't know how that can be, but somehow. Ozzie! This is what we needed to know!"

"Now. It was just a dream," Ozzie cautioned, trying to stay logical. "And it wasn't *my* dream, either," he started to explain. "It was like I was dreaming for someone else, you know?"

"I do know," she said. "Well, where was Georgie at the time?"

Ozzie thought.

Even before he said it, he knew that she knew what the answer was. "See what I mean?" she said.

He smiled, rolling his eyes.

"These cats, with their messages, Ozzie! They must be feeding us dreams. Who can explain that? But of course. I see now that your dream and mine were both about Mars."

Well, then who are the people in the dreams? he wondered.

"This opens the door again. I can start looking into it."

"Hey, why did you call for help?" Ozzie asked.

Silence. "You heard me?"

"Yeah. I think."

A long, pent-up-sounding sigh. "Well, I was just despairing that I was at a dead end, because one of the Icelandic volcanoes started erupting again this morning. I was so worried. I was asking 'Where is someone who can help me do this?' And that was when you called."

It was odd that his mind was drifting right now. He should be listening. He wanted to listen. But it was her voice. He had forgotten while they were in Egypt. Maybe hearing it now all by itself, just her voice, made it show up again, like a piece of amber when it sits alone on black velvet. It was beautiful, full of longing. It made him feel a little dizzy.

"Thank you, Ozzie," she said.

Neither of them said anything more. He was just thinking he should sign off when she said, "Hey?"

"Yeah?"

"Do you know how much I love you?" Her voice was wistful.

The question made his heart stop for a second. *She*

loves me? After all that stuff?

All that stuff flashed through his mind: looking over her shoulder at a map in Egypt, steadying her with his arm as she left the Giza jail, the Memphis vision, her electric kisses, yelling at her from Norm's house... After all that, she was still someone who made him want to be with her right now, all day tomorrow, maybe always. *I guess she really could love me, too, then.*

"Not as much as I love you, I'll bet," he countered, carefully. As if he was bargaining. He felt cowardly. His face was getting hot.

"Really?" Happiness lit her voice. There was a long pause. Then, indulgently: "You are *so dumb* sometimes."

"I am not!" Hotly. *But I am. Single-minded, thick-headed, dumb.*

"Yes you are!" Just as hotly. "Smart but dumb. You love me? But you never say?"

And you are just as dumb as me. Just the same way. We're two of a kind. As the thought came to him, Ozzie knew it was true.

Freya added gently: "Really. I do love you a lot, Ozzie. I can't help it." He tried to speak for a few seconds with no success. He was having trouble breathing. He hoped his voice, when it came out, wouldn't break like a kid's or sound as overpowered as he felt. It took all the courage he had to just tell the scary truth: "I can't help it either, Freya: I love you too."

CHAPTER FORTY-ONE

IT WAS an eye-popping first day of June in New Mexico. The sky was absolute blue. *Bluer than anyone from somewhere else would believe till they got here*, Ozzie thought. Big purple and pink lilac bushes at the porch steps made the air sweet. The cottonwoods were laden with new leaves, green all the way to their towering tops.

The future looked strange, but pretty decent anyway. He had finished the spring term and now he had two weeks till summer term began. And here was Norm, sitting with him on the front porch steps, blinking in the bright sunshine at the sky and the hills.

Norm pushed up his glasses. "Yeah, I've been collecting college offers, and I think I'll take the one from Berkford, but I decided to visit here before I make a final decision. Maybe I'll even wait a year, if they'll hold me a place." He smiled wickedly.

Ozzie rolled his eyes. "You just want to be with

Alexis."

"And why not?"

Why not, really. Ozzie sighed. "You're right. She's a good catch. Smart, funny, pretty..."

"And she likes me," Norm said, grinning. "Important feature."

The mailman drove up to the outer gate. Ozzie ran over to take today's mail from his hand. He shuffled through and held up an envelope as he returned to Norm. "My grades from the Academy," he said.

"Did you ace it? Let's see."

Ozzie sat and opened the envelope. His grades came out but there was a letter with it. Two letters. One on Space Academy letterhead, but they didn't usually send a letter along with your grades unless you were expelled. And one on Grand Galactic paper. Ozzie ran his eyes over it.

"Norm." He held the letter so they could read it together.

The Grand Galactic memo notified the White Sands Space Academy that Oliver S. Reed, 16, had been returned to the list of candidates for apprenticeship on the first Earth-Moon-Mars merchant flight. There was a condition: that he had to get training and experience in advanced robotics design before graduation.

And the Academy letter notified him about the attached memo, urging him to "keep grades and performance high, to continue to uphold the standards of this school..."

Ozzie threw his head back and yelled into the air. "Yeeooww!"

Norm whooped and slapped Ozzie's back. He danced around the yard and tried to climb the tree, which had no reachable branches. "Wait till Alexis hears this!" he crowed.

Well, that won't be long. Ozzie grinned. The day had just become a huge sigh of relief for him.

When she heard about Norm's sudden plans to come to New Mexico, Alexis had asked Ozzie if she could be invited too. She was egged on by Norm, no doubt. Since they both were new graduates, she and Norm, they all should celebrate. To get her here Norm had traded some expensive electronic parts for an unused student-discount flight credit a friend had.

Ozzie got Dad's permission to bunk her in his bedroom while he and Norm used the porch. Dad didn't mind the idea of a girl in the house at all; he seemed to like it. He was out getting the daily ride-through done at the campground so he could be home as host at dinner tonight.

With a couple of weeks till Ozzie's summer term started, there was enough time for some fun showing his friends around Space Valley and the countryside. It wasn't so bad here — kind of interesting and especially for nerds.

Imagine Alexis in New Mexico. "Just bring jeans and

shirts," he had warned her. "None of that British freezer-wear." Now they could see a trail of dust heading out the road — that must be her, in the airshuttle coming from the Las Cruces Airport.

"We could have gone to get her, Norm," Ozzie said again.

"Naw, those airport shuttles are cheap and why bother? Give her time to fix her hair and all."

Ozzie shook his head. Norm knew the real story about girls, he guessed, from long acquaintance with his sisters.

Ozzie raked back his own hair with both sets of fingers. He touched the ring that hung again on the chain around his neck.

"Hey Norm, what do you think of Freya, really?"

Norm's eyebrows went up. There was a funny look on his face. "Well. Charismatic and fairly driven. Dangerous when you try to stop her," he said, ticking these things off on his fingers. Then with a scientific air, he said, "But now that she laughs at my jokes sometimes, I think she'll do for you."

Ozzie gave Norm a shove.

The shuttle drove to the open gate and stopped. Alexis jumped out and ran at both of them, her little arms gathering them in a group hug while the driver dumped her bags and drove off. She did look pretty well turned out, Ozzie thought. Her neat fishtail braid swung happily as she kissed Norm hello.

**

They sat sipping on squeezepaks of local cider at the kitchen table. Alexis said, "I have great news for you both!"

Norm said, "Hey Ozzie, about how much you helped Alexis and me. I just wanna say: you need us, we're there. Pretty much." Alexis nodded and curled her arm behind Norm's waist to demonstrate that they agreed on this matter.

Ozzie knew. But he didn't know what to say to them.

Yes he did. He told Alexis about the memo from Grand Galactic. "It probably happened because of your report," he said. "Thanks."

"Guess what else happened because of my report? Seth got censured by the Contest Board for Improper Conduct!" She scowled fiercely, then gave up and giggled.

"Hey, how's Freya?" Norm asked.

Ozzie answered, "She's been researching, fighting fires again. She's worried a lot about the volcanoes. Can't blame her. Did you know that they let her rejoin the firefighting school now that the volcanic stuff is increasing again over there?" Norm and Alexis just looked at each other.

"Talk to her a lot?" Norm said.

"Almost every day." Ozzie felt both their eyes on him. He'd better get real about this. "I love her voice..." he began, trying hard to say what he meant.

"She calls me too, once a week or so." Alexis smiled knowingly.

Ozzie felt uncomfortable. *Who knows what embarrassing stuff Freya has told Alexis about me.* But he stared bravely back.

A car horn outside startled him. "Who's that?" Ozzie was baffled. "My dad is at the campground..."

They followed him out onto the porch. It was Dad's old aircar, which he never took to the campground, parked at the gate to the front yard. Dad was getting out of it. And at the same time someone stepped out of the passenger side. A woman, blonde with her hair pulled into a knot on top of her head, straightened up and looked at them over the aircar roof with her eyes crinkled and her lips puckered in a sort of delighted smile, as if everything she saw was perfect.

Dad put his arm behind her back to guide her through the gate, to the porch. Ozzie's eyes widened but he was trying not to stare. *A girlfriend? Dad has a girlfriend?* They stopped at the foot of the porch steps. "Hi fellas," Dad said. And you must be Alexis." He beamed at her, and took the hand she offered in his big tanned fingers. Then, "Ozzie, this is my new singing partner, Ilse Arnsdottir."

Ozzie reassembled his scattered wits enough to remember to be polite. He introduced her to his friends. All the while, her name, her looks, her accent, were prodding at something that was still asleep in his mind.

Asleep until another of the aircar doors opened and Freya stepped out.

He woke in a blinding flash.

He must have flown over the fence. He wasn't sure how he got to the car, but now he had her wrapped in his arms. He heard laughter and chatter behind him, then applause as he kissed her — that had to be Norm — then more laughter, before he even remembered where he was — enough to decide he'd better let go of her for now.

**

"We sang together in Iceland, years ago," Dad was saying to Ozzie. They were all crowded around the kitchen table. "When I was looking for a singing partner during the winter, I found Ilse again on the worldweb." He grinned and drained his ice tea. Ozzie had never seen him look so happy. Ever. "Freya was the one who finally figured out that her mother was talking to *your* father. That was just a month ago. But she made us swear we wouldn't tell."

"Made *us* swear, too," Norm said indignantly. Alexis rolled her eyes and launched her sideways smile.

"Ilse and I have a month of bookings already in the Las Cruces area, beginning this weekend..." his father was saying.

"Dad. That's fantastic news," Ozzie answered, and he meant it. But Freya's eyes were shining so brightly that they shot those cool sparks and it was hard for him to take his own eyes off her face.

DREAMERS

*The DREAMERS series continues with **The Singer**, available soon in ebook and print editions.*

*In **The Singer**: Volcanic activity is increasing again on Earth. Although Mars is known to be uninhabited except by recent explorers and colonists, Freya is convinced that a mysterious singer hides there. Because of information she has received in Egypt from one of the Memphis dead, she is also certain that the Singer is the last owner of the music of Osiris, which has the power to stop the volcanoes. Getting to Mars is impossible — but Freya, Ozzie, Alexis and Norm will have to find a way, despite danger and sabotage. They will have to gamble that somewhere on desolate Mars they can find the Singer and get her help.*

By J.K. Stephens

The Ibis Door
The Singer (to be released in early 2019)
Inside the Ring (to be released in 2019)

Your opinion matters

If you enjoyed *The Ibis Door*, please take a minute to leave a short review on the page where you bought this book. Your reviews help readers like you to find books they will enjoy — including this series, I hope.

Connect

I enjoy staying in touch with readers, so please join my mailing list for blogs and periodic updates. If you have joined by release time, I'll provide you with a free electronic copy of the second book in this series: *The Singer.*

To subscribe, just email:

JKStephens@daybreakcreate.com

ABOUT THE AUTHOR

J.K. Stephens lives and writes near Tampa, Florida.

A fan of funny movies, dancing, long walks and bike rides, the author is just as fond of mountains as beaches, and travels at any opportunity — not only to gather ideas for further writing, but also just to enjoy the remarkable people, places, foods and dreams that make the world the way it is.